HUE *and* CRY

HUE *and* CRY

Stories

JAMES ALAN McPHERSON

HarperCollins books may be purchased for educational, business, or sales promotional use. For information, please email the Special Markets Department at SPsales@harpercollins.com.

Originally published in 1968 by The Atlantic Monthly Press.

FIRST ECCO PAPERBACK EDITION PUBLISHED 2001.
SECOND ECCO PAPERBACK EDITION PUBLISHED 2019.

Designed by Michelle Crowe

The Library of Congress has catalogued a previous edition as follows:

McPherson, James Alan, 1943–

Hue and cry: stories / James Alan McPherson—1st pbk. ed.

　p. cm.

　Contents: A matter of vocabulary—On trains—A solo song—Gold Coast—Of cabbages and kings—All the lonely people—An act of prostitution—Private domain—A new place—Hue and cry.

　ISBN 0-06-093647-9 (trade paper)

　1. United States—Social life and customs—20th century—Fiction. 2. African Americans—Fiction. 3. Working class—Fiction. I. Title.

PS3563.A325 H84 2001

813'.54—dc21   2001033146

ISBN 978-0-06-290973-2 (pbk.)

19 20 21 22 23   LSC   10 9 8 7 6 5 4 3 2 1

To my nephew, Woody Miller,
and to Devorah.
And Annie, of P.S. 36

When a felony is committed, the hue and cry (*hutesium et clamor*) should be raised. If, for example, a man comes upon a dead body and omits to raise the hue, he commits an amerciable offense, besides laying himself open to ugly suspicions. Possibly the proper cry is "Out! Out!"

—**POLLOCK AND MAITLAND,**
History of English Law

CONTENTS

PREFACE

I FIRST "MET" JAMES ALAN McPHERSON in the Holy Cross College bookstore in Worcester, Massachusetts, in the fall of 1969. I had come to find something to read beyond the nineteenth-century British novels of the course I was taking. Beyond Dickens. Beyond the Brontës. Beyond Thackeray. It was not that I had not been pleasantly, wonderfully nourished by such authors, but I had spent my teenage years in Washington, D.C., primarily devouring American writers, black and white. The literary world beyond America was still a generally new one to me, still a feast of rich, though unfamiliar food, as it were. And because Dinand Library at the Cross was still several months away from being a place I, a black sophomore at a predominantly white school, could comfortably go and know that I could find something familiar, I went once more to the bookstore.

Familiar, then, was what I began to feel when I came

upon the paperback *Hue and Cry* on the store's shelf. Black cover, orange lettering. And on the back, a black-and-white stamp-sized photograph of Jim, as I, a graduate student, would come to know him, more than ten years later at the University of Virginia. Standing in the bookstore aisle, I had a growing feeling that I knew that man in the photograph in a way that I had not years earlier when seeing pictures of James Baldwin or Ralph Ellison on the backs of their books. Perhaps it was because their photos were those of seasoned, established, older writers. Jim, obviously a long way from being even thirty years old, stood almost shyly in a peacoat, looking as if having his picture taken would never be one of the things he would get used to doing. I felt I knew this man because he looked like me.

I do not now remember how quickly I read all of Jim's stories, but it could not have been more than a day—college work must have been pushed to the side for several hours.

What struck me, as I again read *Hue and Cry*, for perhaps the third or fourth time in 2018, is how powerful and strangely frightening at times the first five stories of the book are with their men and the often crushing burden of their work. Young Thomas Brown of "A Matter of Vocabulary" bagging potatoes in a supermarket. The waiters and sleeping-car porters slaving away on trains in "On Trains" and "A Solo Song: For Doc." Robert the janitor forever lugging his "three overflowing cans of garbage" in "Gold Coast."

The last time I saw Jim, it was winter in Iowa City, nearly fifty years after that sophomore fall of discovering

Hue and Cry. The world and life had done many good and bad things to both of us. He was coming to see me read at the University of Iowa. He could barely walk because of illness, but he still had the look of a wise man with secrets he was more than willing to share. I don't think he knew what part he had played in my getting to that moment in my life.

UPON READING THE FIRST STORIES in *Hue and Cry* in 2018, I was struck, again, at how work can become such a yoke for a black man. Jim has this incredible ability to show how much a black man's work—tied so much to his being—could ultimately contribute to his undoing, no matter how well the job is done. "A Solo Song: For Doc" is a splendid example, well worth, as the worn phrase goes, the price of admission. I always get a feeling of grand relief when I get to the end of "Gold Coast" with Robert's liberation from his garbage cans, with his realization that his world can be a bigger place than a building of sad and failed people. There is a reason why John Updike chose that story as one of the best of the twentieth century.

The first time I met James Alan McPherson in person, it was 1978 in Washington, D.C. He was alone in a corner of someone's home, a few hours before his reading at the Library of Congress. He held a glass of white wine in a living room with ten or so people waiting to go to the reading and he indicated to me with a nod that I should come over, something I would never have done on my own. He had already won praise and prizes for *Elbow Room*, his second book. We talked for some ten or fifteen minutes. He was humble and funny and shy, and it was somehow quietly evident that he knew a lot of things, which was the major reason why I would go to the University of Virginia, where he was then teaching.

With the sixth story in *Hue and Cry*, Jim begins to explore relationships, especially those between black men and white women (not including "An Act of Prostitution")—complicated relationships made even more so by the element of race. What comes through with each page is an empathetic understanding coupled with a writer's knowledge that when dealing with human beings there are no right or wrong answers. There is, to be sure, so much to admire in those final six stories, starting with the dialogue. *This is all true*, a reader wants to say. Those six, like the first four, are to be savored, each word, which is the way a craftsman like Jim would have wanted it.

—**EDWARD P. JONES**
July 2018
Washington, D.C.

HUE *and* CRY

A MATTER of VOCABULARY

THOMAS BROWN STOPPED GOING to church at twelve after one Sunday morning when he had been caught playing behind the minister's pulpit by several deacons who had come up into the room early to count the money they had collected from the other children in the Sunday school downstairs. Thomas had seen them putting some of the change in their pockets and they had seen him trying to hide behind the big worn brown pulpit with the several black Bibles and the pitcher of ice water and the glass used by the minister in the more passionate parts of his sermons. It was a Southern Baptist Church.

"Come on down off of that, little Brother Brown," one of the fat, black-suited deacons had told him. "We see you tryin' to hide. Ain't no use tryin' to hide in God's House."

Thomas had stood up and looked at them; all three

of them, big-bellied, severe and religiously righteous. "I wasn't tryin' to hide," he said in a low voice.

"Then what was you doin' behind Reverend Stone's pulpit?"

"I was praying," Thomas had said coolly.

After that he did not like to go to church. Still, his mother would make him go every Sunday morning; and since he was only thirteen and very obedient, he could find no excuse not to leave the house. But after leaving with his brother Edward, he would not go all the way to church again. He would make Edward, who was a year younger, leave him at a certain corner a few blocks away from the church where Saturday-night drunks were sleeping or waiting in misery for the bars to open on Monday morning. His own father had been that way and Thomas knew that the waiting was very hard. He felt good toward the men, being almost one of them, and liked to listen to them curse and threaten each other lazily in the hot Georgia sun. He liked to look into their faces and wonder what was in their minds that made them not care about anything except the bars opening on Monday morning. He liked to try to distinguish the different shades of black in their hands and arms and faces. And he liked the smell of them. But most of all he liked it when they talked to him and gave him an excuse for not walking down the street two blocks to the Baptist Church.

"Don' you ever get married, boy," Arthur, one of the meaner drunks with a missing eye, told him on several occasions.

The first time he had said it the boy had asked: "Why not?"

"Cause a bitch ain't shit, man. You mind you don' get married now, hear? A bitch'll take all yo' money and then throw you out *in the street!*"

"Damn straight!" Leroy, another drunk much darker than Arthur and a longshoreman, said. "That's all they fit for, takin' a man's money and runnin' around."

Thomas would sit on the stoop of an old deserted house with the men lying on the ground below him, too lazy to brush away the flies that came at them from the urine-soaked dirt on the hot Sunday mornings, and he would look and listen and consider. And after a few weeks of this he found himself very afraid of girls.

Things about life had always come to Thomas Brown by listening and being quiet. He remembered how he had learned about being black, and about how some other people were not. And the difference it made. He felt at home sitting with the waiting drunks because they were black and he knew that they liked him because for months before he had stopped going to church, he had spoken to them while passing, and they had returned his greeting. His mother had always taught him to speak to people in the streets because Southern blacks do not know how to live without neighbors who exchange greetings. He had noted, however, when he was nine, that certain people did not return his greetings. At first he had thought that their silence was due to his own low voice: he had gone to a Catholic school for three years where the black-caped nuns put an academic premium on silence. He had learned that in complete silence lay his safety from being slapped or hit on the flat of the hand with a wooden ruler. And he had been a model student. But even when he raised his voice, intentionally, to certain people in the street they still did not respond. Then he had noticed that while they had different faces like the nuns, whom he never thought of as real people, these nonspeakers were completely different in dress and color from the people he knew. But still, he wondered why they would not speak.

He never asked his mother or anyone else about it: ever since those three years with the nuns he did not like to talk much. And he began to consider certain things about his own person as possible reasons for these slights. He began to consider why it was necessary for one to go to the bathroom. He began to consider whether only people like him had to go to the toilet and whether or not this thing was the cause of his complexion; and whether the other people could know about the bathroom merely by looking at his skin, and did not speak because they knew he did it. This bothered him a lot; but he never asked anyone about it. Not even his brother Edward, with whom he shared a bed and from whom, in the night and dark closeness of the bed, there should have been kept no secret thoughts. Nor did he speak of it to Leroy, the most talkative drunk, who wet the dirt behind the old house where they sat with no shame in his face and always shook himself in the direction of the Baptist Church, two blocks down the street.

"You better go to church," his mother told him when he was finally discovered. "If you don' go, you goin' to hell for sure."

"I don' think I wanna go back," he said.

"You'll be a *sinner* if you don' go," she said, pointing her finger at him with great gravity. "You'll go to hell, sure enough."

Thomas felt doomed already. He had told the worst lie in the world in the worst place in the world and he knew that going back to church would not save him now. He knew that there was a hell because the nuns had told him about it, and he knew that he would end up in one of the little rooms in that place. But he still hoped for some time in Purgatory, with a chance to move into a better room later, if he could be very good for a while before he died. He wanted to be very good and he tried all the time very hard not to have to go to the bathroom. But when his mother talked about hell, he thought again that perhaps he would have to spend all his time, after death, in that great fiery hot burning room she talked about. She had been raised in the Southern Baptist Church and had gone to church, to the same minister, all her life; up until the time she had to start working on Sundays. But she still maintained her faith and never talked, in her conception of hell and how it would be for sinners, about the separate rooms for certain people. Listening to his mother talk about hell in the kitchen while she cooked supper and sweated, Thomas thought that perhaps she did know more than the nuns because there were so many people who believed like her, including the bald Reverend Stone in their church, in that one great burning room, and the Judgment Day.

"The hour's gonna come when the Horn will blow," his mother told him while he cowered in the corner behind her stove, feeling the heat from it on his face. "The Horn's gonna blow all through the world on that Great Morning and all them in the graves will hear it and be raised up," she continued.

"Even Daddy?"

His mother paused, and let the spoon stand still in the pot on the stove. "Everybody," she said, "both the Quick and the Dead and everybody that's alive. Then the stars are gonna fall and all the sinners will be cryin' and tryin' to hide in the corners and under houses. But it won't do no good to hide. You can't hide from God. Then they gonna call the Roll with everybody's name on it and the sheeps are gonna be divided from the goats, the Good on the Right and the Bad on the Left. And then the ground's gonna open up and all them on the Left are gonna fall right into a burnin' pool of fire and brimstone and they're gonna be cryin' and screamin' for mercy but there won't be none because it will be too late. Especially for those who don't repent and go to church."

Then his mother stood over him, her eyes almost red with emotion, her face wet from the stove, and shining black, and very close to tears.

Thomas felt the heat from the stove where he sat in the corner next to the broom. He was scared. He thought about being on the Left with Leroy and Arthur, and all the men who sat on the corner two blocks away from the Baptist Church. He did not think it was at all fair.

"Won't there be no rooms for different people?" he asked her.

"What kind of rooms?" his mother said.

"Rooms for people who ain't done too much wrong."

"There ain't gonna be no separate rooms for any Sinners on the *Left!* Everybody on the Left is gonna fall right into the same fiery pit and the ones on the Right will be raised up into glory."

Thomas felt very hot in the corner.

"Where do you want to be, Tommy?" his mother asked.

He could think of nothing to say.

"You want to be on the Right or on the Left?"

"I don't know."

"What do you mean?" she said. "You still got time, son."

"I don't know if I can ever get over on the Right," Thomas said.

His mother looked down at him. She was a very warm person and sometimes she hugged him or touched him on the face when he least expected it. But sometimes she was severe.

"You can still get on the Right Side, Tommy, if you go to church."

"I don't see how I can," he said again.

"Go on back to church, son," his mother said.

"I'll go," Tommy said. But he was not sure whether he could ever go back again after what he had done right behind the pulpit. But to please her, and to make her know that he was really sorry and that he would really try to go back to church, and to make certain in her mind that he genuinely wanted to have a place on the Right on Judgment Day, he helped her cook dinner and then washed the dishes afterwards.

‖

THEY LIVED ON THE TOP FLOOR of a gray wooden house next to a funeral parlor. Thomas and Edward could look out of the kitchen window and down into the rear door of the funeral parlor, which was always open, and watch Billy Herbs, the mortician, working on the bodies. Sometimes the smell of the embalming fluid would float through the open door and up to them, leaning out the window. It was not a good smell. Sometimes Billy Herbs would come to the back door of the embalming room in his white coat and look up at them, and laugh, and wave for them to come down. They never went down. And after a few minutes of getting fresh air, Billy Herbs would look at them again and go back to his work.

Down the street, almost at the corner, was a police station. There were always two fat, white-faced, red-nosed, blue-suited policemen who never seemed to go anywhere sitting in the small room. These two men had never spoken to Thomas except on one occasion when he was doing some hard thinking about getting on the Right Side on Judgment Day.

He had been on his way home from school in the afternoon. It was fall and he was kicking leaves. His eyes fell upon a green five-dollar bill on the black sand sidewalk, just a few steps away from the station. At first he did not know what to do; he had never found money before. But finding money on the ground was a good feeling. He had picked up the bill and carried it home, to a house that needed it, to his mother. It was not a great amount of money to lose, but theirs was a very poor street and his mother had directed him, without any hesitation, to turn in the lost five dollars at the police station. And he had done this, going to the station himself and telling the men, in a scared voice, how he had found the money, where he had found it, and how his mother had directed him to bring it to the station in case the loser should come in looking for it. The men had listened; they smiled at him and then at each other, and a policeman with a long red nose assured him, still smiling, that if the owner did not call for the five dollars in a week, they would bring the money to his house and it would be his. But the money never came back to his house, and when he saw the red-nosed policeman coming out of the station much, much more than a week later, the man did not even look at him, and Thomas had known that he should not ask what had happened to the money. Instead, in his mind, he credited it against the Judgment Time when, perhaps, there would be some uncertainty about whether he should stand on the Right Side, or whether he should cry with Leroy and Arthur and the other sinners, on the Left.

There was another interesting place on that street. It was across from his house, next to the Michelob Bar on the corner.

It was an old brown house and an old woman, Mrs. Quick, lived there. Every morning, on their way to school, Thomas and Edward would see her washing her porch with potash and water in a steel tub and a little stiff broom. The boards on her porch were very white from so much washing and he could see no reason why she should have to wash it every morning. She never had any visitors to track it except the Crab Lady who, even though she stopped to talk with Mrs. Quick every morning on her route, never went up on the porch. Sometimes the Crab Lady's call would awaken Thomas and his brother in the big bed they shared. "*Crabs! Buy my crabs!*" she would sing, like a big, loud bird, because the words all ran together in her song and it sounded to them like: "*Crabbonnieee crabs!*" They both would race to the window in their underwear and watch her walking on the other side of the street, an old wicker basket balanced on her head and covered with a bright red cloth that moved up and down with the bouncing of the crabs under it as she walked. She was a big, dull-black woman and wore a checkered apron over her dress, and she always held one hand up to the basket on her head as she swayed down the black dirt sidewalk. She did not sell many crabs on that street; they were too plentiful in the town. But still she came, every morning, with her song: "*Crabbonniee crabs!*"

"Wonder why she comes every morning," Thomas said to his brother once. "Nobody never buys crabs here."

"Maybe somebody down the street buys from her," Edward answered.

"Ain't nobody going to buy crabs this early in the morning. She oughta come at night when the guys are over at Michelob."

"Maybe she just comes by to talk to Mrs. Quick," Edward said.

And that was true enough. For every morning the Crab Lady would stop and talk to Mrs. Quick while she washed down her porch. She would never set the basket on the ground while she talked, but always stood with one hand on her wide hip and the other balancing the basket on her head, talking. And Mrs. Quick would continue to scrub her porch. Thomas and his brother would watch them until their mother came in to make them wash and dress for school. Leaving the window, Thomas would try to get a last look at Mrs. Quick, her head covered by a white bandanna, her old back bent in scrubbing, still talking to the Crab Lady. He would wonder what they talked about every morning. Not knowing this bothered him and he began to imagine their morning conversations. Mrs. Quick was West Indian and knew all about roots and voodoo, and Thomas was very afraid of her. He suspected that they talked about voodoo and who in the neighborhood had been fixed. Roots were like voodoo, and knowing about them made Mrs. Quick something to be feared. Thomas thought that she must know everything about him and everyone in the world, because once he and Edward and Luke, a fat boy who worked in the fish market around the corner, had put some salt and pepper and brown sand in a small tobacco pouch, and had thrown it on her white-wood porch, next to the screen door. They had done it as a joke and had run away afterwards, into an alley between his house and the funeral parlor across the street, and waited for her to come out and discover the pouch. They had waited for almost fifteen minutes and still she did not come out; and after all that time waiting it was not such a good joke any more and so they had gone off to the graveyard to gather green berries for their slingshots. But the next morning, on his way to school, Mrs. Quick had looked up from scrubbing her porch and called him over, across the dirt street.

"You better watch yourself, boy," she had said. "You hear me?"

"Why?" Thomas had asked, very frightened and eager

to be running away to join his brother, who was still walking in the wet spring morning, still safe and on his way to school.

Mrs. Quick had looked at him, very intensely. Her face was very black and wrinkled and her hair was white where it was not covered by the white bandanna. Her mouth was small and tight and deliberate and her eyes were dark and red where they should have been white. "You left-handed, ain't you?"

"Yes ma'am."

"Then watch yourself. Watch yourself good, 'less you get fixed."

"I ain't done nothin'," he said. But he knew that she was aware that he was lying.

"You left-handed, ain't you?"

He nodded.

"Then you owe the Devil a day's work and you better keep watch on yourself 'less you get fixed." Upon the last word in this pronouncement she had locked her eyes on his and seemed to look right into his soul. It was as if she knew that he was doomed to stand on the Left Side on that Day, no matter what good he still might do in life. He had said nothing, but her eyes looked so deep into his own that he had no other choice but to hold his head down. He looked away, and far up the street he could see the Crab Lady, swaying along in the dirt. Then he had run.

Late in the night there was another sound Thomas could hear in his bed, next to his brother. This sound did not come every night, but it was a steady sound and it made him shiver when it did come. He would be lying close and warm against his brother's back and the sound would bring him away from sleep.

"Mr. Jones! I love you, Mr. Jones!"

This was the horrible night sound of the Barefoot Lady, who came whenever she was drunk to rummage through the neighborhood garbage cans for scraps of food, and to stand before the locked door of the Herbert L. Jones Funeral Parlor and wake the neighborhood with her cry: "Mr. Jones! I love you, Mr. Jones!"

"Eddie, wake up!" He would push his brother's back. "It's the Barefoot Lady again."

Fully awake, they would listen to her pitiful moans, like a lonely dog at midnight or the faraway low whistle of a night train pushing along the edge of the town, heading north.

"She scares me," he would say to his brother.

"Yeah, Tommy," his brother would say.

There were certain creaking sounds about the old house that were only audible on the nights when she screamed.

"Why does she love Mr. Jones? He's a undertaker," he would ask his brother. But there would be no answer because his brother was younger and still knew how to be very quiet when he was afraid.

"Mr. Jones! I love you, Mr. Jones!"

"It's nighttime," Thomas would go on, talking to himself. "She ought to be scared by all the bodies he keeps in the back room. But maybe it ain't the bodies. Maybe Mr. Jones buried somebody for her a long time ago for free and she likes him for it. Maybe she never gets no chance to see him in the daytime so she comes at night. I bet she remembers that person Mr. Jones buried for her for free and gets drunk and comes in the night to thank him."

"Shut up, Tommy, please," Edward said in the dark. "I'm scared." Edward moved closer to him in the bed and then lay very quiet. But he still made the covers move with his trembling.

"Mr. Jones! I love you, Mr. Jones!"

Thomas thought about the back room of the Herbert L. Jones Funeral Parlor and the blue-and-white neon sign above its door and the Barefoot Lady, with feet caked with dirt and long yellow and black toenails, standing under that neon light. He had only seen her once in the day; but that once had been enough. She wore rags and an old black hat, and her nose and lips were huge and pink, and her hair was long and stringy and hanging far below her shoulders, and she had been drooling. He had come across her one morning digging into their garbage can for scraps. He had felt sorry for her because he and his brother and his mother threw out very few scraps, and had gone back up the stairs to ask his mother for something to give her. His mother had sent down some fresh biscuits and fried bacon, and watching her eat it with her dirty hands with their long black fingernails had made him sick. Now, in his bed, he could still see her eating the biscuits, flakes of the dough sticking to the bacon grease around her mouth. It was a bad picture to see above his bed in the shadows on the ceiling. And it did not help to close his eyes; because then he could see her more vividly, with all the horrible dirty colors of her rags and face and feet made sharper in his mind. He could see her the way he could see the bad men and monsters from *The Shadow* and *Suspense* and *Gangbusters* and *Inner Sanctum* every night after his mother had made him turn off the big brown radio in the living room. He could see these figures, men with long faces and humps in their backs and old women with streaming hair dressed all in black and cats with yellow eyes and huge rats, on the walls in the living room when it was dark there; and when he got into bed and closed his eyes they really came alive and frightened him, the way the present picture in his mind of the Barefoot Lady, her long toenails scratching on the thirty-two stairs as she came up to make him give her more biscuits and bacon, was frightening him. He did not know what to do, and so he moved closer to his brother, who was asleep now. Thomas wanted to wake him up so that he would have help against the Barefoot Lady. He wanted to cut on the light but he was afraid the light would show her where he was. He sweated, and waited. And downstairs, from below the blue-and-white lighted sign above the locked door to the funeral parlor, he heard her scream again; a painful sound, lonely, desperate, threatening, impatient, angry, hungry, he had no word to place it.

"*Mr. Jones! I love you, Mr. Jones!*"

III

THOMAS BROWN GOT HIS FIRST JOB when he was thirteen. Both he and his brother worked at the Feinberg Super Market, owned by Milton Feinberg and his sister, Sarah Feinberg. Between the two of them they made a good third of a man's salary. Thomas had worked himself up from carry-out boy and was now in the Produce Department, while Edward, who was still new, remained a carry-out boy. Thomas enjoyed the status he had over the other boys. He enjoyed not having to be put outside on the street like the other boys up front whenever business was slow and Milton Feinberg wanted to save money. He enjoyed being able to work all week after school while the boys up front had to wait for weekends when there would be sales and a lot of shoppers. He especially liked being a regular boy because then he had to help mop and wax the floors of the store every Sunday morning and could not go to church. He knew that his mother was not pleased when he had been taken into the mopping crew because now he had an excuse not to attend church. But being on the crew meant making an extra three dollars and he knew that she was pleased with the money. Still, she made him pray at night, and especially on Sunday.

His job was bagging potatoes. It was very simple. Every day after school and all day Saturday he would come in the air-conditioned produce room, put on a blue smock, take a fifty-pound sack of potatoes off a huge stack of sacks, slit open the sack and let the potatoes fall into a shopping cart next to a scale, and proceed to put them into five- and ten-pound plastic bags. It was very simple; he could do it in his sleep. Then he would spend the rest of the day bagging potatoes and looking out of the big window, which separated the produce room from the rest of the store, at the customers. They were mostly white, and he had finally learned why they did not speak to him in the street. He had learned that after he came to the supermarket and now he did not mind going to the bathroom, knowing, when he did go, that all of them had to go, just as he did, in the secret places they called home. They had been speaking to him for a long time now, on this business level, and he had formed some small friendships grounded in this.

He knew Fred Burke, the vet who had got a war injury in his back and walked funny. Fred Burke was the butcher's helper who made hamburger from scraps of fat and useless meat cuttings and red powder in the back of the produce room, where the customers could not see. He liked to laugh when he mixed the red powder into the ground white substance, holding gobs of the soft stuff up over the big tub and letting it drip, and then dunking his hands down into the tub again. Sometimes he threw some of it at Thomas, in fun, and Thomas had to duck. But it was all in fun and he did not mind it except when the red and white meat splattered the window and Thomas had to clean it off so that his view of the customers, as he bagged potatoes, would not be obstructed.

He thought of the window as a one-way mirror which allowed him to examine the people who frequented the store without being noticed himself. And it seemed as though he was never really noticed by any of them; no one ever stared back at him as he stood, only his head and shoulders visible behind the glass, looking out at the way certain hands fingered items and the way certain feet moved and the way some faces were set and determined while others laughed with mouths that moved in seemingly pleasant conversation. But none of them ever looked up from what they were about or even casually glanced in his direction. It was as if they could not see beyond the glass.

His line of vision covered the entire produce aisle and he could see the customers who entered the store making their way down that aisle, pushing their carts and stopping, selectively, first at the produce racks, then at the meat counter, then off to the side, beyond his view, to the canned goods and frozen foods and toilet items to the unseen right of him. He began to invent names for certain of the regular customers, the ones who came at a special time each week. One man, a gross fat person with a huge belly and the rough red neck and face of a farmer, who wheeled one shopping cart before him while he pulled another behind, Thomas called Big Funk because, he thought, no one could be that fat and wear the same faded dungaree suit each week without smelling bad. Another face he called the Rich Old Lady, because she was old and pushed her cart along slowly, with a dignity shown by none of the other shoppers. She always bought parsley, and once, when Thomas was wheeling a big cart of bagged potatoes out to the racks, he passed her and smelled a perfume that was light and very fine to smell for just an instant. It did not linger in the air like most other perfumes he had smelled. And it seemed to him that she must have had it made just for her and that it was so expensive that it stayed with her body and would never linger behind her when she had passed a place. He liked that about her. Also, he had heard from the boys up front that she would never carry her own groceries to her house, no more than half a block from the store, and that no matter how small her purchases were, she would require a boy to carry them for her and would always tip a quarter. Thomas knew that there was a general fight among the carry-out boys whenever she checked out. Such a fight seemed worthy of her. And after a while of watching her, he would make a special point of wheeling a cart of newly bagged potatoes out to the racks when he saw her come in the store, just to smell the perfume. But she never noticed him either.

"You make sure you don't go over on them scales now," Miss Hester, the produce manager, would remind him whenever she saw him looking for too long a time out of the window. "Mr. Milton would git mad if you went over ten pounds."

Thomas always knew when she was watching him and just when she would speak. He had developed an instinct for this from being around her. He knew that it worried her when he was silent because she could not know what he was thinking. He knew, even at that age, that he was brighter than she was; and he thought that she must know it too because he could sense her getting uncomfortable when she stood in back of him in her blue smock, watching him lift the potatoes to the plastic bag until it was almost full, and then the plastic bag up to the gray metal scale, and then watching the red arrow fly across to 10. Somehow it almost always stopped wavering at exactly ten pounds. Filling the bags was automatic with him, a conditioned reflex, and he could do it quite easily, without breaking his concentration on things beyond the window. And he knew that this bothered her a great deal; so much so, in fact, that she constantly asked him questions, standing by the counter or the sink behind him, to make him aware that she was in the room. She was always nervous when he did not say anything for a long time and he knew this too, and was sometimes silent, even when he had something to say, so that she could hear the thud and swish of the potatoes going into the bag, rhythmically, and the sound of the bags coming down on the scale, and after a second, the sound, sputtering and silken, of the tops of the bags being twisted and sealed in the tape machine. Edward liked to produce these sounds for her because he knew she wanted something more.

Miss Hester had toes like the Barefoot Lady, except that her nails were shorter and cleaner, and except that she was white. She always wore sandals, was hefty like a man, and had hair under her arms. Whenever she smiled he could not think of her face or smile as that of a woman. It was too tight. And her laugh was too loud and came from too far away inside her. And the huge crates of lettuce or cantaloupes or celery she could lift very easily made her even less a woman. She had short red-brown hair, and whenever he got very close to her it seemed very much unlike the Rich Old Lady's smell.

"What you daydreamin' about so much all the time?" she asked him once.

"I was just thinking, Miss Hester," he had said.

"What about?"

"School and things."

He could sense her standing behind him at the sink, letting her hands pause on the knife and the celery she was trimming.

"You gonna finish high school?"

"I guess so."

"You must be pretty smart, huh Tommy?"

"No. I ain't so smart," he said.

"But you sure do think a lot."

"Maybe I just daydream," Thomas told her.

Her knife had started cutting into the celery branches again. He kept up his bagging.

"Well, anyway, you a good worker. You a good boy, Tommy."

Thomas did not say anything.

"Your brother, he's a good worker too. But he ain't like you, though."

"I know," he said.

"He talks a lot up front. All the cashiers like him a lot."

"Eddie likes to talk," Thomas said.

"Yeah," said Miss Hester. "Maybe he talks too much. Mr. Milton and Miss Martha are watchin' him."

"What for?"

She stopped cutting the celery again. "I donno," she said. "I reckon it's jest that he talks a lot."

IV

ON SATURDAY NIGHTS Thomas and his brother would buy the family groceries in the Feinberg Super Market. Checking the list made out by his mother gave Thomas a feeling of responsibility that he liked. He was free to buy things not even on the list and he liked this too. They paid for the groceries out of their own money, and doing this, with some of the employees watching, made an especially good feeling for him. Sometimes they bought ice cream or a pie or something special for their mother. This made them exceptional. The other black employees, the carry-out boys, the stock clerks, the bag boys, would have no immediate purpose in mind for their money beyond eating a big meal on Saturday nights or buying whiskey from a bootlegger because they were minors, or buying a new pair of brightly colored pants or pointed shoes to wear into the store on their day off, as if to make all the other employees see that they were above being, at least on this one day, what they were all the rest of the week.

Thomas and his brother did not have a day off: they worked straight through the week, after school, and they worked all day on Saturdays. But Edward did not mop on Sunday mornings and he still went to church. Thomas felt relieved that his brother was almost certain to be on the Right Side on That Day because he had stayed in the church and would never be exposed to all the stealing the mopping crew did when they were alone in the store on Sunday mornings with Benny Bills, the manager, who looked the other way when they stole packages of meat and soda and cartons of cigarettes. Thomas suspected that Mr. Bills was stealing bigger things himself, after they had finished mopping and waxing and after he had locked the crew out of the store just after twelve o'clock each Sunday. Thomas also suspected that Milton Feinberg, a big-boned man who wore custom-made shoes and smoked very strong bad-smelling green cigars, knew just what everyone was stealing and was only waiting for a convenient time to catch certain people. He could see it in the way he smiled and rolled the cigar around in his mouth whenever he talked to certain of the bigger stealers; and seeing this, Thomas never stole. At first he thought it was because he was afraid of Milton Feinberg, who had green eyes that could look as deep as Mrs. Quick's; and then he thought to himself that he could not do it because the opportunity only came on Sunday mornings when, if he had never told that first lie, he should have been in church.

Milton and his sister, Sarah Feinberg, liked him. He could tell it by the way Sarah Feinberg always called him up to her office to clean. There were always rolls of coins on her desk, and scattered small change on the floor when he swept. But he never touched any of it. Instead, he would gather what was on the floor and stack the coins very neatly on her desk. And when she came back into the office after he had swept and mopped and waxed and dusted and emptied her wastebaskets, Sarah Feinberg would smile at Thomas from behind her little glasses and say: "You're a good boy, Tommy."

He could tell that Milton Feinberg liked him because whenever he went to the bank for money he would always ask Thomas to come out to the car to help him bring the heavy white sacks into the store, and sometimes up to his office. On one occasion, he had picked Thomas up on the street, after school, when Thomas was running in order to get to work on time. Milton Feinberg had driven him to the store.

"I like you," Milton Feinberg told Thomas. "You're a good worker."

Thomas could think of nothing to say.

"When you quit school, there'll be a place in the store for you."

"I ain't gonna quit school," Thomas had said.

Milton Feinberg smiled and chewed on his green cigar.

"Well, when you finish high school you can come on to work full-time. Miss Hester says you're a good worker."

"Bagging potatoes is easy," said Thomas.

Milton Feinberg smiled again as he drove the car. "Well, we can get you in the stockroom, if you can handle it. Think you can handle it?"

"Yeah," said Thomas. But he was not thinking of the stockroom and unloading trucks and stacking cases of canned goods and soap in the big, musty upstairs storeroom. He was thinking of how far away he was from finishing high school and how little that long time seemed to matter to Milton Feinberg.

V

THOMAS WAS EXAMINING a very ugly man from behind his window one afternoon when Miss Hester came into the produce room from the front of the store. As usual, she stood behind him. Thomas was aware of her eyes on his back. He could feel them on his shoulders as he pushed potatoes into the plastic bags. Miss Hester was silent. And Thomas went on with his work and watching the very ugly man. This man was bald and had a long, thin red nose that twisted down unnaturally, almost to the same level as his lower lip. The man had no chin, but only three layers of skin that lapped down onto his neck like a red cloth necklace. Harry Jackson, one of the stock clerks who occasionally passed through the produce room to steal an apple or a banana, had christened the very ugly man "*Do-funny*," just as he had christened Thomas "Little Brother" soon after he had come to the job when he was thirteen. Looking at Do-funny made Thomas sad: he wondered how the man had lost his chin. Perhaps, he thought, Do had lost it in the war, or perhaps in a car accident. He was trying to picture just how Do-funny would look after the accident when he realized that his chin was gone forever, when Miss Hester spoke from behind him.

"Your brother's in a lotta trouble up front," she said.

Thomas turned to look at her. "What's the matter?"

Miss Hester smiled at him in that way she had, like a man.

"He put a order in the wrong car."

"Did the people bring it back?"

"Yeah," she said. "But some folks is still missin' their groceries. They're out there now mad as hell."

"Was it Eddie lost them?"

"Yeah. Miss Sarah is mad as hell. Everybody's standin' round up there."

He looked through the glass window and up the produce aisle and saw his brother coming toward him from the front of the store. His brother was untying the knot in his blue smock when he came in the swinging door of the air-conditioned produce room. His brother did not speak to him but walked directly over to the sink next to Miss Hester and began to suck water from the black hose. He looked very hot but only his nose was sweating. Thomas turned completely away from the window and stood facing his brother.

"What's the matter up front, Eddie?" he said.

"Nothing," his brother replied, his jaws tight.

"I heard you put a order in the wrong car and the folks cain't git it back," said Miss Hester.

"Yeah," said Eddie.

"Why you tryin' to hide back here?" she said.

"I ain't tryin' to hide," said Eddie.

Thomas watched them and said nothing.

"You best go on back up front there," Miss Hester said.

At that moment Miss Sarah Feinberg pushed through the door. She had her hands in the pockets of her blue sweater and she walked to the middle of the small, cool room and glared at Edward Brown. The door continued swinging back and forth and making a clicking sound in the time she stood there, silent, short of breath and angry. Thomas dropped a half-filled bag of potatoes down into the cart and waited with his brother.

"Why are you back here?" Miss Sarah Feinberg asked Edward.

"I come back for some water."

"You know you lost twenty-seven dollars' worth of groceries up there?"

"It wasn't my fault," said Eddie.

"If you kept your mind on what you're supposed to do this wouldn't have happened. But no! You're always talking, always smiling around, always running your mouth with everybody."

"The people who got the wrong bags might bring them back," Eddie said. His nose was still sweating in the cool room. "Evidently somebody took my cart by mistake."

"*Evidently! Evidently!*" said Miss Sarah Feinberg. "Miss Hester, you should please listen to *that! Evidently.*

You let them go to school and they think they know everything. *Evidently*, you say?"

"Yeah," said Eddie. Thomas saw that he was about to cry.

Miss Hester was still smiling like a man.

Miss Sarah Feinberg stood with her hands in her sweater pockets and braced on her hips, looking Eddie in the face. Eddie did not hold his eyes down and Thomas felt really good but sad that he did not.

"You get back up front," said Miss Sarah Feinberg. And she shoved her way through the door again and out of the cool produce room.

"Evidently, evidently, that sure was funny," said Miss Hester when the fat woman was halfway down the produce aisle. "Lord, was she mad. I ain't never seen her git so mad."

Neither Thomas nor Eddie said anything.

Then Miss Hester stopped smiling. "You best git on back up front, Eddie."

"No," said Eddie. "I'm goin' home."

"You ain't quittin'?" said Miss Hester.

"Yeah."

"What for?"

"I donno. I just gotta go home."

"But don't your folk need the money?"

"No," Eddie said.

He took off his blue smock and laid it on the big pile of fifty-pound potato sacks. "I'm goin' home," he said again. He did not look at his brother. He walked through the door and Thomas watched him walk slowly down the produce aisle and then out the front door, without looking at anything at all.

Then Thomas went over to the stack of potato sacks and pushed the blue smock off the top sack and into a basket on the floor next to the stack. He picked up a fifty-pound sack and lugged it over to the cart and tore it open with his fingers, spilling its contents of big and small dirty brown potatoes into the cart. He could feel Miss Hester's eyes on him, on his arms and shoulders and hands as they moved. He changed the weights on the scale and began to put the potatoes into five-pound bags. He could feel Miss Hester's eyes on his back as he worked. He worked very quickly and looked out the window into the store. Big Funk was supposed to come this afternoon. Thomas had finished seven five-pound bags before Miss Hester moved from where she had been standing behind him, and he knew she was about to speak.

"You going to quit too, Tommy?"

"No," he said.

"I guess your folk *do* need the money now, huh?"

"No," he said. "We don't need the money."

She did not say anything else. Thomas was thinking about Big Funk and what could be done with the time if he did not come. He did not want to think about his brother or his mother or the money, or even the good feeling he got when Milton Feinberg saw them buying the Saturday night groceries. If Big Funk did not come, then perhaps he could catch another glimpse of Do-funny before he left the store. The Rich Old Lady would not come again until next week. He decided that it would be necessary to record the faces and bodies of new people as they wandered, selectively, with their shopping carts beyond the big window glass. He liked it very much now that none of them ever looked up and saw him watching. That way he did not ever have to feel embarrassed or guilty. That way he would never have to feel compelled to nod his head or move his mouth or eyes, or make any indication of a greeting to them. That way he would never have to feel bad when they did not speak back.

VI

IN HIS BED THAT NIGHT, lying very close to his brother's breathing back, Thomas thought again very seriously about the Judgment Day and the Left Side. Now, there were certain people he would like to have with him on the Left Side, on That Day. He thought about church and how he could never go back because of the place where the deacons had made him tell his first great lie. He wondered whether it was because he did not want to have to go back to church on Sunday mornings that he had not quit. He wondered if it was because of the money or going to church or because of the window that he had not walked out of the store with his brother. That would have been good: the two of them walking out together. But he had not done it and now he could not make himself know why. Suddenly, in the night, he heard the Barefoot Lady, under the blue-and-white Herbert L. Jones sign, screaming.

"*Mr. Jones! I love you, Mr. Jones!*"

But the sound did not frighten him now. He pushed against his brother's back.

"Eddie? *Eddie.*"

"Yeah?"

"Wonder why she does it?"

"I donno."

"I wonder why," he said again.

Eddie did not answer. But after the sound of the woman came again his brother turned over in the bed and said to Thomas:

"You gonna quit?"

"No."

"Why not? We could always carry papers."

"I donno. I just ain't gonna quit. Not now."

"Well, *I* ain't goin' back. I'll go back in there one day when I'm rich. I'm gonna go in and buy everything but hamburger."

"Yeah," said Thomas. But he was not listening to his brother.

"Mr. Jones! I love you, Mr. Jones!"

"And I'm gonna learn all the big words in the world too," his brother went on. "When I go back in there I'm gonna be talking so big that fat old Miss Sarah won't even be able to understand me."

"That'll be good," said Thomas. But he was thinking to himself now.

"You'll see," said Eddie. "I'll do it, too."

But Thomas did not answer him. He was waiting for the sound to come again.

"Mr. Jones! I love you, Mr. Jones!"

And then he knew why the Barefoot Lady came to that place almost every night to cry where there was no one alive in the building to hear or care about her sound. He felt what she must feel. And he knew now why the causes of the sound had always bothered him and would always bother him. There was a word in his mind now, a big word, that made good sense of her sound and the burning feeling thing he felt inside himself. It was all very clear, and now he understood that the Barefoot Lady came in the night not because she really loved Mr. Jones or because he had once buried someone for her for free, or even because she liked the blue-and-white lighted sign. She came always in the night to scream because she, like himself, was in misery, and did not know what else to do.

ON TRAINS

THE WAITERS SAY she got on the train in Chicago, after transferring from Dearborn Station. She was plump and matronly and her glasses were tinted so that she might have been a tourist seeking protection from the sun; but there was neither sun nor fresh air on the train and she was very pale and a little wrinkled, the way clerks or indoor people grow after many years of their protected, colorless kind of life. She was, indeed, that nondescript type of person one might be aware of but never really see in a supermarket or at a bargain basement sale, carefully and methodically fingering each item; or on a busy street corner waiting for the light to change while others, with less conscious respect for the letter of the law, flowed around her. She rode for a whole day before coming into the dining car for a meal: then she had the $1.95 Special. She asked for buttermilk and wanted "lightbread" instead of rolls. The black waiters all grinned at each other in their secret way.

When she finished her meal she sat reading a book and looking out at the yellow and green flatlands of North Dakota until the steward had to ask her to leave so that the waiters could clean up the table for the next setting. She did not protest, but left with an indignant flourish of her dress. The automatic door to the car leading to the Pullman section hissed angrily behind her. The steward called her a bitch between his teeth and the waiter who had served her, standing next to the steward with his tray under his arm, grinned broadly, showing his own smoke-stained teeth. But when he saw that she had left no tip he called her a cheap bitch aloud and the steward scowled at him.

After the last setting the waiters sat down to eat their dinner. Two Pullman Porters came in with their coffee cans, begging for handouts. They were very greedy and, if given one can of free coffee, would continue to come back for more during the length of the trip, as if the first can had entitled them to all that they could drink. They sat down at the waiters' table and watched the waiters eat. The waiters were very greedy too. They ate ravenously. The porters watched the waiters for a while, then one of them closed his eyes and began to doze. The other one, an old fellow with aged and tired eyes like an owl's, looked out at the floating gold of the sunset across the passing wheatfields. He watched until the fields became patterns of black and fading gold. Then he turned to the waiters.

"We got a old Southern gal back there," he said.

"We had her up here," one of the waiters said between huge mouthfuls of beef. "She got good service but she didn't leave no tip."

"She had me polishin' her shoes," the porter said, "but I don't reckon she'll pay off when she gets off. I didn't put much work out on it anyway." He stretched his thin legs under the table. They cracked with the sound of dead autumn branches underfoot.

A woman in pants passed through the car. Her hair was cut somewhat like a little girl's Dutch Boy and a ringlet of it curled against her cheek. She blew at it out of the corner of her mouth and smiled knowingly at the men seated around the table. "Which way to the club car?" she asked. Her lipstick was above the line of her mouth so that it looked like a red moustache. She was not at all pretty and not at all young.

"Two cars ahead," one waiter said.

She turned to go, took a few steps and then looked back at the men. The two waiters were looking her over, one porter was still dozing, and the other, the tired one, was seemingly not aware of her.

"How late does it stay open?"

"Till twelve," the same waiter said.

"Chicago time," the other waiter added.

They watched her move through the door.

"She'll tip big tomorrow," one of them said.

"Yeah."

"That old biddy knows where the club car is. She been in there all day. I seen her battin' them greasy eyes at John Perry on the bar."

"Maybe he'll take care of business for her tonight," the

tired Pullman Porter said. But there was no humor in it, and all of their laughs were only polite.

"If he does she'll tip big tomorrow," one of the waiters said again.

The porter with the owl eyes pushed the dozing porter. "Time to get the beds down, Tim," he said. Tim got up slowly and they took their coffee cans and trudged down the aisle toward the Pullman section. As they reached the door it opened and the lady who had transferred from Dearborn came into the car. The two porters stood on either side of the aisle and let her pass between them. They wore white jackets with silver buttons which were embossed: "Pullman Company." Together with their caps with silver plates, which also read "Pullman Porter," and black pants, they looked like two painted black statues before the entrance to some fine suburban home. She did not notice them, but passed directly through the car, leaving behind her a scent of something sweet and strong.

When she entered the club car the woman with the Dutch bob was sitting at the bar talking to John Perry, the bartender, who stood behind the bar leaning with his arms on its waxed red surface. They were very close and the Dutch woman was smiling mysteriously. There was no one else in the car. The Dearborn lady seated herself at a deuce near the far end of the car and began to stare at John Perry as he said something low and soft and smile-provoking to the painted thing on the stool across from him. The Dearborn lady cleared her throat. John Perry placed his dark, thick hand closer to the other, softer hand on the bar and did not look up. The painted woman made a throaty chuckle, like the confusing sound one might hear near a car parked by a frog pond on a summer night.

"I want some service," the lady at the end of the car finally said. "I've been here for ten minutes now and I want some service."

The bartender looked annoyed as he went over to her table. "What'll it be, lady?" he said. His voice was deep and smooth and almost as greasy as the painted woman's lips; and it had that familiar ring of professional servitude, which is peculiar to small, serving people who like their work.

"I want a Benedictine and brandy."

"No Benedictine. This is a train, lady."

She paused. "I'll have a crème de menthe then."

"We don't have that neither."

"Try bourbon and water, honey," the woman at the bar said, and she lifted her glass for the woman to see. "He makes it very good. I'm going to have another one myself." She looked at the bartender as she pushed a five-dollar bill across the bar. "Make yourself one too," she told him.

The lady at the deuce looked at her fiercely.

She finally ordered a rosé, paid for it, and settled back, taking turns watching the immediate reflections of the two at the bar in the window next to her face and the darkness of the passing countryside beyond their reflections. The train lumbered on and it made the only noise, save for an occasional giggle and a deep-throated chuckle from the bar. Finally the woman got up from the stool and said, "See you later on" to the bartender. She said it with a contrived, unnatural seductivity and took her time moving out of the car. The Dearborn lady, still seated at the table and facing the window, saw it all through her tinted glasses.

The bartender began to whistle as he washed the glasses. He was a robust fellow but he moved very gracefully behind the bar, like a dancer. Still, he splashed a great deal of water on the floor. He glanced over at the lady once or twice as she, in turn, looked alternately at the darkness beyond the thick window glass and at him. But only her eyes moved. Then the man moved out from behind the bar and came toward her. She stiffened and gathered her purse and got up, all very quickly. He was wiping the tables and whistling as she hurried out of the car.

II

IN THE PULLMAN CAR, the porter was still making the beds. He shuffled from one roomette to the next, not wasting a single step. The occupants came out of their rooms and stood in the hall while he swished and tucked their sheets. Then he knocked on the Dearborn lady's door. "Porter!" he barked, the way a street-corner concessionaire would say "Hot Dogs!" There was no answer, so he went in and began turning down the bed. She came up behind him and watched his back as he moved about the small compartment. She was breathing very hard.

"What time do you lock the doors to the car?" she asked.

"The doors ain't never locked," he said, not turning to face her.

"How do you keep people out?" She paused, and then said: "My luggage is in the hall. It's very expensive."

"I'll watch out for it. I sit up all night."

"Inside the car?"

"Yes ma'am."

"But I . . . we have to sleep. We have to sleep in here," she said. She was very excited now.

"Yes ma'am." He did not stop his work; nor did he look at her, but answered her questions and made the bed with the proficiency and cool detachment of one used to confronting stupidity in the intelligent. It was bargained and paid for in the price of her ticket and his was a patient and polite endurance of her right to be stupid. "I'm a Pullman Porter," he said. "I been a Pullman Porter for forty-three years." He had finished the bed and he smoothed down a light ripple in the red blanket. His hands were rough and wrinkled and the backs of his fingers were very black. "Forty-three years," he repeated reminiscently, half to himself. She could not see his eyes.

"Well, you can't stay in here tonight," she said, and moved into the small compartment as if to possess it entirely with her presence.

The porter backed out. "It's my job," he said.

She was extremely nervous now and ran her hands lightly over the sides of her dress. Her hands stuck to the thin silk. "You go get the Pullman Conductor," she said. "I can talk to him." She began to pace up and down the little length of the roomette.

The porter returned in a few minutes with the Pullman Conductor. The blue-suited conductor entered the compartment while the porter stood outside the door and watched them, his dark old eyes flashing from one face to the other.

"He sits up in the car, lady," the conductor said. "It's his job. He has to be here if anyone rings for him at night." The conductor was very irritated. He had already started to undress for bed and his tie hung loosely about his neck. The lady was perspiring now and the little beads of sweat glistened on her temples in the glare of the white light overhead.

"I can't and I won't sleep in the same car with that . . . that gentleman!"

"That's your business if you don't sleep, lady," the conductor said. "He stays in the car." The conductor was very mad now. The lines in his forehead grew very red and his nose, which was small, grew larger and redder with his controlled breathing.

"We have a *right* to sleep here without these people coming in *doing* things."

"What's he done to you, lady?"

"He's black! He's black!" And she said it with the exasperation and utter defeat of an inexperienced teacher whose patience has been exhausted and who can only stamp the right answer into the mind of a stupid child.

"He's a porter," the conductor said.

The porter, who stood all the while like a child waiting for punishment, seemed to droop and wither and grow smaller; and his eyes, which had only minutes before flashed brightly from the face of the conductor to the enraged face of the lady, now seemed to dull and turn inward as only those who have learned to suffer silently can turn their eyes inward. He was a very old man and he grew older, even older than his occupation or the oldest and most obsequious Pullman Porter.

People were looking out of their compartments and the Dearborn lady, hearing them, raised her voice in a plea. "He sleeps in here. He sleeps in here with us!" she shouted to them. Down the hall, the painted woman opened the door to Compartment G and listened and smiled and shook her head, and then closed the door again. And the rest listened and weighed the thought, which was a new one deserving some consideration. But the conductor said that it was necessary for comfort and they agreed and returned to their rooms. Only the porter stood outside the door looking guilty.

It was finally decided that the Dearborn lady would take a seat in the coaches for the night. She wanted it that way. The porter would sleep as he had always slept: sitting up in the back of the car with his eyes closed and his mind awake and his coffee can by his side and the small bright night-light over his bowed head, and his ear next to the buzzer in case someone should ring. Everyone agreed that it was the way things should be; it was necessary for comfort, and besides, it was his job.

And later that night, when John Perry, the bartender, who danced and splashed a great deal of water when he washed glasses, stole into the dark sleeping car, he paused for a minute before the bent old man on the porter's seat. The coffee can had fallen over on the seat and John Perry picked it up and placed it on the floor next to the old man's feet. Then he knocked very softly on the door to Compartment G. And after a while it was opened and quickly closed behind him.

A SOLO SONG: FOR DOC

S O YOU WANT TO KNOW THIS BUSINESS, youngblood? So you want to be a Waiter's Waiter? The
Commissary gives you a book with all the rules
and tells you to learn them. And you do, and think that
is all there is to it. A big, thick black book. Poor youngblood.

Look at me. *I* am a Waiter's Waiter. I know all the
moves, all the pretty, fine moves that big book will never
teach you. *I* built this railroad with my moves; and so did
Sheik Beasley and Uncle T. Boone and Danny Jackson,
and so did Doc Craft. That book they made you learn
came from our moves and from our heads. There was a
time when six of us, big men, danced at the same time
in that little Pantry without touching and shouted orders
to the sweating paddies in the kitchen. There was a time
when they *had* to respect us because our sweat and our
moves supported them. We knew the service and the pad-

dies, even the green dishwashers knew that we did and didn't give us the crap they pull on you.

Do you know how to sneak a Blackplate to a nasty cracker? Do you know how to rub asses with five other men in the Pantry getting their orders together and still know that you are a man, just like them? Do you know how to bullshit while you work and keep the paddies in their places with your bullshit? Do you know how to breathe down the back of an old lady's dress to hustle a bigger tip?

No. You are summer stuff, youngblood. I am old, my moves are not so good any more, but I know this business. The Commissary hires you for the summer because they don't want to let anyone get as old as me on them. I'm sixty-three, but they can't fire me: I'm in the Union. They can't lay me off for fucking up: I know this business too well. And so they hire you, youngblood, for the summer when the tourists come, and in September you go away with some tips in your pocket to buy pussy and they wait all winter for me to die. I *am* dying, youngblood, and so is this business. Both of us will die together. There'll always be summer stuff like you, but the big men, the big trains, are dying every day and everybody can see it. And nobody but us who are dying with them gives a damn.

Look at the big picture at the end of the car, youngblood. That's the man who built this road. He's in your history books. He's probably in that big black bible you read. He was a great man. He hated people. He didn't want to feed them but the government said he had to. He didn't want to hire me, but he needed me to feed the people. I know this, youngblood, and that is why that book is

written for you and that is why I have never read it. That
is why you get nervous and jump up to polish the pepper
and salt shakers when the word comes down the line that
an inspector is getting on at the next stop. That is why you
warm the toast covers for every cheap old lady who wants
to get coffee and toast and good service for sixty-five cents
and a dime tip. You know that he needs you only for the
summer and that hundreds of youngbloods like you want
to work this summer to buy that pussy in Chicago and
Portland and Seattle. The man uses you, but he doesn't
need you. But me he needs for the winter, when you are
gone, and to teach you something in the summer about
this business you can't get from that big black book. He
needs me and he knows it and I know it. That is why I am
sitting here when there are tables to be cleaned and linen
to be changed and silver to be washed and polished. He
needs me to die. That is why I am taking my time. I know
it. And I will take his service with me when I die, just like
the Sheik did and like Percy Fields did, and like Doc.

Who are they? Why do I keep talking about them? Let
me think about it. I guess it is because they were the last
of the Old School, like me. We made this road. We got a
million miles of walking up and down these cars under
our feet. Doc Craft was the Old School, like me. He was a
Waiter's Waiter. He danced down these aisles with us and
swung his tray with the roll of the train, never spilling in
all his trips a single cup of coffee. He could carry his tray
on two fingers, or on one and a half if he wanted, and he
knew all the tricks about hustling tips there are to know.
He could work anybody. The girls at the Northland in
Chicago knew Doc, and the girls at the Haverville in Se-

attle, and the girls at the Step-Inn in Portland and all the girls in Winnipeg knew Doc Craft.

But wait. It is just 1:30 and the first call for dinner is not until 5:00. You want to kill some time; you want to hear about the Old School and how it was in my day. If you look in that black book you would see that you should be polishing silver now. Look out the window; this is North Dakota, this is Jerry's territory. Jerry, the Unexpected Inspector. Shouldn't you polish the shakers or clean out the Pantry or squeeze oranges, or maybe change the linen on the tables? Jerry Ewald is sly. The train may stop in the middle of this wheatfield and Jerry may get on. He lives by that book. He knows where to look for dirt and mistakes. Jerry Ewald, the Unexpected Inspector. He knows where to look; he knows how to get you. He got Doc.

Now you want to know about him, about the Old School. You have even put aside your book of rules. But see how you keep your finger in the pages as if the book was more important than what I tell you. That's a bad move, and it tells on you. You will be a waiter. But you will never be a Waiter's Waiter. The Old School died with Doc, and the very last of it is dying with me. What happened to Doc? Take your finger out of the pages, youngblood, and I will tell you about a kind of life these rails will never carry again.

When your father was a boy playing with himself behind the barn, Doc was already a man and knew what the thing was for. But he got tired of using it when he wasn't much older than you, and he set his mind on making money. He had no skills. He was black. He got hungry. On Christmas Day in 1916, the story goes, he wandered

into the Chicago stockyards and over to a dining car waiting to be connected up to the main train for the Chicago-
to-San Francisco run. He looked up through the kitchen
door at the chef storing supplies for the kitchen and said:
"I'm hungry."

"What do you want *me* to do about it?" the Swede chef
said.

"I'll work," said Doc.

That Swede was Chips Magnusson, fresh off the boat
and lucky to be working himself. He did not know yet
that he should save all extra work for other Swedes fresh
off the boat. He later learned this by living. But at that
time he considered a moment, bit into one of the fresh
apples stocked for apple pie, chewed considerably, spit out
the seeds and then waved the black on board the big train.
"You can eat all you want," he told Doc. "But you work
all I tell you."

He put Doc to rolling dough for the apple pies and
the train began rolling for Doc. It never stopped. He fell
in love with the feel of the wheels under his feet clicking
against the track and he got the rhythm of the wheels in
him and learned, like all of us, how to roll with them and
move with them. After that first trip Doc was never at
home on the ground. He worked everything in the kitchen
from putting out dough to second cook, in six years. And
then, when the Commissary saw that he was good and
would soon be going for one of the chef's spots they saved
for the Swedes, they put him out of the kitchen and told
him to learn this waiter business; and told him to learn
how to bullshit on the other side of the Pantry. He was
almost thirty, youngblood, when he crossed over to the

black side of the Pantry. I wasn't there when he made his first trip as a waiter, but from what they tell me of that trip I know that he was broke in by good men. Pantryman was Sheik Beasley, who stayed high all the time and let the waiters steal anything they wanted as long as they didn't bother his reefers. Danny Jackson, who was black and knew Shakespeare before the world said he could work with it, was second man. Len Dickey was third, Reverend Hendricks was fourth, and Uncle T. Boone, who even in those early days could not straighten his back, ran fifth. Doc started in as sixth waiter, the "mule." They pulled some shit on him at first because they didn't want somebody fresh out of a paddy kitchen on the crew. They messed with his orders, stole his plates, picked up his tips on the sly, and made him do all the dirty work. But when they saw that he could take the shit without getting hot and when they saw that he was set on being a waiter, even though he was older than most of them, they settled down and began to teach him this business and all the words and moves and slickness that made it a good business.

His real name was Leroy Johnson, I think, but when Danny Jackson saw how cool and neat he was in his moves, and how he handled the plates, he began to call him "the Doctor." Then the Sheik, coming down from his high one day after missing the lunch and dinner service, saw how Doc had taken over his station and collected fat tips from his tables by telling the passengers that the Sheik had had to get off back along the line because of a heart attack. The Sheik liked that because he saw that Doc understood crackers and how they liked nothing better than knowing that a nigger had died on the job, giving them service. The

Sheik was impressed. And he was not an easy man to impress because he knew too much about life and had to stay high most of the time. And when Doc would not split the tips with him, the Sheik got mad at first and called Doc a barrel of motherfuckers and some other words you would not recognize. But he was impressed. And later that night, in the crew car when the others were gambling and drinking and bullshitting about the women they had working the corners for them, the Sheik came over to Doc's bunk and said: "You're a crafty motherfucker."

"Yeah?" says Doc.

"Yeah," says the Sheik, who did not say much. "You're a crafty motherfucker but I like you." Then he got into the first waiter's bunk and lit up again. But Reverend Hendricks, who always read his Bible before going to sleep and who always listened to anything the Sheik said because he knew the Sheik only said something when it was important, heard what was said and remembered it. After he put his Bible back in his locker, he walked over to Doc's bunk and looked down at him. "Mister Doctor Craft," the Reverend said. "Youngblood Doctor Craft."

"Yeah?" says Doc.

"Yeah," says Reverend Hendricks. "That's who you are."

And that's who he was from then on.

II

I CAME TO THE ROAD away from the war. This was after '41, when people at home were looking for Japs under their beds every night. I did not want to fight because there was no money in it and I didn't want to go overseas to work in a kitchen. The big war was on and a lot of soldiers crossed the country to get to it, and as long as a black man fed them on trains he did not have to go to that war. I could have got a job in a Chicago factory, but there was more money on the road and it was safer. And after a while it got into your blood so that you couldn't leave it for anything. The road got into my blood the way it got into everybody's; the way going to the war got in the blood of redneck farm boys and the crazy Polacks from Chicago. It was all right for them to go to the war. They were young and stupid. And they died that way. I played it smart. I was almost thirty-five and I didn't want to go. But I took *them* and fed them and gave them good times on their way to the war, and for that I did not have to go. The soldiers had plenty of money and were afraid not to spend it all before they got to the ships on the Coast. And we gave them ways to spend it on the trains.

Now in those days there was plenty of money going around and everybody stole from everybody. The kitchen stole food from the company and the company knew it and wouldn't pay good wages. There were no rules in those days, there was no black book to go by and nobody said what you couldn't eat or steal. The paddy cooks used to toss boxes of steaks off the train in the Chicago yards for people at the restaurants there who paid them, cash. These were the days when ordinary people had to have red stamps or blue stamps to get powdered eggs and white lard to mix with red powder to make their own butter.

The stewards stole from the company and from the

waiters; the waiters stole from the stewards and the company and from each other. I stole. Doc stole. Even Reverend Hendricks put his Bible far back in his locker and stole with us. You didn't want a man on your crew who didn't steal. He made it bad for everybody. And if the steward saw that he was a dummy and would never get to stealing, he wrote him up for something and got him off the crew so as not to slow down the rest of us. We had a redneck cracker steward from Alabama by the name of Casper who used to say: "*Jesus Christ*! I ain't got time to hate you niggers, I'm making so much money." He used to keep all his cash at home under his bed in a cardboard box because he was afraid to put it in the bank.

Doc and Sheik Beasley and me were on the same crew together all during the war. Even in those days, as young as we were, we knew how to be Old Heads. We organized for the soldiers. We had to wear skullcaps all the time because the crackers said our hair was poison and didn't want any of it to fall in their food. The Sheik didn't mind wearing one. He kept reefers in his and used to sell them to the soldiers for double what he paid for them in Chicago and three times what he paid the Chinamen in Seattle. That's why we called him the Sheik. After every meal the Sheik would get in the linen closet and light up. Sometimes he wouldn't come out for days. Nobody gave a damn, though; we were all too busy stealing and working. And there was more for us to get as long as he didn't come out.

Doc used to sell bootlegged booze to the soldiers; that was his specialty. He had redcaps in the Chicago stations telling the soldiers who to ask for on the train. He was an open operator and had to give the steward a cut, but he still made a pile of money. That's why that old cracker always kept us together on his crew. We were the three best moneymakers he ever had. That's something you should learn, youngblood. They can't love you for being you. They only love you if you make money for them. All that talk these days about integration and brotherhood, that's a lot of bullshit. The man will love you as long as he can make money with you. I made money. And old Casper had to love me in the open although I knew he called me a nigger at home when he had put that money in his big cardboard box. I know he loved me on the road in the wartime because I used to bring in the biggest moneymakers. I used to handle the girls.

Look out that window. See all that grass and wheat? Look at that big farm boy cutting it. Look at that burnt cracker on that tractor. He probably has a wife who married him because she didn't know what else to do. Back during wartime the girls in this part of the country knew what to do. They got on the trains at night.

You can look out that window all day and run around all the stations when we stop, but you'll never see a black man in any of these towns. You know why, youngblood? These farmers hate you. They still remember when their girls came out of these towns and got on the trains at night. They've been running black men and dark Indians out of these towns for years. They hate anything dark that's not that way because of the sun. Right now there are big farm girls with hair under their arms on the corners in San Francisco, Chicago, Seattle and Minneapolis who got started on these cars back during wartime. The farmers still remember that and they hate you and me for it. But it wasn't for me they got on. Nobody wants a stiff, smelly farm girl when there are sporting women to be got for a dollar in the cities. It was for the soldiers they got on. It was just business to me. But they hate you and me anyway.

I got off in one of these towns once, a long time after the war, just to get a drink while the train changed engines. Everybody looked at me and by the time I got to a bar there were ten people on my trail. I was drinking a fast one when the sheriff came in the bar.

"What are you doing here?" he asks me.

"Just getting a shot," I say.

He spit on the floor. "How long you plan to be here?"

"I don't know," I say, just to be nasty.

"There ain't no jobs here," he says.

"I wasn't looking," I say.

"We don't want you here."

"I don't give a good goddamn," I say.

He pulled his gun on me. "All right, coon, back on the train," he says.

"Wait a minute," I tell him. "Let me finish my drink."

He knocked my glass over with his gun. "You're finished *now*," he says. "Pull your ass out of here *now*!"

I didn't argue.

I was the night man. After dinner it was my job to pull the cloths off the tables and put paddings on. Then I cut out the lights and locked both doors. There was a big farm girl from Minot named Hilda who could take on eight or ten soldiers in one night, white soldiers. These white boys don't know how to last. I would stand by the door and when the soldiers came back from the club car they would pay me and I would let them in. Some of the girls could make as much as one hundred dollars in one night. And I always made twice as much. Soldiers don't care what they do with their money. They just have to spend it.

We never bothered with the girls ourselves. It was just business as far as we were concerned. But there was one dummy we had with us once, a boy from the South named Willie Joe something who handled the dice. He was really hot for one of these farm girls. He used to buy her good whiskey and he hated to see her go in the car at night to wait for the soldiers. He was a real dummy. One time I heard her tell him: "It's all right. They can have my body. I know I'm black inside. *Jesus*, I'm so black inside I wisht I was black all over!"

And this dummy Willie Joe said: "Baby, *don't you ever change!*"

I knew we had to get rid of him before he started trouble. So we had the steward bump him off the crew as soon as we could find a good man to handle the gambling. That old redneck Casper was glad to do it. He saw what was going on.

But you want to hear about Doc, you say, so you can get back to your reading. What can I tell you? The road got into his blood? He liked being a waiter? You won't understand this, but he did. There were no Civil Rights or marches or riots for something better in those days. In those days a man found something he liked to do and liked it from then on because he couldn't help himself. What did he like about the road? He liked what I liked: the money, owning the car, running it, telling the soldiers what to do,

hustling a bigger tip from some old maid by looking under her dress and laughing at her, having all the girls at
the Haverville Hotel waiting for us to come in for stop-
over, the power we had to beat them up or lay them if we
wanted. He liked running free and not being married to
some bitch who would spend his money when he was out
of town or give it to some stud. He liked getting drunk
with the boys up at Andy's, setting up the house and then
passing out from drinking too much, knowing that the
boys would get him home.

I ran with that one crew all during wartime and they,
Doc, the Sheik and Reverend Hendricks, had taken me
under their wings. *I* was still a youngblood then, and
Doc liked me a lot. But he never said that much to me; he
was not a talker. The Sheik had taught him the value of
silence in things that really matter. We roomed together in
Chicago at Mrs. Wright's place in those days. Mrs. Wright
didn't allow women in the rooms and Doc liked that, because after being out for a week and after stopping over
in those hotels along the way, you get tired of women and
bullshit and need your privacy. We weren't like you. We
didn't need a woman every time we got hard. We knew
when we had to have it and when we didn't. And we didn't
spend all our money on it, either. You youngbloods think
the way to get a woman is to let her see how you handle
your money. That's stupid. The way to get a woman is to
let her see how you handle other women. But you'll never
believe that until it's too late to do you any good.

Doc knew how to handle women. I can remember a
time in a Winnipeg hotel how he ran a bitch out of his
room because he had had enough of it and did not need

her any more. I was in the next room and heard every-thing.

"Come on, Doc," the bitch said. "Come on honey, let's do it one more time."

"Hell no," Doc said. "I'm tired and I don't want to any more."

"How can you say you're tired?" the bitch said. "How can you say you're tired when you didn't go but two times?"

"I'm tired of it," Doc said, "because I'm tired of you. And I'm tired of you because I'm tired of it and bitches like you in all the towns I been in. You drain a man. And I know if I beat you, you'll still come back when I hit you again. *That's* why I'm tired. I'm tired of having things around I don't care about."

"What *do* you care about, Doc?" the bitch said.

"I don't know," Doc said. "I guess I care about moving and being somewhere else when I want to be. I guess I care about going out, and coming in to wait for the time to go out again."

"You crazy, Doc," the bitch said.

"Yeah?" Doc said. "I guess I'm crazy all right."

Later that bitch knocked on my door and I did it for her because she was just a bitch and I knew Doc wouldn't want her again. I don't think he ever wanted a bitch again. I never saw him with one after that time. He was just a little over fifty then and could have still done whatever he wanted with women.

The war ended. The farm boys who got back from the war did not spend money on their way home. They did not want to spend any more money on women, and the girls did not get on at night any more. Some of them went into the cities and turned pro. Some of them stayed in the towns and married the farm boys who got back from the war. Things changed on the road. The Commissary started putting that book of rules together and told us to stop stealing. They were losing money on passengers now because of the airplanes and they began to really tighten up and started sending inspectors down along the line to check on us. They started sending in spotters, too. One of them caught that redneck Casper writing out a check for two dollars less than he had charged the spotter. The Commissary got him in on the rug for it. I wasn't there, but they told me he said to the General Superintendent: "Why are you getting on me, a white man, for a lousy son-of-a-bitching two bucks? There's niggers out there been stealing for *years!*"

"Who?" the General Superintendent asked.

And Casper couldn't say anything because he had that cardboard box full of money still under his bed and knew he would have to tell how he got it if any of us was brought in. So he said nothing.

"Who?" the General Superintendent asked him again.

"Why, all them nigger waiters steal, *everybody knows that!*"

"And the cooks, what about them?" the Superintendent said.

"They're white," said Casper.

They never got the story out of him and he was fired. He used the money to open a restaurant someplace in Indiana and I heard later that he started a branch of the Klan in his town. One day he showed up at the station and told Doc, Reverend Hendricks and me: "I'll see you boys get *yours*. Damn if I'm takin' the rap for you niggers."

We just laughed in his face because we knew he could do nothing to us through the Commissary. But just to be safe we stopped stealing so much. But they did get the Sheik, though. One day an inspector got on in the mountains just outside of Whitefish and grabbed him right out of that linen closet. The Sheik had been smoking in there all day and he was high and laughing when they pulled him off the train.

That was the year we got in the Union. The crackers and Swedes finally let us in after we paid off. We really stopped stealing and got organized and there wasn't a damn thing the company could do about it, although it tried like hell to buy us out. And to get back at us, they put their heads together and began to make up that big book of rules you keep your finger in. Still, *we* knew the service and they had to write the book the way we gave the service and at first there was nothing for the Old School men to learn. We got seniority through the Union, and as long as we gave the service and didn't steal, they couldn't touch us. So they began changing the rules, and sending us notes about the service. Little changes at first, like how the initials on the doily should always face the customer, and how the silver should be taken off the tables between meals. But we were getting old and set in our old service, and it got harder and harder learning all those little changes. And we had to learn new stuff all the time because there was no telling when an inspector would get on and catch us giving bad service. It was hard as hell. It was hard because we knew that the company was out to break up the Old School. The Sheik was gone, and we knew that Reverend Hendricks or Uncle T. or Danny Jackson would go soon because they stood for the Old School, just like the Sheik. But what bothered us most was knowing that they would go for Doc first, before anyone else, because he loved the road so much.

Doc was over sixty-five then and had taken to drinking hard when we were off. But he never touched a drop when we were on the road. I used to wonder whether he drank because being a Waiter's Waiter was getting hard or because he had to do something until his next trip. I could never figure it. When we had our layovers he would spend all his time in Andy's, setting up the house. He had no wife, no relatives, not even a hobby. He just drank. Pretty soon the slicksters at Andy's got to using him for a good thing. They commenced putting the touch on him because they saw he was getting old and knew he didn't have far to go, and they would never have to pay him back. Those of us who were close to him tried to pull his coat, but it didn't help. He didn't talk about himself much, he didn't talk much about anything that wasn't related to the road; but when I tried to hip him once about the hustlers and how they were closing in on him, he just took another shot and said:

"I don't need no money. Nobody's jiving me. I'm jiving them. You know I can still pull in a hundred in tips in one trip. I *know* this business."

"Yeah, I know, Doc," I said. "But how many more trips can you make before you have to stop?"

"I ain't never gonna stop. Trips are all I know and I'll be making them as long as these trains haul people."

"That's just it," I said. "They don't *want* to haul people any more. The planes do that. The big roads want freight now. Look how they hire youngbloods just for the busy seasons just so they won't get any seniority in the winter. Look how all the Old School waiters are dropping out. They got the Sheik; Percy Fields just lucked up and died before they got to *him*; they almost got Reverend Hendricks. Even *Uncle T.* is going to retire! And they'll get us too."

"Not me," said Doc. "I know my moves. This old fox can still dance with a tray and handle four tables at the same time. I can still bait a queer and make the old ladies tip big. There's no waiter better than me and I know it."

"Sure, Doc," I said. "I know it too. But please save your money. Don't be a dummy. There'll come a day when you just can't get up to go out and they'll put you on the ground for good."

Doc looked at me like he had been shot. "Who taught you the moves when you were just a raggedy-ass waiter?"

"You did, Doc," I said.

"Who's always the first man down in the yard at train-time?" He threw down another shot. "Who's there sitting in the car every tenth morning while you other old heads are still at home pulling on your longjohns?"

I couldn't say anything. He was right and we both knew it.

"I have to go out," he told me. "Going out is my whole life, I wait for that tenth morning. I ain't never missed a trip and I don't mean to."

What could I say to him, youngblood? What can I say to you? He had to go out, not for the money; it was in his blood. You have to go out too, but it's for the money you go. You hate going out and you love coming in. He loved going out and he hated coming in. Would *you* listen if I told you to stop spending your money on pussy in Chicago? Would he listen if I told him to save *his* money? To stop setting up the bar at Andy's? No. Old men are just as bad as young men when it comes to money. They can't think. They always try to buy what they should have for free. And what they buy, after they have it, is nothing.

They called Doc into the Commissary and the doctors told him he had lumbago and a bad heart and was weak from drinking too much, and they wanted him to get down for his own good. He wouldn't do it. Tesdale, the General Superintendent, called him in and told him that he had enough years in the service to pull down a big pension and that the company would pay for a retirement party for him, since he was the oldest waiter working, and invite all the Old School waiters to see him off, if he would come down. Doc said no. He knew that the Union had to back him. He knew that he could ride as long as he made the trains on time and as long as he knew the service. And he knew that he could not leave the road.

The company called in its lawyers to go over the Union contract. I wasn't there, but Len Dickey was in on the meeting because of his office in the Union. He told me about it later. Those fat company lawyers took the contract apart and went through all their books. They took the seniority clause apart word by word, trying to figure a way to get at Doc. But they had written it airtight back in the days when the company *needed* waiters, and there was nothing in it about compulsory retirement. Not a word. The paddies in the Union must have figured that waiters didn't *need* a new contract when they let us in, and they had let us come in under the old one thinking that all waiters would die on the job, or drink themselves to death when they were still young, or die from buying too much pussy, or just quit when they had put in enough time to draw a pension. But *nothing* in the whole contract could help them get rid of Doc Craft. They were sweating, they were working so hard. And all the time Tesdale, the General Superintendent, was calling them sons-of-bitches for not earning their money. But there was nothing the company lawyers could do but turn the pages of their big books and sweat and promise Tesdale that they would find some way if he gave them more time.

The word went out from the Commissary: "Get Doc." The stewards got it from the assistant superintendents: "Get Doc." Since they could not get him to retire, they were determined to catch him giving bad service. He had more seniority than most other waiters, so they couldn't bump him off our crew. In fact, all the waiters with more seniority than Doc were on the crew with him. There were four of us from the Old School: me, Doc, Uncle T. Boone, and Danny Jackson. Reverend Hendricks wasn't running regular any more; he was spending all his Sundays preaching in his Church on the South Side because he knew what was coming and wanted to have something steady going for him in Chicago when his time came. Fifth and sixth men on that crew were two hardheads who had read the book. The steward was Crouse, and he really didn't want to put the screws to Doc but he couldn't help himself. Everybody wants to work. So Crouse started in to riding Doc, sometimes about moving too fast, sometimes about not moving fast enough. I was on the crew, I saw it all. Crouse would seat four singles at the same table, on Doc's station, and Doc had to take care of all four different orders at the same time. He was seventy-three, but that didn't stop him, knowing this business the way he did. It just slowed him down some. But Crouse got on him even for that and would chew him out in front of the passengers, hoping that he'd start cursing and bother the passengers so that they would complain to the company. It never worked, though. Doc just played it cool. He'd look into Crouse's eyes and know what was going on. And then he'd lay on his good service, the only service he knew, and the passengers would see how good he was with all that age on his back and they would get mad at the steward, and leave Doc a bigger tip when they left.

The Commissary sent out spotters to catch him giving bad service. These were pale-white little men in glasses who never looked you in the eye, but who always felt the plate to see if it was warm. And there were the old maids, who like that kind of work, who would order shrimp or crabmeat cocktails or celery and olive plates because they knew how the rules said these things had to be made. And when they came, when Doc brought them out, they would look to see if the oyster fork was stuck into the thing, and look out the window a long time.

"Ain't no use trying to fight it," Uncle T. Boone told Doc in the crew car one night, "the black waiter is *doomed*. Look at all the good restaurants, the class restaurants in Chicago. *You* can't work in them. Them white waiters got those jobs sewed up fine."

"I can be a waiter anywhere," says Doc. "I know the business and I like it and I can do it anywhere."

"The black waiter is doomed," Uncle T. says again. "The whites is taking over the service in the good places. And when they run you off of here, you won't have no place to go."

"They won't run me off of here," says Doc. "As long as I give the right service they can't touch me."

"You're a goddamn *fool!*" says Uncle T. "You're a nigger and you ain't got no rights except what the Union says you have. And that ain't worth a damn because when the Commissary finally gets you, those niggers won't lift a finger to help you."

"Leave off him," I say to Boone. "If anybody ought to be put off it's you. You ain't had your back straight for thirty years. You even make the crackers sick the way you keep bowing and folding your hands and saying, 'Thank you, Mr. Boss.' Fifty years ago that would of got you a bigger tip," I say, "but now it ain't worth a shit. And every time you do it the crackers hate you. And every time I see you serving with that skullcap on *I* hate you. The Union said we didn't have to wear them *eighteen years ago!* Why can't you take it off?"

Boone just sat on his bunk with his skullcap in his lap, leaning against his big belly. He knew I was telling the truth and he knew he wouldn't change. But he said: "That's the trouble with the Negro waiter today. He ain't got no humility. And as long as he don't have humility, he keeps losing the good jobs."

Doc had climbed into the first waiter's bunk in his longjohns and I got in the second waiter's bunk under him

and lay there. I could hear him breathing. It had a hard
sound. He wasn't well and all of us knew it.

"Doc?" I said in the dark.

"Yeah?"

"Don't mind Boone, Doc. He's a dead man. He just
don't know it."

"We all are," Doc said.

"Not you," I said.

"What's the use? He's right. They'll get me in the end."

"But they ain't done it yet."

"They'll get me. And they know it and I know it. I can
even see it in old Crouse's eyes. He knows they're gonna
get me."

"Why don't you get a woman?"

He was quiet. "What can I do with a woman now, that
I ain't already done too much?"

I thought for a while. "If you're on the ground, being
with one might not make it so bad."

"I hate women," he said.

"You ever try fishing?"

"No."

"You want to?"

"No," he said.

"You can't keep *drinking*."

He did not answer.

"Maybe you could work in town. In the Commissary."

I could hear the big wheels rolling and clicking along
the tracks and I knew by the smooth way we were moving that we were almost out of the Dakota flatlands. Doc
wasn't talking. "Would you like that?" I thought he was
asleep. "Doc, would you like that?"

"Hell no," he said.

"You have to try *something!*"

He was quiet again. "I know," he finally said.

III

JERRY EWALD, THE UNEXPECTED INSPECTOR, got on in Winachee that next day after lunch and we knew that he had the word from the Commissary. He was cool about it: he laughed with the steward and the waiters about the old days and his hard gray eyes and shining glasses kept looking over our faces as if to see if we knew why he had got on. The two hardheads were in the crew car stealing a nap on company time. Jerry noticed this and could have caught them, but he was after bigger game. We all knew that, and we kept talking to him about the days of the big trains and looking at his white hair and not into the eyes behind his glasses because we knew what was there. Jerry sat down on the first waiter's station and said to Crouse: "Now I'll have some lunch. Steward, let the headwaiter bring me a menu."

Crouse stood next to the table where Jerry sat, and looked at Doc, who had been waiting between the tables with his tray under his arm. The way the rules say. Crouse looked sad because he knew what was coming. Then Jerry looked directly at Doc and said: "Headwaiter Doctor Craft, bring me a menu."

Doc said nothing and he did not smile. He brought the menu. Danny Jackson and I moved back into the hall to watch. There was nothing we could do to help Doc and we knew it. He was the Waiter's Waiter, out there by himself, hustling the biggest tip he would ever get in his life. Or losing it.

"Goddamn," Danny said to me. "Now let's sit on the ground and talk about how *kings* are gonna get fucked."

"Maybe not," I said. But I did not believe it myself because Jerry is the kind of man who lies in bed all night, scheming. I knew he had a plan.

Doc passed us on his way to the kitchen for water and I wanted to say something to him. But what was the use? He brought the water to Jerry. Jerry looked him in the eye. "Now, Headwaiter," he said. "I'll have a bowl of onion soup, a cold roast beef sandwich on white, rare, and a glass of iced tea."

"Write it down," said Doc. He was playing it right. He knew that the new rules had stopped waiters from taking verbal orders.

"Don't be so professional, Doc," Jerry said. "It's me, one of the *boys*."

"You have to write it out," said Doc, "it's in the black book."

Jerry clicked his pen and wrote the order out on the check. And handed it to Doc. Uncle T. followed Doc back into the Pantry.

"He's gonna get you, Doc," Uncle T. said. "I knew it all along. You know why? The Negro waiter ain't got no more humility."

"Shut the fuck up, Boone!" I told him.

"You'll see," Boone went on. "You'll see I'm right. There ain't a thing Doc can do about it, either. We're gonna lose all the good jobs."

We watched Jerry at the table. He saw us watching and smiled with his gray eyes. Then he poured some of the water from the glass on the linen cloth and picked up the silver sugar bowl and placed it right on the wet spot. Doc was still in the Pantry. Jerry turned the silver sugar bowl around and around on the linen. He pressed down on it some as he turned. But when he picked it up again, there was no dark ring on the wet cloth. We had polished the silver early that morning, according to the book, and there was not a dirty piece of silver to be found in the whole car. Jerry was drinking the rest of the water when Doc brought out the polished silver soup tureen, underlined with a doily and a breakfast plate, with a shining soup bowl underlined with a doily and a breakfast plate, and a bread-and-butter plate with six crackers; not four or five or seven, but six, the number the Commissary had written in the black book. He swung down the aisle of the car between the two rows of white tables and you could not help but be proud of the way he moved with the roll of the train and the way that tray was like a part of his arm. It was good service. He placed everything neat, with all company initials showing, right where things should go.

"Shall I serve up the soup?" he asked Jerry.

"Please," said Jerry.

Doc handled that silver soup ladle like one of those Chicago Jew tailors handles a needle. He ladled up three good-sized spoonfuls from the tureen and then laid the wet spoon on an extra bread-and-butter plate on the side of the table, so he would not stain the cloth. Then he put a napkin over the wet spot Jerry had made and changed the ashtray for a prayer-card because every good waiter knows that nobody wants to eat a good meal looking at an ashtray.

"You know about the spoon plate, I see," Jerry said to Doc.

"I'm a waiter," said Doc. "I know."

"You're a damn good waiter," said Jerry.

Doc looked Jerry square in the eye. "I know," he said slowly.

Jerry ate a little of the soup and opened all six of the cracker packages. Then he stopped eating and began to look out the window. We were passing through his territory, Washington State, the country he loved because he was the only company inspector in the state and knew that once we got through Montana he would be the only man the waiters feared. He smiled and then waved for Doc to bring out the roast beef sandwich.

But Doc was into his service now and cleared the table completely. Then he got the silver crumb knife from the Pantry and gathered all the cracker crumbs, even the ones Jerry had managed to get in between the salt and pepper shakers.

"You want the tea with your sandwich, or later?" he asked Jerry.

"Now is fine," said Jerry, smiling.

"You're going good," I said to Doc when he passed us on his way to the Pantry. "He can't touch you or nothing."

He did not say anything.

Uncle T. Boone looked at Doc like he wanted to say something too, but he just frowned and shuffled out to stand next to Jerry. You could see that Jerry hated him. But Jerry knew how to smile at everybody, and so he smiled at Uncle T. while Uncle T. bent over the table with his hands together like he was praying, and moved his head up and bowed it down.

Doc brought out the roast beef, proper service. The crock of mustard was on a breakfast plate, underlined with a doily, initials facing Jerry. The lid was on the mustard and it was clean, like it says in the book, and the little silver service spoon was clean and polished on a bread-and-butter plate. He set it down. And then he served the tea. You think you know the service, youngblood, all of you do. But you don't. Anybody can serve, but not everybody can become a part of the service. When Doc poured that pot of hot tea into that glass of crushed ice, it was like he was pouring it through his own fingers; it was like he and the tray and the pot and the glass and all of it was the same body. It was a beautiful move. It was fine service. The iced tea glass sat in a shell dish, and the iced tea spoon lay straight in front of Jerry. The lemon wedge Doc put in a shell dish half-full of crushed ice with an oyster fork stuck into its skin. Not in the meat, mind you, but squarely under the skin of that lemon, and the whole thing lay in a pretty curve on top of that crushed ice.

Doc stood back and waited. Jerry had been watching his service and was impressed. He mixed the sugar in his glass and sipped. Danny Jackson and I were down the aisle in the hall. Uncle T. stood behind Jerry, bending over, his arms folded, waiting. And Doc stood next to the table, his tray under his arm, looking straight ahead and calm because he had given good service and knew it. Jerry sipped again.

"Good tea," he said. "Very good tea."

Doc was silent.

Jerry took the lemon wedge off the oyster fork and squeezed it into the glass, and stirred, and sipped again. "*Very* good," he said. Then he drained the glass. Doc reached over to pick it up for more ice but Jerry kept his hand on the glass. "Very good service, Doc," he said. "But you served the lemon wrong."

Everybody was quiet. Uncle T. folded his hands in the praying position.

"How's that?" said Doc.

"The service was wrong," Jerry said. He was not smiling now.

"How could it be? I been giving that same service for years, right down to the crushed ice for the lemon wedge."

"That's just it, Doc," Jerry said. "The lemon wedge. You served it wrong."

"Yeah?" said Doc.

"Yes," said Jerry, his jaws tight. "Haven't you seen the new rule?"

Doc's face went loose. He knew now that they had got him.

"Haven't you *seen* it?" Jerry asked again.

Doc shook his head.

Jerry smiled that hard, gray smile of his, the kind of smile that says: "I have always been the boss and I am smiling this way because I know it and can afford to give you something." "Steward Crouse," he said. "Steward Crouse, go get the black bible for the headwaiter."

Crouse looked beaten too. He was sixty-three and waiting for his pension. He got the bible.

Jerry took it and turned directly to the very last page.

He knew where to look. "Now, Headwaiter," he said, "*listen* to this." And he read aloud. "Memorandum Number 22416. From: Douglass A. Tesdale, General Superintendent of Dining Cars. To: Waiters, Stewards, Chefs of Dining Cars. Attention: As of 7/9/65 the proper service for iced tea will be (a) Fresh brewed tea in teapot, poured over crushed ice at table; iced tea glass set in shell dish (b) Additional ice to be immediately available upon request after first glass of tea (c) Fresh lemon wedge will be served on bread-and-butter plate, no doily, with tines of oyster fork stuck into *meat* of lemon." Jerry paused.

"Now you know, Headwaiter," he said.

"Yeah," said Doc.

"But why didn't you know before?"

No answer.

"This notice came out last week."

"I didn't check the book yet," said Doc.

"But that's a rule. Always check the book before each trip. *You* know that, Headwaiter."

"Yeah," said Doc.

"Then that's *two* rules you missed."

Doc was quiet.

"Two rules you didn't read," Jerry said. "You're slowing down, Doc."

"I know," Doc mumbled.

"You want some time off to rest?"

Again Doc said nothing.

"I think you need some time on the ground to rest up, don't you?"

Doc put his tray on the table and sat down in the seat across from Jerry. This was the first time we had ever seen

a waiter sit down with a customer, even an inspector. Uncle T., behind Jerry's back, began waving his hands, trying
to tell Doc to get up. Doc did not look at him.

"You *are* tired, aren't you?" said Jerry.

"I'm just resting my feet," Doc said.

"Get up, Headwaiter," Jerry said. "You'll have plenty
of time to do that. I'm writing you up."

But Doc did not move and just continued to sit there.

And all Danny and I could do was watch him from the
back of the car. For the first time I saw that his hair was
almost gone and his legs were skinny in the baggy white
uniform. I don't think Jerry expected Doc to move. I don't
think he really cared. But then Uncle T. moved around
the table and stood next to Doc, trying to apologize for
him to Jerry with his eyes and bowed head. Doc looked at
Uncle T. and then got up and went back to the crew car.
He left his tray on the table. It stayed there all that evening because none of us, not even Crouse or Jerry or Uncle
T., would touch it. And Jerry didn't try to make any of
us take it back to the Pantry. He understood at least that
much. The steward closed down Doc's tables during dinner service, all three settings of it. And Jerry got off the
train someplace along the way, quiet, like he had got on.

After closing down the car we went back to the crew
quarters and Doc was lying on his bunk with his hands
behind his head and his eyes open. He looked old. No one
knew what to say until Boone went over to his bunk and
said: "I feel bad for you, Doc, but all of us are gonna get it
in the end. The railroad waiter is *doomed*."

Doc did not even notice Boone.

"I could of told you about the lemon but he would of

got you on something else. It wasn't no use. Any of it."

"Shut the fuck up, Boone!" Danny said. "The one thing that really hurts is that a crawling son-of-a-bitch like you will be riding when all the good men are gone. Dummies like you and these two hardheads will be working your asses off reading that damn bible and never know a goddamn thing about being a waiter. *That* hurts like a *motherfucker!*"

"It ain't my fault if the colored waiter is doomed," said Boone. "It's your fault for letting go your humility and letting the whites take over the good jobs."

Danny grabbed the skullcap off Boone's head and took it into the bathroom and flushed it down the toilet. In a minute it was half a mile away and soaked in old piss on the tracks. Boone did not try to fight, he just sat on his bunk and mumbled. He had other skullcaps. No one said anything to Doc, because that's the way real men show that they care. You don't talk. Talking makes it worse.

IV

WHAT ELSE IS THERE TO TELL YOU, youngblood? They made him retire. He didn't try to fight it. He was beaten and he knew it; not by the service, but by a book. *That book*, that *bible* you keep your finger stuck in. That's not a good way for a man to go. He should die in service. He should die doing the things he likes. But not by a book.

All of us Old School men will be beaten by it. Danny Jackson is gone now, and Reverend Hendricks put in for his pension and took up preaching, full-time. But Uncle

T. Boone is still riding. They'll get *me* soon enough, with that book. But it will never get you because you'll never be a waiter, or at least a Waiter's Waiter. You read too much.

Doc got a good pension and he took it directly to Andy's. And none of the boys who knew about it knew how to refuse a drink on Doc. But none of us knew how to drink with him knowing that we would be going out again in a few days, and he was on the ground. So a lot of us, even the drunks and hustlers who usually hang around Andy's, avoided him whenever we could. There was nothing to talk about any more.

He died five months after he was put on the ground. He was seventy-three and it was winter. He froze to death wandering around the Chicago yards early one morning. He had been drunk, and was still steaming when the yard crew found him. Only the few of us left in the Old School know what he was doing there.

I am sixty-three now. And I haven't decided if I should take my pension when they ask me to go or continue to ride. I *want* to keep riding, but I know that if I do, Jerry Ewald or Harry Silk or Jack Tate will get me one of these days. I could get down if I wanted: I have a hobby and I am too old to get drunk by myself. I couldn't drink with you, youngblood. We have nothing to talk about. And after a while you would get mad at me for talking anyway, and keeping you from your pussy. You are tired already. I can see it in your eyes and in the way you play with the pages of your rule book.

I know it. And I wonder why I should keep talking to you when you could never see what I see or understand what I understand or know the real difference between my school and yours. I wonder why I have kept talking this long when all the time I have seen that you can hardly wait to hit the city to get off this thing and spend your money. You have a good story. But you will never remember it. Because all this time you have had pussy in your mind, and your fingers in the pages of that black bible.

GOLD COAST

THAT SPRING, when I haD a great deal of potential and no money at all, I took a job as a janitor. That was when I was still very young and spent money very freely, and when, almost every night, I drifted off to sleep lulled by sweet anticipation of that time when my potential would suddenly be realized and there would be capsule biographies of my life on dust jackets of many books, all proclaiming: ". . . He knew life on many levels. From shoeshine boy, freelance waiter, 3rd cook, janitor, he rose to . . ." I had never been a janitor before and I did not really have to be one and that is why I did it. But now, much later, I think it might have been because it is possible to be a janitor without really becoming one, and at parties or at mixers when asked what it was I did for a living, it was pretty good to hook my thumbs in my vest pockets and say comfortably: "Why, I am an apprentice janitor." The hippies would think it degenerate and really dig me and it made me feel good that people in Philosophy and Law and Business would feel uncomfortable trying to make me feel better about my station while wondering how the hell I had managed to crash the party.

"What's an apprentice janitor?" they would ask.

"I haven't got my card yet," I would reply. "Right now I'm just taking lessons. There's lots of complicated stuff you have to learn before you get your card and your own building."

"What kind of stuff?"

"Human nature, for one thing. *Race* nature, for another."

"Why race?"

"Because," I would say in a low voice looking around lest someone else should overhear, "you have to be able to spot Jews and Negroes who are passing."

"That's terrible," would surely be said then with a hint of indignation.

"It's an art," I would add masterfully.

After a good pause I would invariably be asked: "But you're a Negro yourself, how can you keep your own people out?"

At which point I would look terribly disappointed and say: "*I* don't keep them out. But if they get in, it's my job to make their stay just as miserable as possible. Things are changing."

Now the speaker would just look at me in disbelief.

"It's Janitorial Objectivity," I would say to finish the thing as the speaker began to edge away. "Don't hate me," I would call after him to his considerable embarrassment. "Somebody has to do it."

It was an old building near Harvard Square. Conrad Aiken had once lived there and in the days of the Gold Coast, before Harvard built its great Houses, it had been a very fine haven for the rich; but that was a world ago, and this building was one of the few monuments of that era which had survived. The lobby had a high ceiling with thick redwood beams and it was replete with marble floor, fancy ironwork, and an old-fashioned house telephone that no longer worked. Each apartment had a small fireplace, and even the large bathtubs and chain toilets, when I was having my touch of nature, made me wonder what prominent personage of the past had worn away all the newness. And, being there, I felt a certain affinity toward the rich.

It was a funny building; because the people who lived there made it old. Conveniently placed as it was between the Houses and Harvard Yard, I expected to find it occupied by a company of hippies, hopeful working girls, and assorted graduate students. Instead, there were a majority of old maids, dowagers, asexual middle-aged men, homosexual young men, a few married couples and a teacher. No one was shacking up there, and walking through the quiet halls in the early evening, I sometimes had the urge to knock on a door and expose myself just to hear someone breathe hard for once.

It was a Cambridge spring: down by the Charles happy students were making love while sad-eyed middle-aged men watched them from the bridge. It was a time of activity: Law students were busy sublimating. Business School people were making records of the money they would make, the Harvard Houses were clearing out, and in the

Square bearded pot-pushers were setting up their restaurant tables in anticipation of the Summer School faithfuls. There was a change of season in the air, and to comply with its urgings, James Sullivan, the old superintendent, passed his three beaten garbage cans on to me with the charge that I should take up his daily rounds of the six floors, and with unflinching humility, gather whatever scraps the old-maid tenants had refused to husband.

I then became very rich, with my own apartment, a sensitive girl, a stereo, two speakers, one tattered chair, one fork, a job, and the urge to acquire. Having all this and youth besides made me pity Sullivan: he had been in that building thirty years and had its whole history recorded in the little folds of his mind, as his own life was recorded in the wrinkles of his face. All he had to show for his time there was a berserk dog, a wife almost as mad as the dog, three cats, bursitis, acute myopia, and a drinking problem. He was well over seventy and could hardly walk, and his weekly check of twenty-two dollars from the company that managed the building would not support anything. So, out of compromise, he was retired to superintendent of my labor.

My first day as a janitor, while I skillfully lugged my three overflowing cans of garbage out of the building, he sat on his bench in the lobby, faded and old and smoking in patched, loose blue pants. He watched me. He was a chain smoker, and I noticed right away that he very carefully dropped all of the ashes and butts on the floor and crushed them under his feet until there was a yellow and gray smear. Then he laboriously pushed the mess under the bench with his shoe, all the while eyeing me like a cat in silence as I hauled the many cans of muck out to the big disposal unit next to the building. When I had finished, he gave me two old plates to help stock my kitchen and his first piece of advice.

"Sit down, for Chrissake, and take a load off your feet," he told me.

I sat on the red bench next to him and accepted the wilted cigarette he offered me from the crushed package he kept in his sweater pocket.

"Now I'll tell you something to help you get along in the building," he said.

I listened attentively.

"If any of these sons-of-bitches ever ask you to do something extra, be sure to charge them for it."

I assured him that I absolutely would.

"If they can afford to live here, they can afford to pay. The bastards."

"Undoubtedly," I assured him again.

"And another thing," he added. "Don't let any of these girls shove any cat shit under your nose. That ain't your job. You tell them to put it in a bag and take it out them-selves."

I reminded him that I knew very well my station in life, and that I was not about to haul cat shit or anything of that nature. He looked at me through his thick-lensed glasses. He looked like a cat himself. "That's right," he said at last. "And if they still try to sneak it in the trash be sure to make the bastards pay. They can afford it." He crushed his seventh butt on the floor and scattered the mess some more while he lit up another. "I never hauled out no cat shit in the thirty years I been here and you don't do it either."

"I'm going up to wash my hands," I said.

"Remember," he called after me, "don't take no shit from any of them."

I protested once more that, upon my life, I would never, never do it, not even for the prettiest girl in the building. Going up in the elevator, I felt comfortably resolved that I would never do it. There were no pretty girls in the building.

I never found out what he had done before he came there, but I do know that being a janitor in that building was as high as he ever got in life. He had watched two generations of the rich pass the building on their way to the Yard, and he had seen many governors ride white horses thirty times into that same Yard to send sons and daughters of the rich out into life to produce, to acquire, to procreate and to send back sons and daughters so that the cycle would continue. He had watched the cycle from when he had been able to haul the cans out for himself, and now he could not, and he was bitter.

He was Irish, of course, and he took pride in Irish accomplishments when he could have none of his own. He had known Frank O'Connor when that writer had been at Harvard. He told me on many occasions how O'Connor had stopped to talk every day on his way to the Yard. He had also known James Michael Curley, and his most colorful memory of the man was a long-ago day when he and James Curley sat in a Boston bar and one of Curley's runners had come in and said: "Hey Jim, Sol Bernstein the

Jew wants to see you." And Curley, in his deep, memorial voice, had said to James Sullivan: "Let us go forth and meet this Israelite Prince." These were his memories, and I would obediently put aside my garbage cans and laugh with him over the hundred or so colorful, insignificant little details which made up a whole lifetime of living in the basement of Harvard. And although they were of little value to me then, I knew that they were the reflections of a lifetime and the happiest moments he would ever have, being sold to me cheap, as youthful time is cheap, for as little time and interest as I wanted to spend. It was a buyer's market.

II

IN THOSE DAYS I BELIEVED myself gifted with a boundless perception and attacked my daily garbage route with a gusto superenforced by the happy knowledge that behind each of the fifty or so doors in our building lived a story which could, if I chose to grace it with the magic of my pen, become immortal. I watched my tenants fanatically, noting their perversions, their visitors, and their eating habits. So intense was my search for material that I had to restrain myself from going through their refuse scrap by scrap; but at the topmost layers of muck, without too much hand-soiling in the process, I set my perceptions to work. By late June, however, I had discovered only enough to put together a skimpy, rather naïve Henry Miller novel. The most colorful discoveries being:

(1) The lady in #24 was an alumna of Paducah College.

(2) The couple in #55 made love at least five hundred times a week and the wife had not yet discovered the pill.

(3) The old lady in #36 was still having monthly inconvenience.

(4) The two fatsos in #56 consumed nightly an extraordinary amount of chili.

(5) The fat man in #54 had two dogs that were married to each other, but he was not married to anyone at all.

(6) The middle-aged single man in #63 threw out an awful lot of flowers.

Disturbed by the snail's progress I was making, I confessed my futility to James one day as he sat on his bench chain-smoking and smearing butts on my newly waxed lobby floor. "So you want to know about the tenants?" he said, his cat's eyes flickering over me.

I nodded.

"Well, the first thing to notice is how many Jews there are."

"I haven't noticed many Jews," I said.

He eyed me in amazement.

"Well, a few," I said quickly to prevent my treasured perception from being dulled any further.

"A few, hell," he said. "There's more Jews here than anybody."

"How can you tell?"

He gave me that undecided look again. "Where do you

think all that garbage comes from?" He nodded feebly toward my bulging cans. I looked just in time to prevent a stray noodle from slipping over the brim. "That's right," he continued. "Jews are the biggest eaters in the world. They eat the best too."

I confessed then that I was of the chicken-soup generation and believed that Jews ate only enough to muster strength for their daily trips to the bank.

"Not so!" he replied emphatically. "You never heard the expression: 'Let's get to the restaurant before the Jews get there'?"

I shook my head sadly.

"You don't know that in certain restaurants they take the free onions and pickles off the tables when they see Jews coming?"

I held my head down in shame over the bounteous heap.

He trudged over to my can and began to turn back the leaves of noodles and crumpled tissues from #47 with his hand. After a few seconds of digging he unmucked an empty paté can. "Look at that," he said triumphantly. "Gourmet stuff, no less."

"That's from #44," I said.

"What else?" he said all-knowingly. "In 1946 a Swedish girl moved in up there and took a Jewish girl for her roommate. Then the Swedish girl moved out and there's been a Jewish Dynasty up there ever since."

I recalled that #44 was occupied by a couple that threw out a good number of S. S. Pierce cans, Chivas Regal bottles, assorted broken records, and back issues of *Evergreen* and the *Realist*.

"You're right," I said.

"Of course," he replied as if there was never any doubt. "I can spot them anywhere, even when they think they're passing." He leaned closer and said in a you-and-me voice: "But don't ever say anything bad about them in public; the Anti-Defamation League will get you."

Just then his wife screamed for him from the second floor, and the dog joined her and beat against the door. He got into the elevator painfully and said: "Don't ever talk about them in public. You don't know who they are and that Defamation League will take everything you got."

Sullivan did not really hate Jews. He was just bitter toward anyone better off than himself. He liked me because I seemed to like hauling garbage and because I listened to him and seemed to respect what he said and seemed to imply, by lingering on even when he repeated himself, that I was eager to take what wisdom he had for no other reason than that I needed it in order to get along.

He lived with his wife on the second floor and his apartment was very dirty because both of them were sick and old, and neither could move very well. His wife swept dirt out into the hall, and two hours after I had mopped and waxed their section of the floor, there was sure to be a layer of dirt, grease, and crushed-scattered tobacco from their door to the end of the hall. There was a smell of dogs and cats and age and death about their door, and I did not ever want to have to go in there for any reason because I feared something about it I cannot name.

Mrs. Sullivan, I found out, was from South Africa. She loved animals much more than people and there was a great deal of pain in her face. She kept little pans of meat posted at strategic points about the building, and I often came across her in the early morning or late at night throwing scraps out of the second-floor window to stray cats. Once, when James was about to throttle a stray mouse in their apartment, she had screamed at him to give the mouse a sporting chance. Whenever she attempted to walk she had to balance herself against a wall or a rail, and she hated the building because it confined her. She also hated James and most of the tenants. On the other hand, she loved the *Johnny Carson Show*, she loved to sit outside on the front steps (because she could get no further unassisted), and she loved to talk to anyone who would stop to listen. She never spoke coherently except when she was cursing James, and then she had a vocabulary like a sailor. She had great, shrill lungs, and her screams, accompanied by the rabid barks of the dog, could be heard all over the building. She was never really clean, her teeth were bad, and the first most pathetic thing in the world was to see her sitting on the steps in the morning watching the world pass, in a stained smock and a fresh summer blue hat she kept just to wear downstairs, with no place in the world to go. James told me, on the many occasions of her screaming, that she was mentally disturbed and could not control herself. The admirable thing about him was that he never lost his temper with her, no matter how rough her curses became and no matter who heard them. And the second most pathetic thing in the world was to see them slowly making their way in Harvard Square, he supporting her, through the hurrying crowds of miniskirted summer girls,

J-Pressed Ivy Leaguers, beatniks, and bused Japanese tourists, decked in cameras, who would take pictures of every inch of Harvard Square except them. Once, he told me, a hippie had brushed past them and called back over his shoulder: "Don't break any track records, Mr. and Mrs. Speedy Molasses."

Also on the second floor lived Miss O'Hara, a spinster who hated Sullivan as only an old maid can hate an old man. Across from her lived a very nice, gentle, celibate named Murphy who had once served with Montgomery in North Africa and who was now spending the rest of his life cleaning his little apartment and gossiping with Miss O'Hara. It was an Irish floor.

I never found out just why Miss O'Hara hated the Sullivans with such a passion. Perhaps it was because they were so unkempt and she was so superciliously clean. Perhaps it was because Miss O'Hara had a great deal of Irish pride and they were stereotyped Irish. Perhaps it was because she merely had no reason to like them. She was a fanatic about cleanliness and put out her little bit of garbage wrapped very neatly in yesterday's *Christian Science Monitor* and tied in a bow with a fresh piece of string. Collecting all those little neat packages, I would wonder where she got the string and imagined her at night picking meat-market locks with a hairpin and hobbling off with yards and yards of white cord concealed under the gray sweater she always wore. I could even imagine her back in her little apartment chuckling and rolling the cord into a great white ball by candlelight. Then she would stash it away in her breadbox. Miss O'Hara kept her door slightly open until late at night, and I suspected that she heard everything that went on in the building. I had the feeling that I should never dare to make love with gusto for fear that she would overhear and write down all my happy-time phrases, to be maliciously recounted to me if she were ever provoked.

She had been in the building longer than Sullivan, and I suppose that her greatest ambition in life was to outlive him and then attend his wake with a knitting ball and needles. She had been trying to get him fired for twenty-five years or so and did not know when to quit. On summer nights when I painfully mopped the second floor, she would offer me root beer, apples, or cupcakes while trying to pump me for evidence against him.

"He's just a filthy old man, Robert," she would declare in a little-old-lady whisper. "And don't think you have to clean up those dirty old butts of his. Just report him to the Company."

"Oh, I don't mind," I would tell her, gulping the root beer as fast as possible.

"Well, they're both a couple of lushes, if you ask me. They haven't been sober a day in twenty-five years."

"Well, she's sick too, you know."

"Ha!" She would throw up her hands in disgust. "She's only sick when he doesn't give her the booze."

I fought to keep down a burp. "How long have *you* been here?"

She motioned for me to step out of the hall and into her dark apartment. "Don't tell him"—she nodded toward Sullivan's door—"but I've been here for thirty-four years." She waited for me to be taken aback. Then she added: "And it was a better building before those two lushes came."

She then offered me an apple, asked five times if the dog's barking bothered me, forced me to take a fudge brownie, said that the cats had wet the floor again last night, got me to dust the top of a large chest too high for her to reach, had me pick up the minute specks of dust which fell from my dustcloth, pressed another root beer on me, and then showed me her family album. As an afterthought, she had me take down a big old picture of her great-grandfather, also too high for her to reach, so that I could dust that too. Then together we picked up the dust from it which might have fallen to the floor. "He's really a filthy old man, Robert," she said in closing, "and don't be afraid to report him to the property manager any time you want."

I assured her that I would do it at the slightest provocation from Sullivan, finally accepted an apple but refused the money she offered, and escaped back to my mopping. Even then she watched me, smiling, from her half-opened door.

"Why does Miss O'Hara hate you?" I asked James once.

He lifted his cigaretted hand and let the long ash fall elegantly to the floor. "That old bitch has been an albatross around my neck ever since I got here," he said. "Don't trust her, Robert. It was her kind that sat around singing hymns and watching them burn saints in this state."

There was never an adequate answer to my question. And even though the dog was noisy and would surely kill someone if it ever got loose, no one could really dislike the old man because of it. The dog was all they had. In his garbage each night, for every wine bottle, there would be an equally empty can of dog food. Some nights he took the brute out for a long walk, when he could barely walk himself, and both of them had to be led back to the building.

III

IN THOSE DAYS I HAD forgotten that I was first of all a black and I had a very lovely girl who was not first of all a black. We were both young and optimistic then, and she believed with me in my potential and liked me partly because of it; and I was happy because she belonged to me and not to the race, which made her special. It made me special too because I did not have to wear a beard or hate or be especially hip or ultra–Ivy Leaguish. I did not have to smoke pot or supply her with it, or be for any other cause at all except myself. I only had to be myself, which pleased me; and I only had to produce, which pleased both of us. Like many of the artistically inclined rich, she wanted to own in someone else what she could not own in herself. But this I did not mind, and I forgave her for it because she forgave me moods and the constant smell of garbage and a great deal of latent hostility. She only minded James Sullivan and all the valuable time I was wasting listening to him rattle on and on. His conversations, she thought, were useless, repetitive, and promised nothing of value to me. She was accustomed to the old-rich whose conversations meandered around a leitmotiv of how well off they were and how much they would leave behind very soon. She was not at all cold, but she had been taught how to tolerate the old-poor and perhaps toss them a greeting in passing. But nothing more.

Sullivan did not like her when I first introduced them because he saw that she was not a hippie and could not be dismissed. It is in the nature of things that liberal people will tolerate two interracial hippies more than they will an intelligent, serious-minded mixed couple. The former liaison is easy to dismiss as the dregs of both races, deserving of each other and the contempt of both races; but the latter poses a threat because there is no immediacy or overpowering sensuality or "you-pick-my-fleas-I'll-pick-yours" apparent on the surface of things, and people, even the most publicly liberal, cannot dismiss it so easily.

"That girl is Irish, isn't she?" he had asked one day in my apartment soon after I had introduced them.

"No," I said definitely.

"What's her name again?"

"Judy Smith," I said, which was not her name at all.

"Well, I can spot it," he said. "She's got Irish blood, all right."

"Everybody's got a little Irish blood," I told him.

He looked at me cattily and craftily from behind his thick lenses. "Well, she's from a good family, I suppose."

"I suppose," I said.

He paused to let some ashes fall to the rug. "They say the Colonel's Lady and Nelly O'Grady are sisters under the skin." Then he added: "Rudyard Kipling."

"That's true," I said with equal innuendo, "that's why

you have to maintain a distinction by marrying the Colonel's Lady."

An understanding passed between us then, and we
never spoke more on the subject.

ALMOST EVERY NIGHT the cats wet the second floor
while Meg Sullivan watched the *Johnny Carson Show*
and the dog howled and clawed the door. During com-
mercials Meg would curse James to get out and stop
dropping ashes on the floor or to take the dog out or
something else, totally unintelligible to those of us on
the fourth, fifth and sixth floors. Even after the *Carson
Show* she would still curse him to get out, until finally
he would go down to the basement and put away a bottle
or two of wine. There was a steady stench of cat func-
tions in the basement, and with all the grease and dirt,
discarded trunks, beer bottles, chairs, old tools and the
filthy sofa on which he sometimes slept, seeing him there
made me want to cry. He drank the cheapest sherry, the
wino kind, straight from the bottle; and on many nights
that summer at 2:00 A.M. my phone would ring me out
of bed.

"Rob? Jimmy Sullivan here. What are you doing?"

There was nothing suitable to say.

"Come on down to the basement for a drink."

"I have to be at work at eight-thirty," I would protest.

"Can't you have just one drink?" he would say pathetically.

I would carry down my own glass so that I would not
have to drink out of the bottle. Looking at him on the

sofa, I could not be mad because now I had many records for my stereo, a story that was going well, a girl who believed in me and belonged to me and not to the race, a new set of dishes, and a tomorrow morning with younger people.

"I don't want to burden you unduly," he would always preface.

I would force myself not to look at my watch and say: "Of course not."

"My Meg is not in the best health, you know," he would say, handing the bottle to me.

"She's just old."

"The doctors say she should be in an institution."

"That's no place to be."

"I'm a sick man myself, Rob. I can't take much more. She's crazy."

"Anybody who loves animals can't be crazy."

He took another long draw from the bottle. "I won't live another year. I'll be dead in a year."

"You don't know that."

He looked at me closely, without his glasses, so that I could see the desperation in his eyes. "I just hope Meg goes before I do. I don't want them to put her in an institution after I'm gone."

At 2:00 A.M., with the cat stench in my nose and a glass of bad sherry standing still in my hand because I refused in my mind to touch it, and when all my dreams of greatness were above him and the basement and the building itself, I did not know what to say. The only way I could keep from hating myself was to talk about the AMA or the Medicare program or hippies. He was pure hell on all three. To him, the medical profession was "morally bank-rupt," Medicare was a great farce which deprived oldsters like himself of their "rainy-day dollars," and hippies were "dropouts from the human race." He could rage on and on in perfect phrases about all three of his major dislikes, and I had the feeling that because the sentences were so well constructed and well turned, he might have memo-rized them from something he had read. But then he was extremely well read and it did not matter if he had bor-rowed a phrase or two from someone else. The ideas were still his own.

It would be 3:00 A.M. before I knew it, and then 3:30, and still he would go on. He hated politicians in general and liked to recount, at these times, his private catalogue of political observations. By the time he got around to Civil Rights it would be 4:00 A.M., and I could not feel sorry or responsible for him at that hour. I would begin to yawn and at first he would just ignore it. Then I would start to edge toward the door, and he would see that he could hold me no longer, not even by declaring that he wanted to be an honorary Negro because he loved the race so much.

"I hope I haven't burdened you unduly," he would say again.

"Of course not," I would say, because it was over then and I could leave him and the smell of the cats there and sometimes I would go out in the cool night and walk around the Yard and be thankful that I was only an as-sistant janitor, and a transient one at that. Walking in the early dawn and seeing the Summer School fellows sneak out of the girls' dormitories in the Yard gave me a good feeling, and I thought that tomorrow night it would be good to make love myself so that I could be busy when he called.

IV

"WHY DON'T YOU TELL that old man your job doesn't include baby-sitting with him?" Jean told me many times when she came over to visit during the day and found me sleeping.

I would look at her and think to myself about social forces and the pressures massing and poised, waiting to attack us. It was still July then. It was hot and I was working good. "He's just an old man," I said. "Who else would listen to him?"

"You're too soft. As long as you do your work you don't have to be bothered with him."

"He could be a story if I listened long enough."

"There are too many stories about old people."

"No," I said, thinking about us again, "there are just too many people who have no stories."

Sometimes he would come up and she would be there, but I would let him come in anyway, and he would stand in the room looking dirty and uncomfortable, offering some invented reason for having intruded. At these times something silent would pass between them, something I cannot name, which would reduce him to exactly what he was: an old man, come out of his basement to intrude where he was not wanted. But all the time this was being communicated, there would be a surface, friendly conversation between them. And after five minutes or so of being unwelcome, he would apologize for having come, drop a few ashes on the rug and back out the door. Downstairs we could hear his wife screaming.

We endured and aged, and August was almost over. Inside the building the cats were still wetting, Meg was still screaming, the dog was getting madder, and Sullivan began to drink during the day. Outside it was hot and lush and green, and the summer girls were wearing shorter miniskirts and no panties and the middle-aged men down by the Charles were going wild on their bridge. Everyone was restless for change, for August is the month when undone summer things must be finished or regretted all through the winter.

V

BEING IMAGINATIVE PEOPLE, Jean and I played a number of original games. One of them we called "Social Forces," the object of which was to see which side could break us first. We played it with the unknown nightriders who screamed obscenities from passing cars. And because that was her side I would look at her expectantly, but she would laugh and say: "No." We played it at parties with unaware blacks who attempted to enchant her with skillful dances and hip vocabulary, believing her to be community property. She would be polite and aloof, and much later, it then being my turn, she would look at me expectantly. And I would force a smile and say: "No." The last round was played while taking her home in a subway car, on a hot August night, when one side of the car was black and tense and hating and the other side was white and of the same mind. There was not enough room on either side for the two of us to sit and we would not separate; and so we stood, holding on to a steel post through all the stops, feeling all the eyes, between the two sides of the car and the two sides of the world. We aged. And, getting off finally at the stop which was no longer ours, we looked at each other, again expectantly, and there was nothing left to say.

I began to avoid the old man, would not answer the door when I knew it was he who was knocking, and waited until very late at night, when he could not possibly be awake, to haul the trash down. I hated the building then; and I was really a janitor for the first time. I slept a lot and wrote very little. And I did not give a damn about Medicare, the AMA, the building, Meg or the crazy dog. I began to consider moving out.

In that same month, Miss O'Hara finally succeeded in badgering Murphy, the celibate Irishman, and a few other tenants into signing a complaint about the dog. No doubt Murphy signed because he was a nice fellow and women like Miss O'Hara had always dominated him. He did not really mind the dog: he did not really mind anything. She called him "Frank Dear," and I had the feeling that when he came to that place, fresh from Montgomery's Campaign, he must have had a will of his own; but she had drained it all away, year by year, so that now he would do anything just to be agreeable.

One day soon after the complaint, the Property Manager came around to tell Sullivan that the dog had to be taken away. Miss O'Hara told me the good news later, when she finally got around to my door.

"Well, that crazy dog is gone now, Robert. Those two are enough."

"Where is the dog?" I asked.

"I don't know, but Albert Rustin made them get him out. You should have seen the old drunk's face," she said. "That dirty useless old man."

"You should be at peace now," I said.

"Almost," was her reply. "The best thing would be to get rid of those two old boozers along with the dog."

I congratulated Miss O'Hara again and then went out. I knew that the old man would be drinking and would want to talk. I did not want to talk. But very late that evening he called on the telephone and caught me in.

"Rob?" he said. "James Sullivan here. Would you come down to my apartment like a good fellow? I want to ask you something important."

I had never been in his apartment before and did not want to go then. But I went down anyway.

They had three rooms, all grimy from corner to corner. There was a peculiar odor in that place I did not want to ever smell again, and his wife was dragging herself around the room talking in mumbles. When she saw me come in the door, she said: "I can't clean it up. I just can't. Look at that window. I can't reach it. I can't keep it clean." She threw up both her hands and held her head down and to the side. "The whole place is dirty and I can't clean it up."

"What do you want?" I said to Sullivan.

"Sit down." He motioned me to a kitchen chair. "Have you changed that bulb on the fifth floor?"

"It's done."

He was silent for a while, drinking from a bottle of sherry, and he offered me some and a dirty glass. "You're the first person who's been in here in years," he said. "We couldn't have company because of the dog."

Somewhere in my mind was a note that I should never go into his apartment. But the dog had not been the reason. "Well, he's gone now," I said, fingering the dirty glass of sherry.

He began to cry. "They took my dog away," he said. "It was all I had. How can they take a man's dog away from him?"

There was nothing I could say.

"I couldn't do nothing," he continued. After a while he added: "But I know who it was. It was that old bitch O'Hara. Don't ever trust her, Rob. She smiles in your face but it was her kind that laughed when they burned Joan of Arc in this state."

Seeing him there, crying and making me feel unmanly because I wanted to touch him or say something warm, also made me eager to be far away and running hard. "Everybody's got problems," I said. "I don't have a girl now."

He brightened immediately, and for a while he looked almost happy in his old cat's eyes. Then he staggered over to my chair and held out his hand. I did not touch it, and he finally pulled it back. "I know how you feel," he said. "I know just how you feel."

"Sure," I said.

"But you're a young man, you have a future. But not me. I'll be dead inside of a year."

Just then his wife dragged in to offer me a cigar. They were being hospitable and I forced myself to drink a little of the sherry.

"They took my dog away today," she mumbled. "That's all I had in the world, my dog."

I looked at the old man. He was drinking from the bottle.

VI

DURING THE FIRST WEEK OF SEPTEMBER one of the middle-aged men down by the Charles got tired of looking and tried to take a necking girl away from her boyfriend. The police hauled him off to jail, and the girl pulled down her dress tearfully. A few days later another man exposed himself near the same spot. And that same week a dead body was found on the banks of the Charles.

The miniskirted brigade had moved out of the Yard and it was quiet and green and peaceful there. In our building another Jewish couple moved into #44. They did not eat gourmet stuff and, on occasion, threw out pork-and-beans cans. But I had lost interest in perception. I now had many records for my stereo, loads of S. S. Pierce stuff, and a small bottle of Chivas Regal which I never opened. I was working good again and did not miss other things as much; or at least I told myself that.

The old man was coming up steadily now, at least three times a day, and I had resigned myself to it. If I refused to let him in he would always come back later with a missing bulb on the fifth floor. We had taken to buying cases of beer together, and when he had finished his half, which was very frequently, he would come up to polish off mine. I began to enjoy talking about politics, the AMA, Medicare, and hippies, and listening to him recite from books he had read. I discovered that he was very well read in history, philosophy, literature and law. He was extraordinarily fond of saying: "I am really a cut above being a building superintendent. Circumstances made me what I am." And even though he was drunk and dirty and it was very late at night, I believed him and liked him anyway because having him there was much better than being alone. After he had gone I could sleep and I was not lonely in sleep; and it did not really matter how late I was at work the next morning, because when I really thought about it all, I discovered that nothing really matters except not being old and being alive and having potential to dream about, and not being alone.

Whenever I passed his wife on the steps she would say: "That no-good bastard let them take my dog away." And whenever her husband complained that he was sick she said: "That's good for him. He took my dog away."

Sullivan slept in the basement on the sofa almost every night because his wife would think about the dog after the *Carson Show* and blame him for letting it be taken away. He told her, and then me, that the dog was on a farm in New Hampshire; but that was unlikely because the dog had been near mad, and it did not appease her. It was nearing autumn and she was getting violent. Her screams could be heard for hours through the halls and I knew that beyond her quiet door Miss O'Hara was plotting again. Sullivan now had little cuts and bruises on his face and hands, and one day he said: "Meg is like an albatross around my neck. I wish she was dead. I'm sick myself and I can't take much more. She blames me for the dog and I couldn't help it."

"Why don't you take her out to see the dog?" I said.

"I couldn't help it, Rob," he went on. "I'm old and I couldn't help it."

"You ought to just get her out of here for a while."

He looked at me, drunk as usual. "Where would we go? We can't even get past the Square."

There was nothing left to say.

"Honest to God, I couldn't help it," he said. He was not saying it to me.

That night I wrote a letter from a mythical New Hampshire farmer telling them that the dog was very fine and missed them a great deal because he kept trying to run off. I said that the children and all the other dogs liked him and that he was not vicious any more. I wrote that the open air was doing him a lot of good and added that they should feel absolutely free to come up to visit the dog at any time. That same night I gave him the letter.

One evening, some days later, I asked him about it.

"I tried to mail it, I really tried," he said.

"What happened?"

"I went down to the Square and looked for cars with New Hampshire license plates. But I never found anybody."

"That wasn't even necessary, was it?"

"It had to have a New Hampshire postmark. You don't know my Meg."

"Listen," I said. "I have a friend who goes up there. Give me the letter and I'll have him mail it."

He held his head down. "I'll tell you the truth. I carried that letter in my pocket so much it got ragged and dirty and I got tired of carrying it. I finally just tore it up."

Neither one of us said anything for a while.

"If I could have sent it off it would have helped some," he said at last. "I know it would have helped."

"Sure," I said.

"I wouldn't have to ask anybody if I had my strength."

"I know."

"If I had my strength I would have mailed it myself."

"I know," I said.

That night we both drank from his bottle of sherry and it did not matter at all that I did not provide my own glass.

VII

IN LATE SEPTEMBER the Cambridge police finally picked up the bearded pot-pusher in the Square. He had been in a restaurant all summer, at the same table, with the same customers flocking around him; but now that summer was over, they picked him up. The leaves were changing. In the early evening students passed the building and Meg, blue-hatted and waiting on the steps, carrying sofas and chairs and coffee tables to their suites in the

Houses. Down by the Charles the middle-aged men were catching the last phases of summer sensuality before the grass grew cold and damp, and before the young would be forced indoors to play. I wondered what those hungry, spying men did in the winter or at night when it was too dark to see. Perhaps, I thought, they just stood there and listened.

In our building Miss O'Hara was still listening. She had never stopped. When Meg was outside on the steps it was very quiet and I felt good that Miss O'Hara had to wait a long, long time before she heard anything. The company gave the halls and ceilings a new coat of paint, but it was still old in the building. James Sullivan got his yearly two-week vacation and they went to the Boston Common for six hours: two hours going, two hours sitting on the benches, and two hours coming back. Then they both sat on the steps, watching, and waiting.

At first I wanted to be kind because he was old and dying in a special way and I was young and ambitious. But at night, in my apartment, when I heard his dragging feet in the hall outside and knew that he would be drunk and repetitious and imposing on my privacy, I did not want to be kind any more. There were girls outside and I knew that I could have one now because that desperate look had finally gone somewhere deep inside. I was young and now I did not want to be bothered.

"Did you read about the lousy twelve per cent Social Security increase those bastards in Washington gave us?"

"No."

He would force himself past me, trying to block the door with my body, and into the room. "When those old pricks tell me to count my blessings, I tell them, 'You're not one of them.'" He would seat himself at the table without meeting my eyes. "The cost of living's gone up more than twelve per cent in the last six months."

"I know."

"What unmitigated bastards."

I would try to be busy with something on my desk.

"But the Texas Oil Barons got another depletion allowance."

"They can afford to bribe politicians," I would mumble.

"They tax away our rainy-day dollars and give us a lousy twelve per cent."

"It's tough."

He would know that I did not want to hear any more and he would know that he was making a burden of himself. It made me feel bad that it was so obvious to him, but I could not help myself. It made me feel bad that I disliked him more every time I heard a girl laugh on the street far below my window. So I would nod occasionally and say half-phrases and smile slightly at something witty he was saying for the third time. If I did not offer him a drink he would go sooner and so I gave him Coke when he hinted at how dry he was. Then, when he had finally gone, saying, "I hope I haven't burdened you unduly," I went to bed and hated myself.

VIII

If I am a janitor it is either because I have to be a janitor or because I want to be a janitor. And if I do not have to do it, and if I no longer want to do it, the easiest thing in the world, for a young man, is to step up to something else. Any move away from it is a step up because there is no job more demeaning than that of a janitor. One day I made myself suddenly realize that the three dirty cans would never contain anything of value to me, unless, of course, I decided to gather material for Harold Robbins or freelance for the *Realist*. Neither alternative appealed to me.

Toward dawn one day, during the first part of October, I rented a U-Haul truck and took away two loads of things I had accumulated. The records I packed very carefully, and the stereo I placed on the front seat of the truck beside me. I slipped the Chivas Regal and a picture of Jean under some clothes in a trunk I will not open for a long time. And I left the rug on the floor because it was dirty and too large for my new apartment. I also left the two plates given to me by James Sullivan, for no reason at all. Sometimes I want to go back to get them, but I do not know how to ask for them or explain why I left them in the first place. But sometimes at night, when there is a sleeping girl beside me, I think that I cannot have them again because I am still young and do not want to go back into that building.

I saw him once in the Square walking along very slowly with two shopping bags, and they seemed very heavy. As I came up behind him I saw him put them down and exercise his arms while the crowd moved in two streams around him. I had an instant impulse to offer help and I was close enough to touch him before I stopped. I will never know why I stopped. And after a few seconds of standing behind him and knowing that he was not aware of anything at all except the two heavy bags waiting to be lifted after his arms were sufficiently rested, I moved back into the stream of people which passed on the left of him. I never looked back.

OF CABBAGES
and KINGS

CLAUDE SHEATS HAD BEEN in the Brotherhood all his life and then he had tried to get out. Some of his people and most of his friends were still in the Brotherhood and were still very good members, but Claude was no longer a good member because he had tried to get out after over twenty years. To get away from the Brotherhood and all his friends who were still active in it, he moved to Washington Square and took to reading about being militant. But, living there, he developed a craving for whiteness the way a nicely broke-in virgin craves sex. In spite of this, he maintained a steady black girl, whom he saw at least twice a month to keep up appearances, and once he took both of us with him when he visited his uncle in Harlem who was still in the Brotherhood.

"She's a nice girl, Claude," his uncle's wife had told him that night because the girl, besides being attractive, had some very positive ideas about the Brotherhood. Her name was Marie, she worked as a secretary in my office, and it was on her suggestion that I had moved in with Claude Sheats.

"I'm glad to see you don't waste your time on hippies," the uncle had said. "All our young men are selling out these days."

The uncle was the kind of fellow who had played his cards right. He was much older than his wife, and I had the impression, that night, that he must have given her time to experience enough and to become bored enough before he overwhelmed her with his success. He wore glasses and combed his hair back and had that oily kind of composure that made me think of a waiter waiting to be tipped. He was very proud of his English, I observed, and how he always ended his words with just the right sound. He must have felt superior to people who didn't. He must have felt superior to Claude because he was still with the Brotherhood and Claude had tried to get out.

Claude did not like him and always seemed to feel guilty whenever we visited his uncle's house. "Don't mention any of my girls to him," he told me after our first visit.

"Why would I do that?" I said.

"He'll try to psych you into telling him."

"Why should he suspect you? He never comes over to the apartment."

"He just likes to know what I'm doing. I don't want him to know about my girls."

"I won't say anything," I promised.

He was almost twenty-three and had no steady girls,

except for Marie. He was well built, so that he had no trouble in the Village area. It was like going to the market for him. During my first days in the apartment the process had seemed like a game. And once, when he was going out, I said: "Bring back two."

Half an hour later he came back with two girls. He got their drinks and then he called me into his room to meet them.

"This is Doris," he said, pointing to the smaller one, "and I forgot your name," he said to the big blonde.

"Jane," she said.

"This is Howard," he told her.

"Hi," I said. Neither one of them smiled. The big blonde in white pants sat on the big bed and the little one sat on a chair near the window. He had given them his worst bourbon.

"Excuse me a minute," Claude said to the girls. "I want to talk to Howard for a minute." He put on a record before we went outside into the hall between our rooms. He was always extremely polite and gentle, and very soft-spoken in spite of his size.

"Listen," he said to me outside, "you can have the blonde."

"What can I do with that amazon?"

"I don't care. Just get her out of the room."

"She's dirty," I said.

"So you can give her a bath."

"It wouldn't help much."

"Well, just take her out and talk to her," he told me. "Remember, you asked for her."

We went back in. "Where you from?" I said to the amazon.

"Brighton."

"What school?"

"No. I just got here."

"From where?"

"*Brighton!*"

"That's not so far," I said.

"*England*," she said. She looked very bored. Claude Sheats looked at me.

"How did you find Washington Square so fast?"

"I got friends."

She was very superior about it all and seemed to look at us with the same slightly patient irritation of a professional theater critic waiting for a late performance to begin. The little one sat on the chair, her legs crossed, looking up at the ceiling. Her white pants were dirty too. They looked as though they would have been very relieved if we had taken off our clothes and danced for them around the room and across the bed, and made hungry sounds in our throats with our mouths slightly opened.

I said that I had to go out to the drugstore and would be back very soon; but once outside, I walked a whole hour in one direction and then I walked back. I passed them a block away from our apartment. They were walking fast and did not slow down or speak when I passed them.

Claude Sheats was drinking heavily when I came into the apartment.

"What the hell are you trying to pull?" he said.

"I couldn't find a drugstore open."

He got up from the living room table and walked toward me. "You should have asked me," he said. "I got more than enough."

"I wanted some mouthwash too," I said.

He fumed a while longer, and then told me how I had ruined his evening because the amazon would not leave the room to wait for me and the little one would not do anything with the amazon around. He suddenly thought about going down and bringing them back; and he went out for a while. But he came back without them, saying that they had been picked up again.

"When a man looks out for you, you got to look out for him," he warned me.

"I'm sorry."

"A hell of a lot of good *that* does. And that's the last time I look out for *you*, baby," he said. "From now on it's *me* all the way."

"Thanks," I said.

"If she was too much for you I could of taken the amazon."

"It didn't matter that much," I said.

"You could of had Doris if you couldn't handle the amazon."

"They were both too much," I told him.

But Claude Sheats did not answer. He just looked at me.

ll

AFTER TWO MONTHS of living with him I concluded that Claude hated whites as much as he loved them. And he hated himself with the very same passion. He hated the country and his place in it and he loved the country and his place in it. He loved the Brotherhood and all that being in it had taught him and he still believed in what he had been taught, even after he had left it and did not have to believe in anything.

"This Man is going *down*, Howard," he would announce with conviction.

"Why?" I would ask.

"Because it's the Black Man's time to rule again. They had five thousand years, now we get five thousand years."

"What if I don't *want* to rule?" I asked. "What happens if I don't want to take over?"

He looked at me with pity in his face. "You go down with the rest of the country."

"I guess I wouldn't mind much anyway," I said. "It would be a hell of a place with nobody to hate."

But I could never get him to smile about it the way I tried to smile about it. He was always serious. And, once, when I questioned the mysticism in the teachings of the Brotherhood, Claude almost attacked me. "Another man might kill you for saying that," he had said. "Another man might not let you get away with saying something like that." He was quite deadly and he stood over me with an air of patient superiority. And because he could afford to be generous and forgiving, being one of the saved, he sat down at the table with me under the single light bulb and began to teach me. He told me the stories about how it was in the beginning before the whites took over, and about all the little secret significances of black, and about the subtle infiltration of white superiority into everyday objects.

"You've never seen me eat white bread or white sugar, have you?"

"No," I said. He used brown bread and brown sugar.

"Or use bleached flour or white rice?"

"No."

"You know why, don't you?" He waited expectantly.

"No," I finally said. "I don't know why."

He was visibly shocked, so much so that he dropped that line of instruction and began to draw on a pad before him on the living room table. He moved his big shoulders over the yellow pad to conceal his drawings and looked across the table at me. "Now I'm going to tell you something that white men have paid thousands of dollars to learn," he said. "Men have been killed for telling this but I'm telling you for nothing. I'm warning you not to repeat it because if the whites find out you know, you could be killed too."

"You know me," I said. "I wouldn't repeat any secrets."

He gave me a long thoughtful look.

I gave him back a long, eager, honest look.

Then he leaned across the table and whispered: "Kennedy isn't buried in this country. He was the only President who never had his coffin opened during the funeral. The body was in state all that time and they never opened the coffin once. You know why?"

"No."

"Because he's not *in it*! They buried an empty coffin. Kennedy was a Thirty-third Degree Mason. His body is in Jerusalem right now."

"How do you know?" I asked.

"If I told you it would put your life in danger."

"Did his family know about it?"

"No. His lodge kept it secret."

"No one knew?"

"I'm telling you, *no!*"

"Then how did you find out?"

He sighed, more from tolerance than from boredom with my inability to comprehend the mysticism of pure reality in its most unadulterated form. Of course I could not believe him and we argued about it, back and forth; but to absolutely cap all my uncertainties he drew the thirty-three-degree circle, showed me the secret signs that men had died to learn, and spoke about the time when our black ancestors chased an evil genius out of their kingdom and across a desert and onto an island somewhere in the sea; from which, hundreds of years later, this same evil genius sent forth a perfected breed of white-skinned and evil creatures who, through trickery, managed to enslave for five thousand years the one-time Black Masters of the world. He further explained the significance of the East and why all the saved must go there once during their life-times, and possibly be buried there, as Kennedy had been.

It was dark and late at night, and the glaring bulb cast his great shadow into the corners so that there was the sense of some outraged spirit, fuming in the halls and dark places of our closets, waiting to extract some terrible and justifiable revenge from him for disclosing to me, an unbeliever, the closest kept of secrets. But I was aware of them only for an instant, and then I did not believe him again.

The most convincing thing about it all was that he was very intelligent and had an orderly, well-regimented life-style, and yet *he* had no trouble with believing. He believed in the certainty of statistical surveys, which was his work; the nutritional value of wheat germ sprinkled on eggs; the sensuality of gin; and the dangers inherent in smoking. He was stylish in that he did not believe in God, but he was extremely moral and warm and kind; and I wanted sometimes to embrace him for his kindness and bigness and gentle manners. He lived his life so carefully that no matter what he said, I could not help but believe him sometimes. But I did not want to, because I knew that once I started I could not stop; and then there would be no purpose to my own beliefs and no real conviction or direction in my own efforts to achieve when always in the back of my regular thoughts, there would be a sense of futility and a fear of the unknown all about me. So, for the sake of necessity, I chose not to believe him.

He felt that the country was doomed and that the safe thing to do was to make enough money as soon as possible and escape to the Far East. He forecast summer riots in certain Northern cities and warned me, religiously, to avoid all implicating ties with whites so that I might have a chance to be saved when that time came. And I asked him about *his* ties, and the girls, and how it was never a movie date with coffee afterwards but always his room and the cover-all blanket of Motown sounds late into the night.

"A man has different reasons for doing certain things," he had said.

He never seemed to be comfortable with any of the

girls. He never seemed to be in control. And after my third month in the apartment I had concluded that he used his virility as a tool and forged, for however long it lasted, a little area of superiority which could never, it seemed, extend itself beyond the certain confines of his room, no matter how late into the night the records played. I could see him fighting to extend the area, as if an increase in the number of girls he saw could compensate for what he had lost in duration. He saw many girls: curious students, unexpected bus-stop pickups, and assorted other one-nighters. And his rationalizations allowed him to believe that each one was an actual conquest, a physical affirmation of a psychological victory over all he hated and loved and hated in the little world of his room.

But then he seemed to have no happiness, even in this. Even here I sensed some intimations of defeat. After each girl, Claude would almost immediately come out of his room, as if there was no need for aftertalk; as if, after it was over, he felt a brooding, silent emptiness that quickly intensified into nervousness and instantaneous shyness and embarrassment so that the cold which sets in after that kind of emotional drain came in very sharp against his skin, and he could not bear to have her there any longer. And when the girl had gone, he would come into my room to talk. These were the times when he was most like a little boy; and these were the times when he really began to trust me.

"That bitch called me everything but the son of God," he would chuckle. And I would put aside my papers brought home from the office, smile at him, and listen.

He would always eat or drink afterwards and in those early days I was glad for his companionship and the return of his trust, and sometimes we drank and talked until dawn. During these times he would tell me more subtleties about the Man and would re-predict the fall of the country. Once, he warned me, in a fatherly way, about reading life from books before experiencing it; and another night he advised me on how to schedule girls so that one could run them without being run in return. These were usually good times of good-natured arguments and predictions; but as we drank more often he tended to grow more excited and quick-tempered, especially after he had just entertained. Sometimes he would seethe hate, and every drink he took gave life to increasingly bitter condemnations of the present system and our place in it. There were actually flying saucers, he told me once, piloted by things from other places in the universe which would eventually destroy the country for what it had done to the black man. He had run into his room, on that occasion, and had brought out a book by a man who maintained that the government was deliberately withholding from the public overwhelming evidence of flying saucers and strange creatures from other galaxies that walked among us every day. Claude emphasized the fact that the writer was a Ph.D. who must know what he was talking about, and insisted that the politicians withheld the information because they knew that their time was almost up and if they made it public the black man would know that he had outside friends who would help him take over the world again. Nothing I said could make him reconsider the slightest bit of his information.

"What are we going to use for weapons when we take over?" I asked him once.

"We've got atomic bombs stockpiled and waiting for the day."

"How can you believe that crap?"

He did not answer, but said instead: "You are the living example of what the Man has done to my people."

"I just try to think things out for myself," I said.

"You can't think. The handkerchief over your head is too big."

I smiled.

"I know," he continued. "I know all there is to know about whites because I've been studying them all my life."

I smiled some more.

"I ought to know," he said slowly. "I have supernatural powers."

"I'm tired," I told him. "I want to go to sleep now."

Claude started to leave the room, then he turned. "Listen," he said at the door. He pointed his finger at me to emphasize the gravity of his pronouncement. "I predict that within the next week something is going to happen to this country that will hurt it even more than Kennedy's assassination."

"Goodnight," I said as he closed the door.

He opened it again. "Remember that I predicted it when it happens," he said. For the first time I noticed that he had been deadly serious all along.

Two days later several astronauts burned to death in Florida. He raced into my room hot with the news.

"Do you believe in me *now?*" he said. "Just two days and look what happened."

I tried to explain, as much to myself as to him, that in any week of the year something unfortunate was bound to occur. But he insisted that this was only part of a divine plan to bring the country to its knees. He said that he intended to send a letter off right away to Jeane Dixon in D.C. to let her know that she was not alone because he also had the same power. Then he thought that he had better not because the FBI knew that he had been active in the Brotherhood before he got out.

At first it was good fun believing that someone important cared enough to watch us. And sometimes when the telephone was dead a long time before the dial tone sounded, I would knock on his door and together we would run through our telephone conversations for that day to see if either of us had said anything implicating or suspect, just in case they were listening. This feeling of persecution brought us closer together and soon the instruction sessions began to go on almost every night. At this point I could not help but believe him a little. And he began to trust me again, like a tolerable little brother, and even confided that the summer riots would break out simultaneously in Harlem and Watts during the second week in August. For some reason, something very difficult to put into words, I spent three hot August nights on the streets of Harlem, waiting for the riot to start.

In the seventh month of our living together, he began to introduce me to his girls again when they came in. Most of them came only once, but all of them received the same mechanical treatment. He only discriminated with liquor, the quality of which improved with the attractiveness or reluctance of the girl: gin for slow starters, bourbon for momentary strangers, and the scotch he reserved for those he hoped would come again. There was first the trek into his room, his own trip out for the ice and glasses while classical music was played within; then after a while the classical piece would be replaced by several Motowns. Finally, there was her trip to the bathroom, his calling a cab in the hall, and the sound of both their feet on the stairs as he walked her down to the cab. Then he would come to my room in his red bathrobe, glass in hand, for the aftertalk.

THEN IN THE NINTH MONTH the trouble started. It would be very easy to pick out one incident, one day, one area of misunderstanding in that month and say: "That was where it began." It would be easy, but not accurate. It might have been one instance or a combination of many. It might have been the girl who came into the living room, when I was going over the proposed blueprints for a new settlement house, and who lingered too long outside his room in conversation because her father was a builder somewhere. Or it might have been nothing at all. But after that time he warned me about being too friendly with his company.

Another night, when I was leaving the bathroom in my shorts, he came out of his room with a girl who smiled.

"Hi," she said to me.

I nodded hello as I ducked back into the bathroom.

When he had walked her down to the door he came to my room and knocked. He did not have a drink.

"Why didn't you speak to my company?" he demanded.

"I was in my shorts."

"She felt bad about it. She asked what the hell was

wrong with you. What could I tell her—'He got problems'?"

"I'm sorry," I said. "But I didn't want to stop in my shorts."

"I see through you, Howard," he said. "You're just jealous of me and try to insult my girls to get to me."

"Why should I be jealous of you?"

"Because I'm a man and you're not."

"What makes a man anyway?" I said. "Your fried eggs and wheat germ? Why should I be jealous of you *or* what you bring in?"

"Some people don't need a reason. You're a black devil and you'll get yours. I predict that you'll get yours."

"Look," I told him, "I'm sorry about the girl. Tell her I'm sorry when you see her again."

"You treated her so bad she probably won't come back."

I said nothing more and he stood there silently for a long time before he turned to leave the room. But at the door he turned again and said: "I see through you, Howard. You're a black devil."

It should have ended there and it might have with anyone else. I took great pains to speak to his girls after that, even though he tried to get them into the room as quickly as possible. But a week later he accused me of walking about in his room after he had gone out, some two weeks before.

"I swear I wasn't in your room," I protested.

"I saw your shadow on the blinds from across the street at the bus stop," he insisted.

"I've *never* been in your room when you weren't there," I told him.

"I *saw* you!"

We went into his room and I tried to explain how, even if he could see the window from the bus stop, the big lamp next to the window prevented any shadow from being cast on the blinds. But he was convinced in his mind that at every opportunity I plundered his closets and drawers. He had no respect for simple logic in these matters, no sense of the absurdity of his accusations, and the affair finally ended with my confessing that I might have done it without actually knowing; and if I had, I would not do it again.

But what had been a gesture for peace on my part became a vindication for him, proof that I *was* a black devil, capable of lying and lying until he confronted me with the inescapable truth of the situation. And so he persisted in creating situations from which, if he insisted on a point long enough and with enough self-righteousness, he could draw my inevitable confession.

And I confessed eagerly, goaded on by the necessity of maintaining peace. I confessed to mixing white sugar crystals in with his own brown crystals so that he could use it and violate the teachings of the Brotherhood; I confessed to cleaning the bathroom all the time merely because I wanted to make him feel guilty for not having ever cleaned it. I confessed to telling the faithful Marie, who brought a surprise dinner over for him, that he was working late at his office in order to implicate him with the girls who worked there. I confessed to leaving my papers about the house so that his company could ask about them and develop an interest in me. And I pleaded guilty to a record of other little infamies, which multiplied into countless others, and again subdivided into hundreds of little subtleties until my every movement was a threat to him. If I had a girlfriend to dinner, we should eat in my room instead of at the table because he had to use the bathroom a lot and, besides not wanting to seem as if he were making a pass at my girl by walking through the room so often, he was genuinely embarrassed to be seen going to the bathroom.

If I protested he would fly into a tantrum and shake his big finger at me vigorously. And so I retreated, step by step, into my room, from which I emerged only to go to the bathroom or kitchen or out of the house. I tried to stay out on nights when he had company. But he had company so often that I could not always help being in my room after he had walked her to the door. Then he would knock on my door for his talk. He might offer me a drink, and if I refused, he would go to his room for a while and then come back. He would pace about for a while, like a big little boy who wants to ask for money over his allowance. At these times my mind would move feverishly over all our contacts for as far back as I could make it reach, searching and attempting to pull out that one incident which would surely be the point of his attack. But it was never any use; it might have been anything.

"Howard, I got something on my chest and I might as well get it off."

"What is it?" I asked from my bed.

"You been acting strange lately. Haven't been talking to me. If you got something on your chest, get it off now."

"I have nothing on my chest," I said.

"Then why don't you talk?"

I did not answer.

"You hardly speak to me in the kitchen. If you have something against me, tell me now."

"I have nothing against you."

"Why don't you talk, then?" He looked directly at me. "If a man doesn't talk, you think *something's* wrong!"

"I've been nervous lately, that's all. I got problems and I don't want to talk."

"Everybody's got problems. That's no reason for going around making a man feel guilty."

"For God's sake, I don't want to talk."

"I know what's wrong with you. Your conscience is bothering you. You're so evil that your conscience is giving you trouble. You got everybody fooled but *me*. I know you're a black devil."

"I'm a black devil," I said. "Now will you let me sleep?"

He went to the door. "You dish it out but you can't take it," he said. "That's *your* trouble."

"I'm a black devil," I said.

I lay there, after he left, hating myself but thankful that he hadn't called me into his room for the fatherly talk as he had done another time. That was the worst. He had come to the door and said: "Come out of there, I want to talk to you." He had walked ahead of me into his room and had sat down in his big leather chair next to the lamp with his legs spread wide and his big hands in his lap. He had said: "Don't be afraid. I'm not going to hurt you. Sit down. I'm not going to argue. What are you so nervous about? Have a drink," in his kindest, most fatherly way, and that had been the worst of all. That was the time he had told me to eat in my room. Now I could hear him pacing about in the hall and I knew that it was not over for the night. I began to pray that I could sleep before he came and that he would not be able to wake me, no matter what he did. I did not care what he did as long as I did not have to face him. I resolved to confess to anything he accused me of if it would make him leave sooner. I was about to go out into the hall for my confession when the door was kicked open and he charged into the room.

"You black son-of-a-bitch!" he said. "I ought to *kill* you." He stood over the bed in the dark room and shook his big fist over me. And I lay there hating the overpowering cowardice in me, which kept my body still and my eyes closed, and hoping that he would kill all of it when his heavy fist landed.

"First you insult a man's company, then you ignore him. I been *good* to you. I let you live here, I let you eat my uncle's food, and I taught you things. But you're a ungrateful motherfucker. I ought to *kill* you right now!"

And I still lay there, as he went on, not hearing him, with nothing in me but a loud throbbing which pulsed through the length of my body and made the sheets move with its pounding. I lay there secure and safe in cowardice for as long as I looked up at him with my eyes big and my body twitching and my mind screaming out to him that it was all right, and I thanked him, because now I truly believed in the new five thousand years of Black Rule.

It is night again. I am in bed again, and I can hear the new blonde girl closing the bathroom door. I know that in a minute he will come out in his red robe and call a cab. His muffled voice through my closed door will seem very tired, but just as kind and patient to the dispatcher as it is to everyone, and as it was to me in those old times. I am afraid because when they came up the stairs earlier they caught me working at the living room table with my back to them. I had not expected him back so soon; but then I should have known that he would not go out. I had turned around in the chair and she smiled and said hello and I said "Hi" before he hurried her into the room. I *did* speak and I know that she heard. But I also know that I must have done something wrong; if not to her, then to him earlier today or yesterday or last week, because he glared at me before following her into the room and he almost paused to say something when he came out to get the glasses and ice. I wish that I could remember just what it was. But it does not matter. I *am* guilty and he knows it.

Now that he knows about me I am afraid. I could move away from the apartment and hide my guilt from him, but I know that he would find me. The brainwashed part of my mind tells me to call the police while he is still busy with her, but what could I charge him with when I know that he is only trying to help me. I could move the big, ragged yellow chair in front of the door, but that would not stop him, and it might make him impatient with me. Even if I pretended to be asleep and ignored him, it would not help when he comes. He has not bothered to knock for weeks.

In the black shadows over my bed and in the corners I can sense the outraged spirits who help him when they hover about his arms as he gestures, with his lessons, above my bed. I am determined now to lie here and take it. It is the price I must pay for all the black secrets I have learned, and all the evil I have learned about myself. I *am* jealous of him, of his learning, of his girls. I am not the same handkerchief-head I was nine months ago. I have Marie to thank for that, and Claude, and the spirits. They know about me, and perhaps it is they who make him do it and he cannot help himself. I believe in the spirits now, just as I believe most of the time that I am a black devil.

They are going down to the cab now.

I will not ever blame him for it. He is helping me. But I blame the girls. I blame them for not staying on afterwards, and for letting all the good nice happy love talk cut off automatically after it is over. *I* need to have them there, after it is over. And he needs it; he needs it much more and much longer than they could ever need what he does for them. He should be able to teach them, as he has taught me. And he should have their appreciation, as he has mine. I blame them. I blame them for letting him try and try and never get just a little of the love there is left in the world.

I can hear him coming back from the cab.

ALL *the*
LONELY PEOPLE

*Deep, deep down and far away it lies, waiting, dormant,
lazily latent and still waiting, confined, measuring the
time, conditions and touching circumstances; imprisoned,
but marking life and time with its own violent beats
against suppressing strictures and rectitudes, and
estimating the chances of being reborn.*

*Sometimes, in the night, it is expectant and therefore
eager to be out. It has slept too long and is restless, fighting
the force that keeps it patient. Years of internal slumber
have drugged it, but not decisively, so that, once slightly
touched, it starts and quivers and attempts to announce
itself so strongly that, occasionally, a man's mind will
wake in his bed and ask itself: "Who is there?"*

WHY DO THEY ALWAYS FAIL ME, DENNIS?" he said.
"I'm sure I don't know," I said.

"They never pay me back; but they always want to borrow again."

"You're too generous, Alfred," I said. "Save your money."

"Sometimes they won't even speak to me on the street. And when I try to speak to them they get mad."

"That proves they're not your friends," I said. "Don't lend them anything else."

Alfred looked at me across the table. He spread his bony fingers flat on the plastic surface of the table and looked me full in the face. "You wouldn't fail me, would you, Dennis?"

I looked again under the dress of a careless girl, at another table across the room, who had now noticed me and was pumping her knees up and down under the table, telling me to forget about the fellow who sat too intellectual and confident across from her.

"Of course not, Alfred," I said.

"Thank you," Alfred said.

He was a coffee-shop fag, to use a local expression, who was getting older and desperate so that his teeth were not wet when he smiled, as is their custom, because his mouth was so dry from his daily decreasing expectations. He was also losing most of the hair from the top of his head and his eyes were soft and scared, like a trapped animal who does not know how to fight. Doubtless he had been in that place before and had some unpleasant experience, because he kept looking over at the counterman, a rednecked fellow who picked at his chin, as if he expected to be thumbed out at any moment for some past sin against the establishment. He smiled very little, in fact, and leaned too far across the table when talking so that the entire clientele of the café, if they cared enough to look, could easily surmise what we were about. I had come into that place for coffee.

"Do you know Rudy Smith?" he breathed across the table almost passionately.

I recalled Rudy Smith, sometime stud, dope-pusher, and freelance hip black who wore a great head of natural hair and an African costume in order to work part-time as a shill in one of the mod shops. "No," I said.

"You should. Everybody knows Rudy."

"It's a common name."

"Well, he's a friend of mine." He paused to allow me to become sufficiently impressed. "He owes me money, too."

"You must have lots of money to lend it out so freely."

"I have a trust fund," he said quickly. Then he added, somewhat more casually: "I'm really a poet."

"Published?"

"I've a book almost finished. It's on Melville's poetry."

"Did he write poetry?"

"Very little. It's a small book. I'm trying to put all his poems in chronological order by tracing the deterioration of his handwriting in the original manuscripts. I had to take a course in handwriting analysis just to do that," he said very proudly. "And I guess I have to do something scholarly to justify my own self as a poet."

"Why?"

"People have this impression that poets just go around sniffing little girls' bicycle seats." He laughed. "It's my private Holy Crusade."

"Of course," I said, looking at the bobbing knees again.

The intellectual friend was now explaining some very fine point to her. I heard him mention Nietzsche as he made little progressive motions on the table with his hand, and I knew that he was lost. He did not notice her smiling at me, he was so enraptured with his ideas.

"Are we going to be friends, Dennis?" Alfred Bowles was asking.

"Sure," I said, not looking at him.

"You do like me?"

"Of course." The friend had finally noticed her smiling and was now talking faster and making the motions on the table with both his hands.

"She's got the clap," said Alfred. He had been watching me all along.

I looked back at him. "How do you know?"

He looked pleased. "Rudy Smith told me when we were here last. She hangs out here all the time."

"I guess *he would* know," I said.

"I thought you didn't know him?"

"I don't. But I guess he would know all right."

"Rudy gets around," Alfred said. He considered for a moment and then said very carefully: "Let's have a drink."

Our coffee was cold by this time. "All the bars are closed now," I said.

"I've got scotch at my place?" he offered.

"Not tonight," I said. "I have something to do."

"Please have just one. I don't live far from here." He leaned closer and said more intimately: "We could have some *grass* if you want."

Bobbing Knees was looking hard at her watch and making sure that I saw her. "I've got to go," I told Alfred.

"You'll get clap," he warned me.

"Maybe not."

"What about him?"

"She knows what to do. Besides, we're not after the same thing. He wants to impress her with his mind."

"And you?"

"There're too many good minds here to bother with exercises," I said. "I can impress her with my lack of one." I picked up my check very conspicuously. The girl pushed her watch close to the intellectual's face. He looked at her watch and then at his own, and then he threw up his hands in what might have been exasperation or an over-dramatized apology. She got up quickly, motioned for him to stay and paused while he wrote something in his note-book. Then she left him and walked past us and toward the door.

"Goodbye," I said to Alfred Bowles. "I really enjoyed the talk."

"At least take my card," he said. He handed me a homemade, handwritten quarter of a lined index card. "Everything's on there," he said. I glimpsed a wad of simi-lar cards in his wallet before he put it back into his pocket. "Please call," he said in a voice that made me look at him, really, for what was probably the first time in the whole hour we had spent at the table. The tone was sad and lack-ing optimism, as if he did not expect me to call but, deep inside himself, pleadingly wished that I would.

"I will," I told him.

He gave me that last-hope look directly in the eyes and said: "Please don't fail me, Dennis. Don't be like all the others."

"Look," I said, trying to be sincere and trying not to be hard all in the same voice, "we'll have a drink or something. That's all. We'll talk, that's all. We'll be friends, that's all."

"Good," he said, somewhat slowly. "But do call."

"I will," I assured him. "I promise to call."

I left him there looking over the brim of his empty coffee cup, holding it up to his face with both hands as if he were hiding, possibly searching the room for others who had not yet found their bobbing knees. I met mine outside on the street, cigarette in mouth, being patient and selective about who she would ask for a match. I gave her a light and then walked away. She had only been for the benefit of Alfred, a convenient and manly excuse for getting out of that shop without having to give an aging fairy specific reasons why I would not have a scotch with him. Also, there was a certain affirmation of something, a certain pride, a sense of some small and sensual accomplishment in it for me.

II

FOR THOSE WHO CHOOSE to live their lives as animals, life is really very simple. In the human jungle there are only the hunters and the hunted. The idea of social classes is a mythical invention, I suspect, manufactured like religion by successful hunters who have found their prey and who want to maintain what they have already won from other hunters. And successful hunters are a higher order; for once their prey is secure in their caves, other, less fortunate hunters begin to sniff around and smell them out and they then become the hunted. We all begin as hunters, uncertain and fumbling until we gain sufficient confidence in our weapons and equipment so that we can afford to rest, and let others seek us out. Sometimes, like the lion, we fight to keep other hunters away; and sometimes we share, out of generosity or kindness but most often out of unconcern and sated appetites, a small part of our prey. And this sharing also serves as a declaration, in the jungle of things, that one has passed the hunter stage and recognizes his coming into the ranks of the very select few who are hunted. A man is my friend and seeks me out either because he wants something I have acquired or he hopes to get closer to something to which I alone have the necessary access. Unsuccessful hunters are weaker than the hunted because they declare, by their searching, their inability to be self-sufficient; they have nothing to guard from others, they are always seeking, they have very little to lose. In nature, the stronger animals are not really the hunters; they are called so merely because they have the ability to fend for themselves. Those who follow the lion for the scraps he may leave, and not the lion himself, are the real hunters. The lion is all-confident and certain that he will always be able to bring down his meat, and allows jackals to follow him, at a safe distance, to see that he can very well survive on his own and needs them only to feed his own ego. Sometimes I want to be a lion because I have many friends who have grown strong that way.

On the subway in the early-morning going-to-work hours I met Alfred again. His eyes were not the same as they had been that first night: they were very bright and open, and only his mouth, when he talked and occasionally wet his lips might have suggested to the straphangers around us in the jostling car who he really was. We talked of politics, poetry, our jobs, and certain other things. He was a teacher by day, he told me; poetry was only his nighttime thing. He was professionally cool and detached from me, his card, and anything of that night now more than two weeks old. "We might have lunch downtown some noon," he said to me just before his station.

"That would be fine," I said.

"I'd really like to know you," he said sincerely, his eyes not looking at mine. "Truthfully, I really like talking to you."

I gave him my number and address, knowing the risk of midnight desperation and sudden drop-ins, because he looked so changed and different from that night.

"I'll make it a point to call you someday for lunch," he said.

"Please do," I told him.

He went away with the crowd and was one of them in an instant. I wondered how many others like him went that same way to work each morning without disclosing by their movements or eyes the secret thoughts or interludes of the night before.

III

HE KNOCKED ON MY DOOR very late at night when I had been expecting a girl. Opening the door and seeing him there, nervous and sweating and a little funny because he was relieved and afraid at the same time, irritated me.

"Oh God!" he said. "Please can I talk to you!"

"Come in," I said, resigned to tolerate him for the little time until the girl came. He moved into the room and sat on the sofa with the timidity of a child carefully exercising properly taught manners for the first time.

"Have a cup of coffee, Alfred," I said.

He accepted and I heated water while he sat on the sofa, his face in his hands. "Oh my God! Oh my God!" he kept repeating.

"What's wrong?" I asked from the kitchen when I knew he was waiting for me to respond.

"Nothing. Everything. I haven't a friend in the world. Are you my friend, Dennis? Are you really?"

"Of course," I said. "You know I am."

"Do you like me?"

"Of course."

"I like *you*. I love you."

Not knowing how to respond, I handed him the cup of hot water and the jar of instant coffee. His hands shook as he put them on the coffee table and continued to stare at me.

"What happened?" I finally asked.

"It's Rudy," he said. "He won't pay me. I went over to his place to talk about it—just to talk about the money—and he called me all kinds of names. Now, that wasn't right. You know it wasn't right."

"No, it wasn't," I said.

"And he had a bitch there, and they *both* laughed at me. A bleached-blonde bitch, and she laughed at *me!*"

"It wasn't right," I said again.

"Now I love your people," he said. "I think they're all beautiful. I think it's a dirty shame the way they treat you people down South."

"I've never been South," I lied, drinking my own coffee busily.

"But Rudy owes me money and he and that bitch laughed at me."

"I'm sorry about it," I said. I looked at my watch. "Just don't lend him any more money."

He made a great effort to look deep into my eyes. I looked into his. They were his nighttime eyes now; the hurt there was that of a wounded animal, almost tearful and brightly moist and desperate for a life that was fast leaving him.

"I love your people," he declared again. Then he paused and continued to look directly at me. And then he held out both his arms. "Dennis," he said, "Dennis, Dennis, Dennis. Oh come to me."

I looked at him, not quite in amazement. I had been expecting it all along, but I was disgusted by his lack of finesse or tact.

"You're such a beautiful man, Dennis. You're all so beautiful. Oh, God! You're *so* beautiful!"

I got up from the chair and began to walk about the room and away from him. "Now look," I said, with all the manhood in my voice I could muster. "I understand your position but you've got to see mine. I'm straight. I can't do what Rudy does."

"Come to me," he said again, his arms still raised in a Christly pose.

"You have to go," I said decisively.

"Please, Dennis, oh please, please, don't leave me alone."

"Finish your coffee and just cut it out."

He mixed his coffee, which was now cold and undrinkable, and kept his eyes moving over my face, my legs, my body, all the while he was stirring. He drank it in gulps, glancing up at me as if I were holding a gun on him or had some great reward to be given as soon as the coffee was finished. It was a terrible power to have; and having it weakened me, made me want to give him reasons for not doing the thing he wanted. I hated Rudy Smith for having this power, I hated him for using it the way he had; and I hated and pitied Alfred, both at the same time, for forcing me to fall victim to his own inability to cope with himself and for forcing an invasion of his dignity onto me.

"Isn't there some bar you could go to?" I asked.

"No. The vice squad men all know me and I'd have to pay them money."

"Would it help if we just talked some—about your poems?"

He had that dying look again. "Please, Dennis, oh please help me!" he moaned, again with his head in his hands.

"I'm sorry, Alfred. I really am," I said.

He kept his head pressed into his spread palms and commenced to sob. He sounded like a rooting pig, smothering great sniffles and coughs in his two hands. I could not touch him, although I wanted to; I dared not touch him, although he needed just the slightest touch, the merest sign at that moment more than anything else in the world. But my rooms were not the world, and his world was surely not there, in that room. And so I opened the door for him and stood outside it, and waited for him to come out because I had, all at once, the greatest fear of having him behind me. "Come and talk whenever you want," I told him. He still sat on the sofa, his eyes red, his face blotched with very red and very white areas; sniffing, he sat there. I stepped out further into the hall. "I want you to know that you can come back to talk—to talk—whenever you want."

He rose meekly from the sofa and came out the door, toward me. I backed away. He looked hurt, even more, and I was sorry.

"I'm all right now, Dennis," he said. He looked awfully tired. He looked at me a long moment longer, as if daring himself to say something more, and then he turned and went away down the hall.

I lay on my bed after I had made sure that he was not standing around in the hall and waiting before he knocked again. I lay on the bed and wondered at how close I had come to touching him. I thought about Betty and how late she was getting there and how I needed to ask her to spend the night, for company and for something else. I hated to have Betty in my bed in the morning: it was a small bed and she did not know what to do with her legs. Besides, she was a huge feeder and it disgusted me to have to eat with her and watch her eat breakfast. Still, I needed to have her there and I could endure anything as long as I had a girl there—for other things.

I thought about those other things.

Jeffrey is the only boy in our high-school class who has already got a moustache. We all envy him.

Sometimes he lets us touch it. Sometimes he lets me buy lunch for him. Then we hang around together after school. When I make Jeffrey laugh he slaps me on the back very hard. I like it. I try to make him laugh all the time. At graduation time he lets me autograph his yearbook. I use a whole page for a poem I write on friendship. Then the other kids come to autograph the book and see the poem and begin to look at me. I see them talking and laughing in the corners and Jeffrey is embarrassed and laughs too. The teacher knows about it and comes over to me and says, "Never mind, that's a good poem," but it does not help. I do not have anything to say to him. That last week of school I begin to find written on my desk the kind of words they put above the toilets in men's rooms of bus stations.

"WHAT HAPPENED TO YOU?" I asked Betty over the telephone. It was 2:00 A.M.

"I got tied up," she said.

"Can you still come?"

"It's too late."

"You could have called."

"I know," she said. "I guess I'm no good for you."

I could not lose her tonight and was prepared to lie relentlessly just to have her there that one night. "You're *too* good for me. Come on over."

"Look," she said. "It's late. We can have a drink some other time. Let's both just get some sleep."

"We could do that together."

"I'm tired. And I'm sorry that I didn't call or come but I just didn't. Can't you accept that?"

"Goodbye," I said and pushed down the button.

It is very hard to push down a button that way when that little, little expenditure of strength cuts off forever the source of what has kept me from touching Alfred Bowles or from being on the streets like him, a hunter, with different, desperate eyes, reserved for the night, looking into back alleys and risking every degradation to solicit strangers in search of an affirmation of what he thought was himself. I lay back on my bed and thought of him, where he was now, whether he was still crying and to whom, or on what hard ear his pleas were falling. I thought of what must be his deep determination to get whatever it was he wanted, his desperate acceptance of whatever a hustler demanded for his company, his endurance of blows and laughs and insinuations, all for what? I had the feeling that I might have gone into Alfred's arms earlier and that would have been all he really wanted, even though he might have tried to do something else, perhaps for no other reason than because he was expected to.

I took out my wallet and found his card, wondering how many other of these crude, homemade, handwritten offerings of himself were moving through the city, forgotten in wallets, left on the floors of men's rooms or coffee shops or taverns or dormitories, or even libraries. I looked at the writing for the first time. It read: Alfred Bowles: 17 Brewster Street, Apartment Number 21, Telephone Number: 351–5210, Poet. Nothing was abbreviated; nothing that might misdirect the holder of the card was left to chance. It was a sad summation of himself, a crudely pleading invitation to invade a privacy he did not want. The card was a limited, almost secret, declaration of himself, cut and set and written, not by his own hands, but by the subtler, more powerful hands of men who had discovered girls very early in life in closets and school play areas, and who had learned, as he had not, that a man's place in life must necessarily be that of the hunted and he must hurry through the hunter stages before something stops him from becoming a lion.

IV

MY FRIEND GERALD IS ONE of the hunted. His specialty is girls. Although his reputation is firmly established as one of those to be sought out, he modestly prefers to call himself a cock-hound; and when in private company, but especially in the company of girls, he takes great pleasure in getting down on his knees and crawling around on the floor and declaring: "I am a cock-hound, gimme-some, gimme-some" in a voice very much like a bark. He is not crude, because he drinks good scotch and only does his dog thing in the company of honest girls who, he is always confident, will laugh immediately and not later, when they arc alone. He has a keen eye for these girls, a virtue with which I was never blessed. He is a lion and is quite successful. Like me, he is a bachelor; unlike me, he knows how to live by his wits. He is my source. Whenever I do not have a girl, it is only necessary to call Gerald and he will arrange for me to meet one, usually the rare ones who do not laugh at his cock-hound bits.

"I need one," I told Gerald that Thursday in our favorite barroom. "I need a date bad."

He looked at me, thinking. Gerald is the kind of person who believes in the credit-debit system of life. He does not give anything away.

"I drove you to the airport last week," I reminded him.

"Yeah," he said from his carefully trimmed moustache. "You did. Well, all I have for you is a dog."

"Your kind?" I asked.

He laughed. "No, a real dog. I already had it. She's a real bitch. A real community chest. Do *you* want it?"

"Sure," I said, knowing that Gerald dislikes immensely anyone with tastes different from his own. "How do I play it?"

"Just be cool," he said. "She's such a dog your natural reaction to the way she looks will make you look cool. But don't say anything intelligent; she's also a dummy and can't stand intelligence."

"That's *all* you got?"

"That's it," he said. "But it's a sure thing. Take it or go horny all week."

"It's not the pussy, Gerald," I said.

"Like hell," said Gerald. "You can't bullshit me. You just like to talk a lot before you get into it just to make yourself suffer."

"You're a real Freud," I said.

"Like hell," he said. "Freud knew the shit and went horny. I know it and don't."

"But it's really not the pussy that matters."

Gerald looked at his watch. "Do you want the dog or don't you?" he said.

I thought about the weekend and some other things. "O.K.," I said. "I'll take the dog."

Gerald smiled, and for a second his eyes and big teeth behind his moustache were laughing at me in the worst way. "Her name is Gloria," he said. "I'm screwing her roommate Friday night so I'll take you over when I go to pick her up."

"Shouldn't I call her myself?"

"Hell no," said Gerald. "I told you she's not that kind of girl. Look," he said, eyeing me seriously for a moment, "this girl is a shortcoat. If you go over there longcoating you'll fuck up and not get anything. Play it my way. Play it cool."

"O.K.," I said. "I'll play it shortcoat."

"Now you're being hip," said Gerald.

Certain people I do not know always speak to me on the street. They are very neat boys in tight pants and impeccable shirts; they are men who walk in fast, sometimes nervous steps, men with suggestive, sensitive mouths. They seem to recognize me or nod or stare, and know me; but I do not know them, although their eyes, passing over my face, say that I do. I make a point of not speaking to them, but I cannot help looking back whenever they recognize me. And whenever I do, I see that their eyes are frightened, always frightened, and I know that my own are. But I do not know why. Once, drinking beer in a bar with a friend, one of them comes over to our booth and ignores my friend and looks directly at me, and says: "What happened to you? They're all waiting for you at the party." I wink at my friend and he winks back and I begin to put the fellow on. "I stepped out for a while for a beer," I say. "Tell them I'll be back in an hour."

"Take your time," he says. "It's been going on for days, it'll last awhile longer."

"Why did you leave?" I ask him.

"I'll tell you later," he says, noticing my friend for the first time. "But do hurry back. They'll miss us both."

"I'll be there," I say.

He walks back to the bar.

"Who was that?" my friend Norris asks.

"I don't know," I say honestly. "I was just putting him on."

"He probably mistook you for somebody else," says Norris.

"Yeah," I say. "This is a crazy bar."

"Wasn't he gay?" asks Norris.

I think a minute. "He probably was," I say at last. "There're more fairies here than in the Brothers Grimm."

Norris laughs and drinks his beer. I look at mine on the table and see how round and big my face looks reflected in the brown liquid. All at once I do not feel like drinking.

She was a real dog. I really expected her to bark, but she only held out her hand and looked very unhappy to see me. Gerald, of course, was very pleased to introduce us. His date was pretty, with smooth, dark brown skin and a genuine smile, and I could see that Gloria hated him, perhaps not so much for screwing her and then taking out her roommate, as for insinuating in his wide, toothy smiles and sly asides to me, that he was passing her body on to someone who had need of it for a night.

"Watch out for the curves, if you can find them," Gerald said to me in his most obvious aside. Gloria was watching us as we stood by the door. I knew that she hated both of us.

"God help the dogs," I said to Gerald, trying, in my own way, to be hip.

He laughed heartily.

"What's funny?" said Gloria.

"You are," Gerald said. "You are one funny chick."

"You know what I think of *you*," she said.

"Yeah," said Gerald. "And *you* know that I don't give a good goddamn."

The odd thing was that they were both smiling, which gave me the feeling that they had long ago arrived at some silent agreement, of which this scene was merely the verbal part.

The roommate came out of her room. She was very pretty, especially when she stood next to Gloria. She was wearing a white miniskirt, which complemented her skin. Out of the corner of my eye, I could see Gerald watching me watching her and laughing, and knew that he would not introduce me to her.

"Stay cool," he said, still smiling and taking the roommate out the door. And then the dog and I were alone.

We talked. She was from the South and was ashamed of it. "I left when I was real young," she said.

We drank. Scotch. Because, she said, that was all she ever drank. "It doesn't get me drunk," she said, watching me.

"What sort of music do you like?"

"I like Maggie and the Vaudevilles," she said. "I like all their stuff. I like the Impressions a lot too."

"That's all you like?"

"Yeah," she said defensively. "What about it?"

"Nothing. I like them too."

We were both silent. "What do you think of Gerald?" I said just to hear myself speak.

"He's a real son-of-a-bitch," she said. "He's a no-good bastard, if you ask me."

"Oh," I said.

"I'll tell you something about Gerald. He uses people. He don't give a damn about anybody but hisself."

"Oh," I said.

I had been sitting all this time in a cushioned chair, allowing her to sit by herself on the sofa, her thick legs open, her long girdle showing far below the hemline of her dress. I had been waiting all this time for her to become attractive; because everyone, even the worst dog or most colorless person, can become attractive almost immediately if they are touched in the right place. Even a round, hard face like hers can, almost magically, become interesting if the mind gives the eyes sufficient reason to come alive. Her magic spot was her utter helplessness and her dull inability to defend herself against it. She had been used, probably, all her life by people like Gerald and I suspected that she did not know or could never accept any other way to live. I pitied her for this. And because I pitied her, I remained in the chair while she shifted her legs on the sofa in a pathetic effort to be seductive, a grotesque display of all she had in the world to make her interesting. I did not want to play dumb in order to impress her because I did not want her. I wanted to brush her short, wiry hair with my hands and hold her hands and tell her that she would always be used and passed from body to body by men like Gerald and myself, and cry with her for all of us.

"What's wrong with you?" she said.

"Nothing."

"Why are you looking at me that way?" She was smiling, expecting a momentary movement over to where she sat on the sofa.

"I am looking at you this way, Gloria, because I do not know any other way to look."

"You're funny," she said.

"I might as well be," I said.

"You want to dance?"

She put on one of the records, a slow one, and I got to touch her hair the way I wanted and then she laid her head on my shoulder and waited for me to execute the thing high-school boys do in the dark to girls at chaperoned dances. I could not bring myself that close to her.

She looked up at me, her small eyes uncertain, cloudy, questioning, her face big and hanging below me on the brink of something. "You're queer," she said.

I looked down at that face and felt something go far away from me. "I might as well be," was all that I could say.

V

SHE WAS SITTING ON THE SOFA and I was back in my cushioned chair when Gerald and his date came in, early. We had not spoken to each other for almost twenty minutes when they came. Gerald called me out into the kitchen. "Man, I got fucked up tonight," he said.

"What happened?"

"This is her night to be a bitch. She won't do anything."

"I thought you were going to a movie?"

Gerald looked at me, disgusted. "I never take a bitch out until afterwards. First we go to my apartment. That way if she won't go, I save my money." He looked as if I should have known that. And I should have, since I know him.

"How did you make out?"

"O.K.," I said.

"Did you get over?"

I considered my reputation and esteem in Gerald's eyes. "No," I finally said.

"*You weak cat!*" he said. "I told you that chick belongs to everybody. A real community chest. I told you, play it cool. Don't pull that longcoat shit on her."

"I know," I said.

"And you just blew it?"

"Yeah."

"You know your trouble?" Gerald said. "You're trying to be a martyr."

"That's me," I said. "A martyr."

He thought for a minute. "Look man," he said, "do you want it or not?"

"No," I said flatly.

"Do you mind if I take it?"

"How can you when she hates you?"

"That bitch? She isn't smart enough to hate anybody."

"What about the other girl?"

"I'll take Gloria out when she goes to bed. Don't worry about it."

I just looked at him.

"Now watch this," he said. He went to the refrigerator and searched the bottom drawers until he found a large, thick cucumber. "Come on," he told me, slamming the refrigerator door. He led me back into the living room. Both girls were now sitting on the sofa and the proximity was making Gloria a dog again. Gerald sat in my chair directly in front of them and I stood against the wall and watched. Gloria made a point of not looking at me.

Gerald put the big cucumber in his lap and commenced to tell his penis jokes. I knew them all from drinking beer with him. In a few minutes both girls were laughing with Gerald. I looked at Gloria. She was laughing much harder than the other girl or even harder than Gerald, who always laughs loudest at his own jokes. And even when the other girl said, "Oh come on, Jerry, that joke's as old as the hills," Gloria was so convulsed with laughter that she could not stop herself or stop the tears which were flowing from her eyes.

VI

THERE ARE CERTAIN GREEN AREAS in every city given to the citizens for recreational purposes. Of course there are rapes and muggings and homeless men sleeping in them on summer nights, but for the daring, for the careless, for those who want to be alone, these are very good places to walk, or recreate, or think. At certain times, very well into the night, a smell comes up from the grass that is worth any dangers present in these free areas. And there is a certain cleanliness, hard to distinguish, but just present, and there. There are also birds walking in these places in the late night, pecking in the ground for things only they can see, absolutely free of the popcorn bribes of children and well-meaning daytime bench-sitters. These animals are themselves at night and seem to unlearn all the daytime tricks they use to lure their daily doles of popcorn and bits of bread from some office girl's lunchbag: they do not wander near the benches; they do not flutter up into the air and down again to tantalize a potential crumb-thrower; they do not coo gratefully when they swallow whatever it is they pull from the dark green, wet earth. They have earned it themselves, and they swallow without a sound. And continue to peck, again in silence, for more.

I called Alfred Bowles from a telephone booth at the far end of the park. Of course he was not in: it was only 2:00 A.M. and Alfred was, of necessity, a night hunter. If he had been in, I would have restated, over the telephone, my position, and would have required him to restate his. Of course it would not have mattered, being over the telephone, but we might have laid some ground rules for our talk and our drink that night. After the drink, I might have asked him about the crusade for Melville's poetry, as if the man needed it, and his own crusade for himself as a poet and whatever else he wanted to be. I might even have let him touch me, in some inconsequential place. Certainly the most important thing I wanted to ask him was why certain people recognize me on the street and speak to me in bars when I am positive that in all my life I have never seen them before. Perhaps he might know.

At 3:00 A.M. I sat in the same coffee shop, at the same table, and recognized some of the same faces. Alfred was not there. Behind the counter, the rednecked waiter, it seemed, gave me the same look he had given Alfred that night. I did not care. At the next table sat an intellectual, pandering his readings late into the night to a girl whose legs I could not see. That did not matter either. *My* readings will always be safe with me, never pandered, never used without a legitimate purpose. That is the way I am. But sitting there, at that table, with the eyes of the counterman occasionally checking the direction of my own eyes, I began to wonder about the way I am.

AN ACT *of* PROSTITUTION

WHEN HE SAW THE WOMAN, the lawyer put down his pencil and legal pad and took out his pipe.

"Well," he said. "How do you want to play it?"

"I wanna get outta here," the whore said. "Just get me outta here."

"Now get some sense," said the lawyer, puffing on the pipe to draw in the flame from the long wooden match he had taken from his vest pocket. "You ain't got a snowball's chance in hell."

"I just want out," she said.

"You'll catch hell in there," he said, pointing with the stem of his pipe to the door which separated them from the main courtroom. "Why don't you just get some sense and take a few days on the city."

"I can't go up there again," she said. "Those dike matrons in Parkville hate my guts because I'm wise to them.

They told me last time they'd really give it to me if I came back. I can't do no time up there again."

"Listen," said the lawyer, pointing the stem of his pipe at her this time, "you ain't got a choice. Either you cop a plea or I don't take the case."

"*You* listen, you two-bit Jew shyster." The whore raised her voice, pointing her very chubby finger at the lawyer. "*You* ain't got no choice. The judge told you to be my lawyer and you got to do it. I ain't no dummy, you know that?"

"Yeah," said the lawyer. "You're a real smarty. That's why you're out on the streets in all that snow and ice. You're a real smarty, all right."

"You chickenshit," she said. "I don't want you on my case anyway, but I ain't got no choice. If you was any good, you wouldn't be working the sweatboxes in this court. I ain't no dummy."

"You're a real smarty," said the lawyer. He looked her up and down: a huge woman, pathetically blonde, big-boned and absurd in a skirt sloppily crafted to be mini. Her knees were ruddy and the flesh below them was thick and white and flabby. There was no indication of age about her. Like most whores, she looked at the same time young but then old, possibly as old as her profession. Sometimes they were very old but seemed to have stopped aging at a certain point so that ranking them chronologically, as the lawyer was trying to do, came hard. He put his pipe on the table, on top of the police affidavit, and stared at her. She sat across the room, near the door in a straight chair, her flesh oozing over its sides. He watched her pull her mini-skirt down over the upper part of her thigh, modestly, but with the same hard, cold look she had when she came in the room. "You're a real smarty," he commented, drawing on his pipe and exhaling the smoke into the room.

The fat woman in her miniskirt still glared at him. "Screw you, Yid!" she said through her teeth. "Screw your fat mama and your chubby sister with hair under her arms. Screw your brother and your father and I hope they should go crazy playing with themselves in pay toilets."

The lawyer was about to reply when the door to the consultation room opened and another man came into the small place. "Hell, Jimmy," he said to the lawyer, pretending to ignore the woman, "I got a problem here."

"Yeah?" said Jimmy.

The other man walked over to the brown desk, leaned closer to Jimmy so that the woman could not hear and lowered his voice. "I got this kid," he said. "A nice I-talian boy that grabbed this Cadillac outta a parking lot. Now he only done it twice before and I think the Judge might go easy if he got in a good mood before the kid goes on, this being Monday morning and all."

"So?" said Jimmy.

"So I was thinking," the other lawyer said, again lowering his voice and leaning much closer and making a sly motion with his head to indicate the whore on the chair across the room. "So I was thinking. The Judge knows Philomena over there. She's here almost every month and she's always good for a laugh. So I was thinking, this being Monday morning and all and with a cage-load of nigger drunks out there, why not put her on first, give the old man a good laugh and then put my I-talian boy on. I know he'd get a better deal that way."

"What's in it for me?" said Jimmy, rapping the ashes from his pipe into an ashtray.

"Look, I done *you* favors before. Remember that Chinaman? Remember the tip I gave you?"

Jimmy considered while he stuffed tobacco from a can into his pipe. He lit the pipe with several matches from his vest pocket and considered some more. "I don't mind, Ralph," he said. "But if she goes first the Judge'll get a good laugh and then he'll throw the book at her."

"*What the hell, Jimmy?*" said Ralph. He glanced over at the whore, who was eyeing them hatefully. "Look, buddy," he went on, "you know who that is? Fatso Philomena Brown. She's up here almost every month. Old Bloom knows her. I tell you, she's good for a laugh. That's all. Besides, she's married to a nigger anyway."

"Well," said Jimmy. "So far she ain't done herself much good with me. She's a real smarty. She thinks I'm a Jew."

"There you go," said Ralph. "Come on, Jimmy. I ain't got much time before the Clerk calls my kid up. What you say?"

Jimmy looked over at his client, the many pounds of her rolled in great logs of meat under her knees and around her belly. She was still sneering. "O.K." He turned his head back to Ralph. "O.K., I'll do it."

"Now look," said Ralph, "this is how we'll do. When they call me up I'll tell the Clerk I need more time with my kid for consultation. And since you follow me on the docket you'll get on pretty soon, at least before I will. Then after everybody's had a good laugh, I'll bring my I-talian on."

"Isn't *she* Italian?" asked Jimmy, indicating the whore with a slight movement of his pipe.

"Yeah. But she's married to a nigger."

"O.K.," said Jimmy, "we'll do it."

"What's that?" said the whore, who had been trying to listen all this time. "What are you two kikes whispering about anyway? What the hell's going on?"

"Shut up," said Jimmy, the stem of his pipe clamped far back in his mouth so that he could not say it as loud as he wanted. Ralph winked at him and left the room. "Now listen," he said to Philomena Brown, getting up from his desk and walking over to where she still sat against the wall. "If you got a story, you better tell me quick because we're going out there soon and I want you to know I ain't telling no lies for you."

"I don't want you on my case anyway, kike," said Philomena Brown.

"It ain't what *you* want. It's what the old man out there says you gotta do. Now if you got a story let's have it *now*."

"I'm a file clerk. I was just looking for work."

"Like *hell!* Don't give *me* that shit. When was the last time you had your shots?"

"I ain't never had none," said Mrs. Brown.

Now they could hear the Clerk, beyond the door, calling the Italian boy into court. They would have to go out in a few minutes. "Forget the story," he told her. "Just pull your dress down some and wipe some of that shit off your eyes. You look like hell."

"I don't want you on the case, Moses," said Mrs. Brown.

"Well, you got me," said Jimmy. "You got me whether you want me or not." Jimmy paused, put his pipe in his coat pocket, and then said: "And my name is *Mr. Mulligan!*"

The woman did not say anything more. She settled her weight in the chair and made it creak.

"Now let's get in there," said Jimmy.

II

THE JUDGE WAS IN HIS MONDAY MORNING MOOD. He was very ready to be angry at almost anyone. He glared at the Court Clerk as the bald, seemingly consumptive man called out the names of six defendants who had defaulted. He glared at the group of drunks and addicts who huddled against the steel net of the prisoners' cage, gazing toward the open courtroom as if expecting mercy from the rows of concerned parties and spectators who sat in the hot place. Judge Bloom looked as though he wanted very badly to spit. There would be no mercy this Monday morning and the prisoners all knew it.

"*Willie Smith!* Willie Smith! Come into Court!" the Clerk barked.

Willie Smith slowly shuffled out of the prisoners' cage and up to the dirty stone wall, which kept all but his head and neck and shoulders concealed from the people in the musty courtroom.

From the bench the Judge looked down at the hungover Smith.

"You know, I ain't never seen him sitting down in that

chair," Jimmy said to one of the old men who came to court to see the daily procession, filling up the second row of benches, directly behind those reserved for court-appointed lawyers. There were at least twelve of these old men, looking almost semi-professional in faded gray or blue or black suits with shiny knees and elbows. They liked to come and watch the fun. "Watch old Bloom give it to this nigger," the same old man leaned over and said into Jimmy Mulligan's ear. Jimmy nodded without looking back at him. And after a few seconds he wiped his ear with his hand, also without looking back.

The Clerk read the charges: Drunkenness, Loitering, Disorderly Conduct.

"You want a lawyer, Willie?" the Judge asked him. Judge Bloom was now walking back and forth behind his bench, his arms gravely folded behind his back, his belly very close to pregnancy beneath his black robe. "The Supreme Court says I have to give you a lawyer. You want one?"

"No sir," the hungover Smith said, very obsequiously.

"Well, what's your trouble?"

"Nothing."

"You haven't missed a Monday here in months."

"Yes sir."

"All that money you spend on booze, how do you take care of your family?"

Smith moved his head and shoulders behind the wall in a gesture that might have been a shuffle.

"When was the last time you gave something to your wife?"

"Last Friday."

"You're a liar. Your wife's been on the City for years."

"I help," said Smith, quickly.

"You help, all right. You help her raise her belly and her income every year."

The old men in the second row snickered and the Judge eyed them in a threatening way. They began to stifle their chuckles. Willie Smith smiled.

"If she has one more kid she'll be making more than me," the Judge observed. But he was not saying it to Smith. He was looking at the old men.

Then he looked down at the now bashful, smiling Willie Smith. "You want some time to sleep it off or you want to pay?"

"I'll take the time."

"How much you want, Willie?"

"I don't care."

"You want to be out for the weekend, I guess."

Smith smiled again.

"Give him five days," the Judge said to the Clerk. The Clerk wrote in his papers and then said in a hurried voice: "Defendant Willie Smith, you have been found guilty by this court of being drunk in a public place, of loitering while in this condition, and of disorderly conduct. This court sentences you to five days in the House of Correction at Bridgeview and one month's suspended sentence. You have, however, the right to appeal, in which case the suspended sentence will not be allowed and the sentence will then be thirty-five days in the House of Correction."

"You want to appeal, Willie?"

"Naw sir."

"See you next week," said the Judge.

"Thank you," said Willie Smith.

A black fellow in a very neatly pressed Army uniform came on next. He stood immaculate and proud and clean-shaven with his cap tucked under his left arm while the charges were read. The prosecutor was a hard-faced black police detective, tieless, very long-haired in a short-sleeved white shirt with wet armpits. The detective was tough but very nervous. He looked at his notes while the Clerk read the charges. The Judge, bald and wrinkled and drooping in the face, still paced behind his bench, his nose twitching from time to time, his arms locked behind his back. The soldier was charged with assault and battery with a dangerous weapon on a police officer; he remained standing erect and silent, looking off into the space behind the Judge until his lawyer, a plump, greasy black man in his late fifties, had heard the charges and motioned for him to sit. Then he placed himself beside his lawyer and put his cap squarely in front of him on the table.

The big-bellied black detective managed to get the police officer's name, rank, and duties from him, occasionally glancing over at the table where the defendant and his lawyer sat, both hard-faced and cold. He shuffled through his notes, paused, looked up at the Judge, and then said to the white officer: "Now, Officer Bergin, would you tell the Court in your own words what happened?"

The white policeman put his hands together in a prayer-like gesture on the stand. He looked at the defendant, whose face was set and whose eyes were fixed on the officer's hands. "We was on duty on the night of July twenty-seventh driving around the Lafayette Street area when we got a call to proceed to the Lafayette Street subway station because there was a crowd gathering there and they thought it might be a riot. We proceeded there, Officer Biglow and me, and when we got there sure enough there was a crowd of colored people running up and down the street and making noise and carrying on. We didn't pull our guns because they been telling us all summer not to do that. We got out of the car and proceeded to join the other officers there in forming a line so's to disperse the crowd. Then we spotted that fellow in the crowd."

"Who do you mean?"

"That fellow over there." Officer Bergin pointed to the defendant at the table. "That soldier, Irving Williams."

"Go on," said the black detective, not turning to look at the defendant.

"Well, he had on this red costume and a cape, and he was wearing this big red turban. He was also carrying a big black shield right outta Tarzan and he had that big long cane waving it around in the air."

"Where is that cane now?"

"We took it off him later. That's it over there."

The black detective moved over to his own table and picked up a long brown leather cane. He pressed a small button beneath its handle and then drew out from the interior of the cane a thin, silver-white rapier, three feet long.

"Is this the same cane?"

"Yes sir," the white officer said.

"Go on, Officer."

"Well, he was waving it around in the air and he had a whole lot of these colored people behind him and it looked to me that he was gonna charge the police line. So me and Tommy left the line and went in to grab him before he could start something big. That crowd was getting mean. They looked like they was gonna try something big pretty soon."

"Never mind," said the Judge. He had stopped walking now and stood at the edge of his elevated platform, just over the shoulder of the officer in the witness box. "Never mind what you thought, just get on with it."

"Yes sir." The officer pressed his hands together much tighter. "Well, Tommy and me, we tried to grab him and he swung the cane at me. Caught me right in the face here." He pointed his finger to a large red and black mark under his left eye. "So then we hadda use force to subdue him."

"What did you do, Officer?" the black detective asked.

"We hadda use the sticks. I hit him over the head once or twice, but not hard. I don't remember. Then Tommy grabbed his arms and we hustled him over to the car before these other colored people with him tried to grab us."

"Did he resist arrest?"

"Yeah. He kicked and fought us and called us lewd and lascivious names. We hadda handcuff him in the car. Then we took him down to the station and booked him for assault and battery."

"Your witness," said the black detective without turning around to face the other lawyer. He sat down at his own table and wiped his forehead and hands with a crumpled white handkerchief. He still looked very nervous but not as tough.

"May it please the Court," the defendant's black lawyer said slowly, standing and facing the pacing Judge. "I move . . ." And then he stopped because he saw that the Judge's small eyes were looking over his head, toward the back of the courtroom. The lawyer turned around and looked, and saw that everyone else in the room had also turned their heads to the back of the room. Standing against the back walls and along the left side of the room were twenty-five or so stern-faced, cold-eyed black men, all in African dashikis, all wearing brightly colored hats, and all staring at the Judge and the black detective. Philomena Brown and Jimmy Mulligan, sitting on the first bench, turned to look too, and the whore smiled but the lawyer said, "Oh hell," aloud. The men, all big, all bearded and tight-lipped, now locked hands and formed a solid wall of flesh around almost three-quarters of the courtroom. The Judge looked at the defendant and saw that he was smiling. Then he looked at the defendant's lawyer, who still stood before the Judge's bench, his head down, his shoulders pulled up toward his head. The Judge began to pace again. The courtroom was very quiet. The old men filling the second rows on both sides of the room leaned forward and exchanged glances with each other up and down the row. "Oh hell," Jimmy Mulligan said again.

Then the Judge stopped walking. "Get on with it," he told the defendant's lawyer. "There's justice to be done here."

The lawyer, whose face was now very greasy and wet, looked up at the officer, still standing in the witness box, but with one hand now at his right side, next to his gun.

"Officer Bergin," said the black lawyer. "I'm not clear about something. Did the defendant strike you *before* you asked him for the cane or *after* you attempted to take it from him?"

"Before. It was before. Yes sir."

"You *did* ask him for the cane, then?"

"Yes sir. I asked him to turn it over."

"And what did he do?"

"He hit me."

"But if he hit you before you asked for the cane, then it must be true that you asked him for the cane *after* he had hit you. Is that right?"

"Yes sir."

"In other words, after he had struck you in the face you were still polite enough to keep your hands off him and ask for the weapon."

"Yes sir. That's what I did."

"In other words, he hit you twice. Once *before* you requested the cane and once *after* you requested it."

The officer paused. "No sir," he said quickly. "He only hit me once."

"And when was that again?"

"I thought it was before I asked for the cane but I don't know now."

"But you did ask for the cane before he hit you?"

"Yeah." The officer's hands were in prayer again.

"Now, Officer Bergin, did he hit you *because* you asked for the cane or did he hit you in the process of giving it to you?"

"He just hauled off and hit me with it."

"He made no effort to hand it over?"

"No, no sir. He hit me."

"In other words, he struck you the moment you got

close enough for him to swing. He did not hit you as you were taking the cane from him?"

The officer paused again. Then he said: "No sir." He touched his face again, then put his right hand down to the area near his gun again. "I asked him for the cane and he hauled off and hit me in the face."

"Officer, are you telling this court that you did not get hit until you tried to take the cane away from this soldier, this Vietnam veteran, or that he saw you coming and immediately began to swing the cane?"

"He swung on me."

"Officer Bergin, did he swing on you, or did the cane accidentally hit you while you were trying to take it from him?"

"All I know is that he *hit me*." The officer was sweating now.

"Then you don't know just when he hit you, before or after you tried to take the cane from him, do you?"

The black detective got up and said in a very soft voice: "I object."

The black lawyer for the defendant looked over at him contemptuously. The black detective dropped his eyes and tightened his belt, and sat down again.

"That's all right," the oily lawyer said. Then he looked at the officer again. "One other thing," he said. "Was the knife still inside the cane or drawn when he hit you?"

"We didn't know about the knife till later at the station."

"Do you think that a blow from the cane by itself could kill you?"

"Object!" said the detective. But again his voice was low.

"*Jivetime Uncle Tom motherfucker!*" someone said from the back of the room. "Shave that Afro off your head!"

The Judge's eyes moved quickly over the men in the rear, surveying their faces and catching what was in all their eyes. But he did not say anything.

"The prosecution rests," the black detective said. He sounded very tired.

"The defense calls the defendant, Irving Williams," said the black lawyer.

Williams took the stand and waited, head high, eyes cool, mouth tight, militarily, for the Clerk to swear him in. He looked always toward the back of the room.

"Now, Mr. Williams," his lawyer began, "tell this court in your own words the events of the night of July twenty-seventh of this year."

"I had been to a costume party." Williams's voice was slow and deliberate and resonant. The entire courtroom was tense and quiet. The old men stared, stiff and erect, at Irving Williams from their second-row benches. Philomena Brown settled her flesh down next to her lawyer, who tried to edge away from touching her fat arm with his own. The tight-lipped Judge Bloom had reassumed the pacing behind his bench.

"I was on leave from the base," Williams went on, "and I was coming from the party when I saw this group of kids throwing rocks. Being in the military and being just out of Vietnam, I tried to stop them. One of the kids had that cane and I took it from him. The shield belongs to me. I got it in Taiwan last year on R and R. I was trying to break up the crowd with my shield when this honkie cop begins to beat me over the head with his club. Police brutality. I tried to tell . . ."

"That's enough," the Judge said. "That's all I want to hear." He eyed the black men in the back of the room. "This case isn't for my court. Take it upstairs."

"If Your Honor pleases," the black lawyer began.

"I don't," said the Judge. "I've heard enough. Mr. Clerk, make out the papers. Send it upstairs to Cabot."

"This court has jurisdiction to hear this case," the lawyer said. He was very close to being angry. "This man is in the service. He has to ship out in a few weeks. We want a hearing today."

"Not in my court you don't get it. Upstairs, and that's *it!*"

Now the blacks in the back of the room began to berate the detective. "Jivetime cat! Handkerchief-head flunky! Uncle Tom motherfucker!" they called. "We'll get *you*, baby!"

"Get them out of here," the Judge told the policeman named Bergin. "Get them the hell out!" Bergin did not move. "Get them the hell out!"

At that moment Irving Williams, with his lawyer behind him, walked out of the courtroom. And the twenty-five bearded black men followed them. The black detective remained sitting at the counsel table until the Clerk asked him to make way for counsel on the next case. The detective got up slowly, gathered his few papers, tightened his belt again and moved over, his head held down, to a seat on the right side of the courtroom.

"Philomena Brown!" the Clerk called. "Philomena Brown! Come into Court!"

The fat whore got up from beside Jimmy Mulligan and walked heavily over to the counsel table and lowered herself into one of the chairs. Her lawyer was talking to Ralph, the Italian boy's counsel.

"Do a good job, Jimmy, please," Ralph said. "Old Bloom is gonna be awful mean now."

"Yeah," said Jimmy. "I got to really work on him."

One of the old men on the second row leaned over the back of the bench and said to Jimmy: "Ain't that the one that's married to a nigger?"

"That's her," said Jimmy.

"She's gonna catch hell. Make sure they give her hell."

"Yeah," said Jimmy. "I don't see how I'm gonna be able to try this with a straight face."

"Do a good job for me, please, Jimmy," said Ralph. "The kid's name is Angelico. Ain't that a beautiful name? He ain't a bad kid."

"Don't you worry, I'll do it." Then Jimmy moved over to the table next to his client.

The defendant and the arresting officer were sworn in. The arresting officer acted for the state as prosecutor and its only witness. He had to refer to his notes from time to time while the Judge paced behind his bench, his head down, ponderous and impatient. Then Philomena Brown got in the witness box and rested her great weight against its sides. She glared at the Judge, at the Clerk, at the officer in the box on the other side, at Jimmy Mulligan, at the old men smiling up and down the second row, and at everyone in the courtroom. Then she rested her eyes on the officer.

"Well," the officer read from his notes. "It was around

one-thirty A.M. on the night of July twenty-eighth. I was working the night duty around the combat zone. I come across the defendant there soliciting cars. I had seen the defendant there soliciting cars on previous occasions in the same vicinity. I had then on previous occasions warned the defendant there about such activities. But she kept on doing it. On that night I come across the defendant soliciting a car full of colored gentlemen. She was standing on the curb with her arm leaning up against the door of the car and talking with these two colored gentlemen. As I came up they drove off. I then arrested her, after informing her of her rights, for being a common streetwalker and a public nuisance. And that's all I got to say."

Counsel for the whore waived cross-examination of the officer and proceeded to examine her.

"What's your name?"

"Mrs. Philomena Brown."

"Speak louder so the Court can hear you, Mrs. Brown."

She narrowed her eyes at the lawyer.

"What is your religion, Mrs. Brown?"

"I am a Roman Catholic. Roman Catholic born."

"Are you presently married?"

"Yeah."

"What is your husband's name?"

"Rudolph Leroy Brown, Jr."

The old men in the second row were beginning to snicker and the Judge lowered his eyes to them. Jimmy Mulligan smiled.

"Does your husband support you?"

"Yeah. We get along all right."

"Do *you* work, Mrs. Brown?"

"Yeah. That's how I make my living."

"What do you do for a living?"

"I'm a file clerk."

"Are you working now?"

"No. I lost my job last month on account of a bad leg I got. I couldn't move outta bed."

The men in the second row were grinning and others in the audience joined them in muffled guffaws and snickerings.

"What were you doing on Beaver Avenue on the night of July twenty-eighth?"

"I was looking for a job."

Now the entire court was laughing and the Judge glared out at them from behind his bench as he paced, his arms clasped behind his back.

"Will you please tell this court, Mrs. Brown, how you intended to find a job at that hour?"

"These two guys in a car told me they knew where I could find some work."

"As a file clerk?"

"Yeah. What the hell else do you think?"

There was here a roar of laughter from the court, and when the Judge visibly twitched the corners of his usually severe mouth, Philomena Brown saw it and began to laugh too.

"Order! Order!" the Clerk shouted above the roar. But he was laughing.

Jimmy Mulligan bit his lip. "Now, Mrs. Brown, I want you to tell me the truth. Have you ever been arrested before for prostitution?"

"Hell no!" she fired back. "They had me in here a coupla times but it was all a fluke. They never got nothing on me. I was framed, right from the start."

"How old are you, Mrs. Brown?"

"Nineteen."

Now the Judge stopped pacing and stood next to his chair. His face was dubious: very close and very far away from smiling. The old men in the second row saw this and stopped laughing, awaiting a cue from him.

"That's enough of this," said the Judge. "I know you. You've been up here seven times already this year and it's still summer. I'm going to throw the book at you." He moved over to the left end of the platform and leaned down to where a husky, muscular woman Probation Officer was standing. She had very short hair and looked grim. She had not laughed with the others. "Let me see her record," said the Judge. The manly Probation Officer handed it up to him and then they talked together in whispers for a few minutes.

"All right, *Mrs. Brown*," said the Judge, moving over to the right side of the platform near the defendant's box and pointing his finger at her. "You're still on probation from the last time you were up here. I'm tired of this."

"I don't wanna go back up there, Your Honor," the whore said. "They hate me up there."

"You're going back. That's it! You got six months on the State. Maybe while you're there you can learn how to be a file clerk so you can look for work during the day."

Now everyone laughed again.

"Plus you get a one-year suspended sentence on probation."

The woman hung her head with the gravity of this punishment.

"Maybe you can even learn a *good* profession while you're up there. Who knows? Maybe you could be a ballerina dancer."

The courtroom roared with laughter. The Judge could not control himself now.

"And another thing," he said. "When you get out, keep off the streets. You're obstructing traffic."

Such was the spontaneity of laughter from the entire courtroom after the remark that the lawyer Jimmy Mulligan had to wipe the tears from his eyes with his finger and the short-haired Probation Officer smiled, and even Philomena Brown had to laugh at this, her final moment of glory. The Judge's teeth showed through his own broad grin, and Ralph, sitting beside his Italian, a very pretty boy with clean, blue eyes, patted him on the back enthusiastically between uncontrollable bursts of laughter.

For five minutes after the smiling Probation Officer led the fat whore in a miniskirt out of the courtroom, there was the sound of muffled laughter and occasional sniffles and movements in the seats. Then they settled down again and the Judge resumed his pacings and the Court Clerk, very slyly wiping his eyes with his sleeve, said in a very loud voice: "Angelico Carbone! Angelico Carbone! Come into Court!"

PRIVATE DOMAIN

RODNEY FINISHED HIS BEER in slow, deliberate swallows, peering over the rim of his mug at the other black, who, having polished off three previous mugs of draft, now sat watching Rodney expectantly, being quite obvious with his eyes that he held no doubt that more beer was forthcoming. Rodney ignored his eyes. He licked his lips. He tabled the empty mug. "Now give it to me again," he said to the heavily bearded beer-hungry black still eyeing him, now demandingly, from across the small booth. "Let me see if I have it all down."

"How 'bout throwing some more suds on me?" said the black.

"In a minute," said Rodney.

The black considered. "I'm dry again. Another taste."

Rodney sighed, considered his position from behind the sigh, made himself look annoyed and then grudgingly raised his hand until the cigar-chewing bartender noticed, stopped his stooped glass-washing dance behind the counter, and nodded to the waitress, sitting on a stool at the bar, to replenish them. She was slow about getting up. It was a lazy day: the two men in the booth were the only customers.

"Now," said Rodney. "Give it to me again."

The other man smiled. He had won again. "It's this way," he said to Rodney.

Rodney ignored the waitress as she pushed the two fresh mugs onto the table while his companion paused to consider her ass bouncing beneath the cloth of her blue dress. Lighting another cigarette, Rodney observed that the waitress wore no stockings and felt himself getting uncomfortable.

"Well?" he said.

"It's this way," his companion said again. "Your *bag* is where you keep whatever you do best. Whatever is in your bag is your *thing*. Some cats call it your *stick*, but it means the same. Now, when you know you got your thing going all right, you say 'I got myself together' or 'I got my game together.'"

"All right, all right," said Rodney. "I've got it down now." He was growing very irritated at the other man, who smiled all the time in a superior way and let the beer wet his gold tooth before he swallowed, as if expecting Rodney to be impressed with its gleam. Rodney was not impressed. He disliked condescension, especially from Willie, whom he regarded in most respects as his inferior.

"Anything else I should know?" Rodney snapped.

"Yeah, baby-boy," Willie said slow and matter-of-factly, implying, in his accents, a whole world of essential instruction being overlooked for want of beer and money and mind and other necessities forever beyond Rodney's reach. "There's lots. There's lots and lots."

"Like what?"

Willie drained his mug. "You know about the big 'I Remember Rock 'n Roll' Memorial in Cleveland last week?"

"No." Rodney was excited. "Who was there?"

"All the cats from the old groups."

"Anything special happen?"

"Hell yes!" Willie smiled again and looked very pleased with himself. "Fatso Checkers didn't show. The cats would have tore the place down but Dirty Rivers filled in for him. He made up a song right on stage. Man, the cats dug it, they went wild they dug it so."

"What's the song?"

"I donno."

"Is it on record?"

"Not yet. He just made it up."

"There's no place I can check it out?"

Again Willie smiled. "You can follow the other squares and check out this week's issue of *Soul*. They might have a piece on it."

"I don't have *time*," Rodney said. "I've got my studies to do."

"You don't have to, then; just be cool."

Rodney got up. "That's it," he said to Willie. "I'll check you out later." He put two dollars down on the table and turned to go. Willie reached over and picked up the bills. "That's for the beer," Rodney cautioned him.

"Sure," said Willie.

Rodney walked toward the door. "Be cool," he heard

Willie say from behind him. He did not look back. He knew that Willie and possibly the waitress and even the bartender would be smiling.

Although he felt uncomfortable in that area of the city, Rodney decided to walk around and digest all that he had been told before driving back to the University. He had parked and locked his car on a small side street and felt relatively protected from the rows and rows of aimless men who lined the stoops of houses and posts and garbage cans on either side of the street, their eyes seemingly shifty, their faces dishonest, their broad black noses alert and sniffing, feeling the air for the source of the smell which Rodney half believed rose from the watch and the wallet and the valuables stored in his pocket. He walked faster. He felt their eyes on his back and he was very uncomfortable being there, in the rising heat from the sidewalk, amid the smells of old food and wine and urine which rose with the heat.

He passed two boys with gray-black, ashy faces and running noses who laughed as they chased a little black girl up and down the steps of a tenement. "Little Tommy Tucker was a bad motherfucker," one of the boys half sang, half spoke, and they all laughed. Rodney thought it obscene and a violation of a protective and sacred barrier between two distinctively different age groups. But after a few more steps he began to think that it was very clever. He stopped. He looked back. He began to memorize it. Then he began to walk back toward them, still at play on the steps, having already forgotten the inventiveness of a moment before. Rodney was about to call to them to repeat the whole verse when a robust and short-haired dark woman in a tight black dress that was open at the side came out of the tenement and down the stairs and began to undulate her way, sensually, toward him. The three children followed her, laughing as they each attempted to imitate her walk. Just when he was about to pass her, a light blue Ford pulled over to the curb next to her and a bald-headed white man leaned, questioningly, out of the driver's window toward the big woman. She stopped, and looking the man directly in the eye with a hint of professional irritation on her round, hard face, asked, "How much?"

"Ten," the man said.

"Hell no," she said turning to go in a way that, while sharp and decisive, also suggested that there was a happy chance that, upon the occurrence of certain conditions, as yet unnamed, she might not go at all.

"Twelve," said the man.

The woman looked at Rodney for a moment; then she looked the leaning man full in the face with fierce eyes. "Fuck you!" she said matter-of-factly.

"Well, damn if you're worth more than that," the man said, ignoring Rodney and the children.

"Get the hell on," said the woman, and began to walk slowly and sensually in the direction in which the car was pointed.

"She ain't got no drawers on," exclaimed one of the children.

"Can you see her cunt?"

"Yeah" was the answer. They all ran after her and the car, which was now trailing her, leaving Rodney alone on that part of the hot sidewalk. But he was not mind-ing the heat now, or the smells, or the lounging men, or even Willie's condescension; he only minded that he had not thought to bring a notebook because he was having difficulty arranging all this in his head for memorization.

Returning to his car at last, Rodney paused amid afternoon traffic to purchase a copy of *Muhammad Speaks* from a conservatively dressed, cocoa-brown Muslim on a street corner. Rodney tried to be very conspicuous about the transaction, doing his absolute best to engage the fellow in conversation while the homebound cars, full of black and white workers, passed them. "What made you join?" he asked the Muslim, a striking fellow who still retained the red eyes of an alcoholic or drug addict.

"Come to see us and find out for yourself," said the fellow, his eyes not on Rodney but on the moving traffic lest he should miss the possibility of a sale.

"Are you happy being a Muslim?" asked Rodney.

"Come to our mosque, brother, and find out."

"I should think you'd get tired of selling papers all the time."

The Muslim, not wanting to insult Rodney and lose a possible conversion and at the same time more than slightly irritated, struck a compromise with himself, hitched his papers under his arms and moved out into the street between the two lanes of traffic. "Come to our mosque, brother, and gain all knowledge from the lips of the Messenger," he called back to Rodney. Rodney turned away and walked to his car. It was safe; the residents had not found it yet. Still, he inspected the doors and windows and keyholes for jimmy marks, just to feel secure.

II

"WHERE HAVE YOU BEEN?" Lynn asked as he opened the door to his apartment. She was sitting on the floor, her legs crossed, her panties showing—her favorite position, which always embarrassed Rodney when they relaxed with other people. He suspected that she did it on purpose. He had developed the habit of glancing at all the other fellows in a room, whenever she did it, until they saw him watching them discovering her and directed their eyes elsewhere in silent respect for his unexpressed wish. This always made Rodney feel superior and polished.

"Put your legs down," he told her.

"For what?" she said.

"You'll catch cold."

"Nobody's looking. Where you been?"

Rodney stood over her and looked down. He looked severe. He could not stand irritation at home too. "Go sit on the sofa," he ordered her. "Only white girls expose themselves in public."

"You prude," she said. "This isn't public." But she got up anyway and reclined on the sofa.

"That's better," said Rodney, pulling off his coat. "If sitting like that is your thing, you should put it in a separate bag and bury it someplace."

"What do you know about *my thing?*" Lynn said.

Rodney did not answer her.

"Where you been, *bay-bee?*"

Rodney said nothing. He hated her when she called him that in private.

"We're going to be late for dinner, *bay-bee*," she said again.

"I've been out studying," Rodney finally said.

"What?"

"Things."

"Today's Saturday."

"So? God made Saturdays for students."

"Crap," she said. Then she added: "*Bay-bee!*"

"Oh, shut up," said Rodney.

"You can give me orders when we're married," said Lynn.

"That'll be the day," Rodney muttered.

"Yeah," Lynn repeated. "That'll be the day."

Rodney looked at her, legs miniskirted but sufficiently covered, hair natural but just a little too straight to be that way, skin nut-brown and smooth and soft to touch and feel against his mouth and arms and legs, body well built and filled, very noticeable breasts and hips, also good to touch and feel against his body at night. Rodney liked to make love at night, in the dark. He especially did not like to make sounds while making love, although he felt uneasy if the girl did not make any. He was considering whether or not it was dark enough in the room to make love when the telephone rang. Lynn did not move on the sofa and so he answered it himself. It was Charlie Pratt.

"What's happening, baby?" said Rodney.

"Not much," said Charlie. "Listen, can you make dinner around seven? We got some other cats coming over at nine we don't want to feed nothin' but beer."

"Cool," said Rodney. He looked at his watch. "We can make it as soon as Lynn gets herself together." He glanced over at Lynn still stretched out on the sofa.

"Great," said Charlie Pratt. "Later."

Rodney hung up. "What do you have to do to get ready?" he asked Lynn.

"Nothing."

"You *could* put on another skirt."

"Go to hell," she said, not lifting her head from the sofa. "This skirt's fine."

"You could at least comb your hair or something."

Lynn ignored him. Rodney began to reconsider the sufficiency of the darkness in the room. Then he thought better of the idea. Instead, he went out of the room to shave and take a bath.

These days Rodney found himself coming close to hating everyone. Still, he never allowed himself to recognize it, or call what he felt toward certain people genuine hate. He preferred to call it differing degrees of dislike, an emotion with two sides like a coin, which was constantly spinning in his mind. Sometimes it landed, in his brain, heads up, signifying a certain affinity; sometimes it landed tails up, signifying a slight distaste or perhaps a major objection to a single person and his attitudes. He refused to dislike absolutely because, he felt, dislike was uncomfortably close to bigotry and Rodney knew too many different people to be a practicing bigot. Sometimes, very frequently in fact, he disliked Willie immensely. On the other hand, he sometimes felt a bit of admiration for the fellow and, occasionally, footnoted that admiration by purchasing an extra beer for him. This gesture served to stamp those rare moments onto his memory, a reminder that, because he had done this on enough occasions in the past, there would always be a rather thick prophylactic between how he really felt and how Willie assumed he felt.

Talking to Willie was informative and amusing to Rodney up to the point when Willie began to smile and to seem to know that what he was telling Rodney had some value. After he could see when that point was reached in Willie's face, Rodney was not amused any more. Sometimes he was annoyed and sometimes, when Willie smiled confidently and knowledgeably and condescendingly, Rodney began to almost hate him. He felt the same about Lynn and her panties and her *bay-bee* and the loose ways she had, Rodney assumed, picked up from living among whites for too long. Sometimes she made him feel really uncomfortable and scared. He began to say *bay-bee, bay-bee* to himself in the shower. Thinking about it, he suddenly realized that he felt exactly the same way about Charlie Pratt.

Pratt made Rodney feel uncomfortable because he did not fit either side of the coin. The fellow had well over two thousand records: some rhythm and blues, some jazz, some folk, some gospels, but all black. And Charlie Pratt was not. He knew the language and was proud to use the vocabulary Rodney had been trying to forget all his life. He was pleasantly chubby with dark blond hair and a fuzzy Genghis Khan moustache which hung down on either side of his chin. Sometimes the ends dangled when he moved. And sometimes Pratt dangled when he moved. Sometimes Charlie Pratt, his belly hanging over his belt and his chin going up and down in talk, dangled when he did not move. Drying his legs with a towel, Rodney thought of himself and Charlie locked in mortal combat. Rodney had no doubt that he would win; he was slim and wiry, he was quick, he had a history of natural selection in his ancestry. Besides, Charlie was fat. He never used his body. Thinking about him, Rodney realized that he had never seen Charlie dance or move to the rhythm of any one of his two thousand records. He had never seen him snap his fingers once, or voluntarily move any part of his body besides his arms and legs; and even these movements were not rhythmic but something close to an unnatural shuffle.

Rodney did a quick step with his feet as he brushed his teeth in front of the mirror. He moved back from the mirror in order to see his feet. He did the step again, grinning at himself and at the white-foamed toothbrush hanging loosely from his mouth. The foam covered his lips and made them white, and, remembering a fast song in his head, Rodney snapped his fingers and did the step again. And again.

III

"WHEN YOU FINISH," said Charlie Pratt in between chews on a pork-chop bone, "I'll let you hear some of the stuff I picked up yesterday."

Rodney wiped his mouth carefully before answering. "What'd you get this time?" he asked, knowing what to expect.

"Some vintage Roscoe and Shirley stuff," said Charlie.

"We found it in Markfield's back room. It was just lying there under a stack of oldies full of dust. We figure it must be their only LP. Jesus, what a find!" Both Charlie and his wife smiled pridefully.

"How about that," said Rodney. But he did not say it with enthusiasm.

Charlie stood up from the table and began to shift his bulk from foot to foot, a sort of safe dance, but more like the movements of someone who wants desperately to go to the bathroom.

"Whatever happened to them?" asked Lynn.

Both the Pratts smiled together. "They broke up in '52 because the girl was a lesbian," his wife said. She had gone to Vassar, and Rodney always noticed how small and tight her mouth became whenever she took the initiative from her husband, which was, Rodney had noticed over a period of several dinners and many beer parties with them, very, very often. She was aggressive, in keeping with the Vassar tradition, and seemed to play a very intense, continuous game of one-upmanship with her husband.

"That's not what happened at all," her husband said. "After they hit the big time with 'I Want to Do It,' it was in '53, Roscoe started sleeping around. One night she caught him in a hotel room with a chick and razored his face. His face was so cut up he couldn't go onstage any more. I saw him in Newark in '64 when he was trying to make a comeback. He still looked razored. He looked bad."

Rodney felt tight inside, remembering that in '64 he had been trying desperately to make up for a lifetime of not knowing anything about Baroque. Now he knew all about it and he had never heard of Roscoe and Shirley.

"There was an 'I Remember Rock 'n Roll' Memorial in Cleveland last week," he said.

"Yeah," said Charlie. "Too bad Fatso couldn't make it. But that was one hell of a song Dirty Rivers made up. Jesus, right on the spot too! Jesus, right on the stage! He sang for almost two hours. Christ! I was lucky to get it taped, the cats went wild. They almost overran the stage."

"How did you get the tape?" asked Rodney, now vaguely disgusted.

"We knew about the show for months," Peggy Pratt broke in. "We planned to go but there was an Ashy Williamson Revue in the Village that same night. We couldn't make both so we called up this guy in Cleveland and got him to tape the show for us." She paused. "Want to hear it?"

"No," said Rodney, somewhat flatly. Then he added: "Not right now."

"Want to hear the Roscoe and Shirley?"

"No."

"I got a new Baptist group," said Charlie Pratt. "Some new freedom songs. Lots of finger-poppin' and hand jive."

"That's not my stick," said Rodney.

"You mean that ain't your *thing*," said Charlie.

"Yeah," said Rodney. "That's what I mean."

IV

THEY WERE DRINKING BEER and listening to the Dirty Rivers tape when the other people came in. Rodney had been sitting on the sofa, quietly, too heavy to keep time with his feet and too tight inside to care if the Pratts did. Lynn was in her best position, on the floor, cross-legged. The two girls with names he did not catch sat in chairs and crossed their legs, keeping time to the music and smoking. Looking at Lynn on the floor and looking at them on the chairs made Rodney mad. Listening to the Pratts recount, to the two white fellows, how they got the Cleveland tape made Rodney mad too. He drained his beer can and then began to beat time to the music with his foot and both hands on the arm of the sofa with a heavy, controlled deliberation that was really off the beat. Still, he knew that, since he was the only black male in the room, the others would assume that he alone knew the proper beat, even if it was out of time with their own perception of it, and would follow him. The two bearded fellows did just that when they sat down on the floor with Lynn; but the two girls maintained their original perception of the beat. Nevertheless, watching the fellows, Rodney felt the return of some sense of power.

"Some more suds," he said to Peggy Pratt.

She went out of the room.

"You've had enough," said Lynn.

Rodney looked at her spitefully. "Just be cool," he told her. "You just play your own game and stay cool."

The two girls looked at him and smiled. Their dates looked at Lynn. They did not smile. Dirty Rivers was moaning, "*Help me! Help me! Help me!*" now, and Rodney felt that he had to feel more from the music than any of them. "*Mercy! Mercy! Mercy!*" he exclaimed as Peggy Pratt handed him another can of beer. "This cat is *together!*"

The girls agreed and smiled again. One of them even reconciled her beat to Rodney's. Lynn just looked at him.

"He's just a beautiful man," the reconciled girl said.

"He's got more soul than anybody," said Rodney. "Nobody can touch him." He got up from the sofa, put his hands in his pockets and began to exercise a slow, heavy grind to the music without moving his feet. Charlie, who had been standing by the recorder all this time with his hands locked together, smiled his Genghis Khan smile. "Actually," he said rather slowly, "I think Ashy Williamson is better."

"You jivetime cat," said Rodney. "Williamson couldn't touch Dirty Rivers with a stick,"

"Rivers couldn't adapt," said Charlie.

"What do you mean?"

"He's just an old man now, playing the toilets, doing his same thing. Williamson's got class. He's got a new sound everybody digs. Even the squares."

"What do you know?" said Rodney.

Charlie Pratt smiled. "Plenty," he said.

After more beer and argument all around, and after playing Williamson's oldest and latest LP's by way of proof, it was decided that they should put it to a vote. Both the Pratts were of the same mind: Ashy Williamson was better than Dirty Rivers. The two fellows on the floor agreed with them. And also one of the girls. The other girl, however, the skinny brunette who had reconciled her beat to Rodney's, observed that she had been raised on Rivers and felt, absolutely, that he had had in the past, and still had now, a very good thing going for him. But Rodney was not impressed. She had crooked teeth and was obviously out to flatter her date with her maintenance of an independent mind in spite of her looks. Rodney turned to Lynn, still sitting cross-legged and exposed on the floor, but saving Rodney from utilizing his cautioning eye by having the beer can conveniently placed between her open legs. "Well, what do you say?" he asked, standing over her in his usual way.

She looked up at him. Casually sipping her beer, she considered for a long moment. The room was now very quiet, the last cut having been played on the Williamson record. The only sound was Lynn sipping her beer. It grated in Rodney's mind. The only movement was Charlie Pratt doing his rubber shift from foot to foot. That also irritated Rodney. "Well?" he said.

Lynn placed the can between her legs again, very carefully and neatly. "Dirty Rivers is an old man," she said.

"What the hell does that mean?"

"He's got nothing new going for him, *bay-bee*," she said in a way that told Rodney she had made up her mind about it long before her opinion had been asked. She looked up at Rodney, her face resolved and, it seemed to him, slightly victorious.

"There you go, mother," Charlie said.

Rodney could see them all smiling at him, even Lynn, even the ugly brunette who had reconciled. He sat down on the sofa and said nothing.

"Now I'll play my new Roscoe and Shirley for you," Charlie told the others.

"Wasn't she a lesbian?" one of the fellows asked.

"Absolutely not!" said Charlie Pratt.

Rodney was flipping the coin in his mind again now.

He flipped it faster and faster. After a while it was spinning against Willie and the cigar-chewing bartender and
Lynn and especially the Pratts. Finishing the beer, Rodney
found that the coin had stopped spinning; and from where
his mind hung on the bad side of it, somewhere close to
the place where he kept his bigotry almost locked away, he
could hear the Pratts battling back and forth for the right
to tell the others about a famous movie star who sued her
parents when she found out that she was a mulatto. He
got to his feet and walked over to the stacks and stacks
of records that lined the wall. Aimlessly going through
them, he considered all the black faces on their covers and
all the slick, praising language by white disc jockeys and
white experts and white managers on their backs. Then
he commenced to stare at the brunette who had agreed
with him. She avoided his eyes. He stared at Lynn too; but
she was looking at Charlie Pratt, very intentionally. Only
once did she glance up at him and smiled in a way that
said "*bay-bee.*" And then she looked away again.

Rodney leaned against the wall of records, put his
hands in his pockets and wet his lips. Then he said: "Little
Tommy Tucker was a *bad* motherfucker!"

They all looked up at him.

"What?" said Peggy Pratt, smiling.

He repeated it.

V

DRIVING HOME, Rodney went slower than required and
obeyed traffic signals on very quiet, very empty streets.

Lynn sat against the door, away from him. She had her legs crossed.

"You were pretty good tonight," she said at last.

Rodney was looking at a traffic light changing back to red.

"You were the life of the party."

Rodney inspected a white line of bird shit running down the top of the window, between him and the red light. It would have to come off in the morning.

"I knew you would let that color come through if you had enough beer," Lynn said.

"Oh shut the hell up!" said Rodney. He was not mad. She had just interrupted his thinking. He was thinking of going over to buy some more beer for Willie and talk some more before the usual Saturday time. He was thinking about building up his collection of Ashy Williamson LP's. He was thinking about driving Lynn directly home and not going up with her to make love to her in her bed, which was much wider than his own, no matter how much she apologized later and no matter how dark and safe and inviting her room would be.

A NEW PLACE

AT FIRST ALL WE HAD growing was a potted plant that Ellen had brought over and put in the window. But it didn't get enough sun and the air was too heavy for it and after a bird shit on it, God knows how at that angle, we had to pick off all the splattered leaves because we couldn't clean the leaves without breaking them. Jack was pissed off and so was Ellen when she came back over and saw what was left of the plant.

"Why did you two pigs have to eat it?" she asked us.

"We didn't eat it," I said. "We were just trying to save it."

"Save it!" she said. "How can you save a plant by pulling off the leaves? Just tell me that."

I was going to tell her about how the bird had shit on the leaves but Jack got to her before me. He was sitting on the floor in his underwear. He had been sitting there like that most of the day, doing nothing, and I knew he was just as pissed off over the thing as Ellen was. "Don't make such a big deal out of it," he told her. "It wasn't grass or anything important. It was just a stupid plant."

"I raised that plant in my own bathroom from just some seeds," said Ellen. "And you two pigs had to go and eat it."

"You're a real mother," said Jack. "You're such a mother you ought to sell soap on television."

"Come on and cool it now," I told Jack. Ellen was my piece and I knew that once he got to going good they would be at it all afternoon. She was my piece and I had to protect her. I went over to the window and threw the plant downstairs. But then Ellen got pissed at me too and stalked out the door, that long brown hair trailing behind her in the breeze she made.

"What a real cool head you've got there," said Jack, as Ellen was slamming the door. "She's uptight and it wasn't even grass. Just a lousy pile of leaves."

"You don't understand her," I said.

"You don't either," said Jack.

So we sat around and wondered what we should do next. We had a whole summer to do whatever we wanted and all we had to do was figure it out. Then, that next morning, Jack had the idea that we should go to Newport, start our beards growing, sleep in the open, and sweat and not bother to wash until we got back. It sounded great to me and that night we drove down in my VW. But when we hit the town we saw that there were a million kids around with the same idea and all of us looked alike, and the local pig-cops wouldn't let us sleep on the ground. They had a lot of sawdust on the ground and we dragged our feet through it and threw it up in the air and on each other. Jack even tried to stuff some of it in his pockets to bring back with us and make our place smell better, but the pigs stopped us there too. The Festival was on that weekend and a lot of the little rock groups were singing "I Can't Get No Satisfaction," a real oldie. It seemed to catch on, though, and even way up on the stage, about a hundred benches from us, Christopher Robin and the Sparrows, a new group in from the Coast, were singing it too. It was our first night there and I looked around in the bright white outdoor lamplight and at all the faces and there was this girl, a Jew with a big nose trying to keep warm in a blanket, and she was singing it too, right next to me on the bench, and she was crying.

I nudged Jack. "Let's get the hell out of here," I said.

"All right," Jack said. He was as set to go as me: our beards had not grown as much as some of the others there. We left the benches but Jack thought we should wander around some to pick up a couple of girls to bring back with us. I was thinking about Ellen and the plant.

"I don't want to," I told him.

"Why not?"

"Let's just get the hell out, alone."

Jack didn't push it or bitch about it much. I guess he didn't mind that either.

So we came back to the city with some groovy saw-dust in our shoes that we had managed to pick up. But that night in our place when we poured it out of our shoes on the floor it looked too much like dirt. And we had to throw that out too.

"I'm tired of this shit," said Jack.

"What's wrong?" I asked him.

"I don't know," he said.

"Want to call Ellen and Katie over and get laid?"

"If *you* want to," Jack said.

"I don't really want any unless you need some."

"No. I don't want any."

"What *do* you want?"

"I don't know," Jack said.

He was always that way. He never knew what he wanted. Sometimes I thought he was pretty deep because he never knew, because sometimes *I* don't know what *I* want. But sometimes I thought he was square and pretty stupid. Like for instance the way he wouldn't dress in the morning; he'd just mope around in his underwear all day as if he was trying to make up his mind whether he wanted to put clothes on or not before it was time to go to bed again. Sometimes he could be really weird, like he was being that night. I looked at him. "Look," I said. "That Newport thing was crap anyway. We should've left the crowd and cut out on our own, up to one of the beaches or something."

"Yeah," said Jack.

He was laying on the floor with his hands behind his head and he was looking up at the way the lovebeads dangled from the string on the light. I felt bad because it had been my decision to come back so soon.

"You sure you don't want some pussy?" I asked him.

"I'm sure I don't want some pussy," he said.

"Want to turn on?"

"No."

"Want to go to bed?"

Jack just looked up at the lovebeads. Finally he got up and went over to the box and got a couple of beers. We sat drinking them.

Now I know Jack, mind you, and I knew that when he didn't know what it was he wanted he would always think about it over beer. We had been in the place two years together and I had got used to the way he was. Sometimes, for no reason at all, he would get moody and just flake out. We would be laughing about something or we would have a couple of broads over and I would look up all at once and Jack would be turned off, completely. Now, I tend to mind my own business and I usually do a good job of it, but seeing him all uptight or flaked out or whatever he was, kind of bothered me. I remembered one time he went away, just before he finally quit school for good. Jack had been in Philosophy and he used to really think about it and read a lot of it before he saw where it was at, and put it down. I remember seeing him there, at his desk, not even turning the pages of his book or not even smiling when I was talking funny about some far-out cat we both knew who was trying to be hip. It was real funny. But Jack wasn't listening to me. I stopped talking for a few minutes and he never even noticed it. Then I said:

"Hey, man, where are you?"

He didn't even look up at me. He just stared blank-like at the wall behind his desk.

"What are you writing?" I said in a louder voice.

"I can't do this paper," he finally said.

"Why not?"

"Too goddamn many footnotes. I can't put my own ideas in."

"Well, what ideas you got?"

Jack sighed. "None," he said. "But I refuse to use anybody else's."

"What does it matter?" I said. "All you want is the grade anyway."

"It matters," he said. "It matters to me. And I don't give a damn about the grade. I just want to do something with my ideas."

"But you don't *have* any ideas!"

"What's wrong with that?" he snapped.

"It's weird, that's what's wrong."

"So I'm weird," he said. He slammed his hand down on the desk, hard. He even turned around in the chair and looked at me, mean.

"And another thing," he said. "When you see me thinking don't ever interrupt me."

I started to tell him just where he could go but then I changed my mind. I had just been in the loft with him three months then and I didn't want to provoke him because I was thinking that he was a real nut.

"All right," I said to Jack. "If that's the way you want it."

"That's the way," Jack said.

And that's the way it had been for almost two years. I knew when to talk to Jack and when to leave him alone. I learned to leave him alone when he was quiet and wanted to be left alone, and I learned to get him to start talking when he wanted to talk but didn't want to begin the thing. But seeing him that night, on the floor drinking the second can of beer and looking up at the lovebeads, made me feel responsible because it had been my idea to leave the sawdust at Newport.

"Tell you what," I said to him. "We'll do it again."

"Do what?" said Jack.

"We'll go back to Newport tomorrow. The Festival's still on and some new group'll be in and there'll always be plenty of girls around."

"I don't want to go back," said Jack. "It bothers me being there."

"But you dug it tonight?"

"That was tonight. I don't want to go back. There'll be new things tomorrow but it'll be the same place."

"You want a new place, is that what you want?"

"Yeah," he said. "That's what I want, a new place."

I thought about a new scene. I thought very hard about someplace new to go. I almost blew my mind thinking about a new scene. But it was no good. We had been everywhere.

"I've had it," I said after a while. "There's no place left to go to. Unless you want to fly somewhere."

Jack sat up on the floor and knocked over the can of beer he had put next to his arm. He was smiling and I knew he had one of his ideas.

"Bryan Dillworth has a place in the woods," he said. "I know where it is, up in New Hampshire. I was up there with him last winter. It's a groovy place in the woods and I know it's open because it's way back in the sticks and you have to walk to get to it."

"You out of your nut, Jack?" I said. "What could *we* do in the woods?"

"Just *go* and sit around."

"I don't think Ellen and Katie would go for that," I said. "Even if Katie *did* decide to speak to you again."

"The hell with them," Jack said. "We don't want to take girls along anyway. They would just spoil things."

"Then what do you plan to *do* at night?"

"Just sit around."

"That's pretty weird, Jackie," I said. "Who wants to sit around and listen to crickets making out all night?"

"The hell with you too," he said. "I'll go by myself."

But I knew he wouldn't do it alone. I knew that much about Jack. He didn't say anything else and he lay back on the floor and started mumbling to himself about the stuff he was going to take up with him. He didn't even look up at me and I knew he was waiting for me to throw in the towel and say I would go. But I didn't know whether I should or not. No one wants to be stuck out in the woods with a nut; and I was coming around to thinking that Jack was blowing more of his mind every day. Still, I had made him come in from Newport before he wanted to and I knew he would try to make me feel guilty about that if I didn't go along with him. Jack was very good about doing that.

"Can I take the VW if you're not going?" he asked all at once from the floor.

"I don't want my car going down no country roads," I told him. "If it got stuck you'd never be able to get it out by yourself."

"So, O.K., I'll walk."

"You're really out of your nut, you know that?"

"What the hell?" said Jack. "I'll walk."

And it was still my fault about the Newport thing. I felt guilty. Jack was playing with me and waiting and I was pissed off because I couldn't help myself. He had me.

"All right," I told him. "We'll go. But I'll be damned if I'm driving."

Jack looked over at me and smiled.

||

WE GOT AN EARLY START that next morning. Jack was driving my car and he refused to take the turnpike. I thought he was doing it just to make me get mad and say something, so I kept my cool. But after a while of going down that little road with a drag-ass ahead of us slowing us down I decided to risk it. "Look," I said to him. "This way it'll take at least seven hours to get there. Be logical and take the pike, for the love of Jesus."

"If you want to be logical and drive on the pike, go ahead," he told me, "but if *I* drive we go all the way on back roads."

"But think of all the extra gas we'll use?"

"So?"

"And we'll waste a lot of time too, going this way."

Jack thought a minute. I thought he was finally seeing the light. Then he said: "That's what you think."

"O.K.," I said. "We'll do it your way. But I'm not paying a fucking cent for the extra gas."

Jack stepped on the brakes right in the middle of traffic on that road. I was lucky to have my seat belt locked.

"Get out," he said to me.

"What the fuck do you mean?" Cars were honking behind us.

"Just get the hell out of the car." He had his lips tight and he was looking through the windshield.

"We're way out in the middle of the goddamn sticks already."

"I don't give a good goddamn. Get out *now* and thumb a ride back."

"Be logical," I said to Jack. "At least pull over to the side of the road."

"*Everybody's* logical," he said. "I'm tired. Get *out!*"

I just sat there looking at Jack's face. It was tight and turning red and the two sides of his nose were moving real fast like he was out of breath. I didn't move from the seat beside him. I mean, it was *my* car. More traffic was honking now, but Jack just sat there, his hands locked on the wheel, looking out the window down the empty road. I was getting hot as hell then but I knew I had to keep my cool because Jack was just waiting for an excuse to throw me out of the car and I was scared to fight him. I don't think I would have fought him anyway. You can't win fighting a crazy man.

We sat there quiet-like, waiting for me to get out or the car to start. It was really tense. I knew that I wasn't about to leave my own car in the hands of a madman. And I was thinking about playing it cool and safe and apologizing to him, when this pig-faced trucker leaned into the window on Jack's side of the car and said: "How much longer you guys gonna take for your coffee break?"

"We don't have coffee," Jack told him.

"I don't neither," said the pig. "In fact, I ain't got nothin' but a truckloada overripe peaches back there. But

I figure since you guys are sittin' here and ain't got no cof-fee I might as well offer you some peaches, since I can't move my truck anyways."

"Thanks," Jack told him.

The trucker slammed his hands down on the roof of the car like he really had to hit something. Then he reached in the car and grabbed Jack by the arm. "All right, smart-ass," he said. "Get the *fuck* outta the road. You got five seconds, and if you ain't outta here before then I'm gonna pull that hair off your chin one piece atta time!" He was wearing this unhip plaid shirt that was open at the chest and the thick red hair under it was moving up and down real fast, like he was about to really explode.

"Please, Jackie," I said. "We don't want trouble. Let's go."

"You tell him, Willie," the trucker said. "You young punks *need* some trouble anyway. I'd like to see one of you guys bleed anyway 'cause I got this bet with a buddy that you ain't human."

Jack still had his hands on the wheel and all at once he gave the VW the gas, right down to the floor. He al-most ran over the pig trucker's feet, he pulled out so fast. "Schmuck!" he called back at the trucker out the window. He gave the guy the finger with his left arm and almost lost control of the car. I knew better than to say anything. I was sure now that Jack was losing it. But he was smart enough to do eighty until we came to a place where we could turn off that back road and onto the pike. The pig trucker was really pouring it on behind us but it didn't do any good. We were way out front, and after we got on the pike Jack kept her at eighty.

"Hey, slow down," I told him. "You'll run into something going this fast."

Jack seemed to ignore me. Then, after a while, he said: "What the hell. Why should you worry? You belong to Allstate anyway. You don't have to be responsible for anything."

"I worry," I said. "I haven't paid for the car yet."

Jack smiled. "Why worry about that either? You're *Allstate's*."

But after a while he finally slowed her down to a smooth sixty and we settled back for some steady driving and neither one of us said anything. I couldn't say anything. I was thinking about moving the hell out of the apartment just as soon as we got back.

III

IT WAS REALLY BEAUTIFUL in those woods that first evening. The water in the pond was too muddy and had too many bugs in it for us to drink it, and so we had to find our own source. Jack liked that. We went off into the woods just before sunset, and all the leaves on the ground were hit by this kind of white-red sunlight coming through the trees and it made them look browner and redder and greener than they actually were. Walking on them made a good sound. The sound was so good, in fact, that we didn't even look very hard for water. We just walked around some and listened to the sound our feet made in the leaves. It was much better than the sawdust and I really began to feel good that Jack had made me come up. I even began to feel a little bit good about Jack. But I was still thinking about moving the hell out of the loft as soon as we got back. Then Jack found a little stream and we followed it until we came to a place where the white water flowed down over some clean black stones, and we filled our bottles with the water without collecting a single bug.

Going back to the cabin, Jack said to me: "I'm awfully sorry about today, Joe. I just got kind of pissed off."

"Forget it," I said.

"I didn't mean to be a shit about the thing."

"Don't think about it," I said.

"I feel closer to you than anybody in the world and I don't want you to feel bad about me. About the way I am."

It was getting dark and the woods were not so beautiful then.

"Let's get back to the cabin," I said.

"You don't feel bad towards me, do you, Joe?"

"Hell no," I told him. "But let's get back to the cabin."

We had to cut wood for the stove and the fireplace because with the sun down it got awfully cold in the cabin all of a sudden. Jack insisted on cutting all the wood; he wouldn't let me help him cut any or even bring any in the cabin. He didn't even want to stop when both the woodboxes were full and he was sweating. "For the love of Jesus," I told him from the cabin door, "don't be a mule. That's enough. We're only going to be here for one night. Leave something standing for the woodpeckers."

"I like it," Jack called back to me, swinging the axe

high over his head and coming down hard on a log. He didn't even split that log; it was hard work.

"But we don't *need* all that."

"*I* need it," said Jack.

"What the hell for?"

"For me."

I couldn't get him to stop it, and finally I went on back inside the cabin and started the fire in the big old rusty pot-bellied iron stove. I took a can of beans out of my bundle and opened it and thought about Jack. Something was always eating him up inside and I didn't think it was something that I caused. After you live with a fellow for almost two years you kind of know what he thinks and what bothers him and what doesn't. I knew it wasn't being around me or Ellen that bothered Jack. And it wasn't Kay either. He didn't give a damn about her; she was just something he liked to have around because she was so stupid that having her around made him feel better. I knew that much. But I didn't understand what else there was to it. Outside, Jack was still cutting wood and it was really dark. I didn't see the sense of it but I wasn't about to go out to stop him. One man has his bag and another man has his own. Jack was into his now, and there must have been some good things in it for him, whatever they were.

He came in later with three loads of wood. The cabin was warm from the stove then and he was sweating in his beard and on his forehead.

"We might as well stay the winter," I told him. "We've got enough wood now, anyway."

He dumped the last armload on the pile next to the big fireplace and turned around and looked at me.

"We *could* stay the winter," I said again, nodding to the big pile of wood behind him on the cement part of the fireplace. I was trying to find a way to make him smile or talk, at least, because the quiet bothered me. "We *could*, with all *that*."

"Maybe we will," he said.

"We could bring up Ellen and Katie, or maybe big Susan Slussman. She likes to cook. You could chop wood all winter and Susan could cook while Ellen and I made out all the time."

"That's all you think about, making out, isn't it?"

"Yeah," I said. "Then you wouldn't have to worry about footnotes or somebody else's ideas all the time. You wouldn't even have to worry about what to do next or feel guilty about dropping out of school. You could just chop wood all the time."

"That would be real good," said Jack.

"Of course we couldn't get grass or acid this far out in the sticks. The best we could hope for would be airplane glue or extract. But whatever we got, this would be one hell of a good place to trip."

"I think I'll put acid down anyway," he said. "I'm through with tripping."

"Man," I said, "you can't mean that. How would you live?"

"I'll cut wood."

"I was only putting you on with that bit," I said. "This is an O.K. scene for a night or so, but it's weird if you really get into it."

"I still like it," Jack said.

"Well, don't forget, we're pulling out tomorrow morning."

"Yeah," he said. Then he got down in front of the fire-place and began to light the smallest sticks for the fire. I watched him. And he didn't even try to use the lighter fluid we brought. He just kept trying to do this Davy Crockett bit with a box of wooden matches. They didn't work but he kept striking them and watching them burn out before the wood caught. It was really frustrating watching him. But I knew he was just waiting for me to suggest the fluid so he could start some shit. I just watched him. We didn't even need the fireplace now but he kept on with this frontier jazz. I knew then that it was time for me to pack my things when we got back to the place.

IV

WE WERE JUST LAYING AROUND the fire after we had eaten the beans and I got to feeling kind of concerned about Jack again. I got to thinking about the last few months before the summer and how he had started to all at once cut people off, about how he cut off Katie.

He had had a good thing going with her. Katie was a real slave. She did all of those spade things for him like cooking, washing his things, keeping the loft clean, even sewing his sandals. A real slave. And she was nice to him in the sack too. From the sound of them, she must have been much better than Ellen. Sometimes at night, when she was sleeping over in Jack's room, there were lots of good things to hear. They really had a good time and, I admit, sometimes, listening to them go, I got a little jealous of Jack. And many times, in my bed in the next room, I caught myself thinking about how nice it would be to try Katie for a change, just to see if Ellen measured up to her. But I never got a chance because Jack fucked it up for both of us with another of his weird ideas.

He wouldn't let Katie use the pill. He made a big thing about wanting everything to be natural and uncomplicated. He said he wanted her to be *original*. Of course Katie didn't go for it, and neither did Ellen, and neither did any of us. But Jack said it was his show because she was his piece and he was going to run it his way. The *natural* way. Then Katie took to staying away at her time every month. And that really pissed Jack off. It was like he *wanted* her to get pregnant, just to see if he could do it. He must have thought he was a real cool head, really hip, because all of us knew that he wouldn't marry her if she did get pregnant. Katie knew it too, and even though she really dug Jack, she told him that she was going to put him down if he didn't come off the God bit. But Jack wouldn't cool it, and pretty soon we got the word that Katie was sleeping around with some spade cat she had picked up. That really got to Jack. And that was when he took to laying around and thinking, and that was when he finally put school down.

Now, looking at him spread out by the fire and looking up at the big, dusty moose head over the fireplace, it kind of came to me just what it was that was eating him and why he wanted to get me way out in the sticks, alone with him.

"Hey, Jack?" I said.

"Yeah."

"Tell me something honestly."

"What?"

"You turning queer?"

"*What?*"

I had to swallow hard and brace myself before I could say it again. I expected him to jump on me. "Do you think you're going into a gay period?"

He didn't answer.

"I want you to know, it's nothing to me if you are. Everybody's gotta live."

"Suppose I am?" he said. He was still eyeing that moose head.

"I just wanted to know, that's all."

"Well, maybe," he said.

I propped my head up on my arm and looked into the fire. "What's it like?"

"I don't know. I just don't feel anything. I don't want anything. I just feel like nothing all the time."

"That's normal," I said. "When was the last time you tripped?"

"Acid?"

"Yeah."

"Last spring, I guess."

"Why don't you get some from Solly when we get back and go again? That's probably all you need."

"That's not it," said Jack. "It won't be any good. I just feel useless." He stopped talking and thought for a while. I could tell he was thinking because his eyes were moving from the fire up the moose head and the firelight was flashing in them. "Maybe you're right," he finally went on. "Maybe that's the start of a gay period."

"Katie's worried about you, you know that?"

"Yeah, I know."

"Everybody's worried about you," I said. "If you keep acting this way the word'll get out that you *are* gay."

"So what if I am?"

"So nothing," I told him. "It makes no difference to me. I just want you to know how I feel about it."

Now Jack began to smile, and his teeth and his beard and the shadows from the fire and the moose head made him look really wicked.

"How *do* you feel about it, Joe?"

"I'm *not* gay. *That's* how I feel about it."

Now Jack laughed aloud. And he looked directly at me in the firelight and scared me, he looked so wicked. "You're not missing much," he said.

I got up and went over to the cot against the wall. It was the only one in the cabin but it was big enough for two. Jack was still laying at the fireplace looking at me and smiling. It was really weird.

"You want to sleep by the fire or you want to take the cot?" I asked him.

"Is it big enough for both of us?"

"No. Take your choice."

Jack smiled again in the firelight. He took a long time smiling and then he looked up at the moose head. "I'll stay here," he said.

And he slept there all night because I laid awake in the cot all night and watched him.

V

I DROVE STRAIGHT THROUGH all the way back to the city. Jack just sat on the seat most of the way back and said nothing. Once we stopped for gas at a station with a little restaurant on the side and I was really hungry but I didn't get out because I was afraid that Jack might take the car and leave me there. You don't know how to handle a queer all the time, especially if you're not used to knowing he's a queer. I have nothing against fags, mind you, some of the best men in the country are fags, but nobody wants to drive across country with one who, just the day before, was straight. At least in your mind he was. I didn't want to be mean to Jack; I understood him now. I just wanted to get back to the place so we could decide which one of us was going to move out. I was scared to mention it in the car, and I figured that our loft was the best spot.

But when we got into the city, Jack wanted to get out downtown instead of going all the way in with me.

"I'll come in after a while," he told me when I let him out. "I want to do some things first."

"Sure," I said. "Come on in when you want."

"And I'll have a surprise for you tonight when I come in."

"I'll bet," I said.

Jack looked hurt. He stood outside the car and put his hand on the door next to me. "Look, Joe," he said. "Back there, last night, I thought about it and I figure I was only kidding about being gay."

"Sure," I said.

"You don't think I'm really gay, do you, Joe?"

"I don't know," I said. "I honestly don't know what happened to you."

"I don't know either," said Jack. "But I know I'm not gay."

"So you're not gay," I said. "I'll see you later."

"I'm *not!*" he said again. But I was already driving away.

Ellen was at the loft waiting for me when I got there. She was still pissed off about the plant and about how I had gone off without telling her. Then she was hot about Jack and how he had made fun of the plant. And the place was filthy with beer bottles and cigarette ashes and socks and dirt all over, and she was hot about that too.

"Don't worry about Jack," I told her. "He's leaving before next weekend or else I'm leaving."

"What happened?"

"Nothing," I said. "We just can't make it together any more."

"I could've told you *that* three months ago when he put Kay down. He's turning into a real nut."

"That's not all," I said. "He's turning into something else too."

"What?"

"Never mind," I said. "He's leaving anyway." Then I pulled her down on my lap and we fooled around some before we hit the sack. Being with her again was really good after a night in the woods with Jack. But I was sleepy and I could tell that I wasn't too good for her then. Ellen is a tolerant girl, though. And, I guess, a lot more understanding than Katie. She knew there would be better times coming; so afterwards she let me sleep without asking me more about where I'd been or what had happened between Jack and me. I dreamed about her too while I was sleeping. And I dreamed about Jack. I dreamed that I was back to feeling sorry for him again and I was back in the cabin and letting him get in the bunk with me because he kept telling me that it was cold on the floor because the fire had gone out and the moose head was about to fall down on him. He was still getting in the bed and talking about how cold it was on the floor and how glad he was that he didn't have to sleep there when I woke up and he was still talking, but in a different voice now. I heard him saying: "Bitch! Bitch!" and it wasn't part of the dream.

I jumped out of bed and ran into the living room. Jack and Ellen were standing there screaming at each other. Jack kept calling her a bitch and Ellen was almost crying but still managing to call him a few choice things too.

When Jack saw me he pointed his finger at Ellen and said: "Look what she's done. *Look what she did to the place!*"

I looked. Ellen had given it a really good cleaning. She had thrown out all the old beer cans and bottles and cleaned out the ashtrays and swept the floor. She had even washed the windowsills. And from where I stood in the living room I could see that she had done the same good job in the kitchen. That's all she had done; but Jack was standing there like a crazy man pointing his finger at her and cursing.

"She just cleaned up," I told him. "What's wrong with that?"

Jack stopped cursing and just stood in the middle of the clean room and glared at both of us. Ellen had been crying hard. Some of that long brown hair of hers was stuck to her face where it was wet.

"I just thought that since this *pig* was leaving soon I'd just clean up some and get the smell out of here."

"You don't even live here," said Jack. "You just come here to get laid. Isn't that enough for you?"

"*Now shut the fuck up!*" I told him. I started to move toward him and he grabbed one of the wooden chairs from the table and lifted it high in the air. Ellen screamed and when he looked over at her I rushed him and tripped him to the floor. I had to hit him once or twice, and I really didn't want to. But he kept trying to get up and I couldn't take a chance on letting him. You can't give a queer the same breaks you'd give a real man, no matter how sorry you feel for him. Finally I managed to pin him to the floor by lying on top of him and pushing both his arms down with both of mine. Ellen got the chair away from us.

"Now, what's your trouble?" I said to him. I was breathing hard and I was ready to let him have it again if he started some more shit.

Jack went all limp under me, like a girl would after that last big moment, and I felt really uneasy lying on top of him that way. I got off and let him get up. But he only got up as far as his knees.

"What's got into you?" I asked him.

"Nothing," he said.

"If you wanted to raise hell couldn't you find some better excuse than her cleaning up the place?"

Jack just stayed there on his knees. I was beginning to

feel bad again, about the whole thing. Ellen was sitting on the chair, still crying.

"Look at the place," I told him. "Look around. See how clean it is. It looks better than it's looked in months. Is that something to bitch about?"

"*I* wanted to do it," Jack said. "I wanted to clean up the loft."

"Whatever the hell for?"

Jack did not answer.

"You've never wanted to do it before."

"I wanted to do it," Jack said again.

"You always kept it pretty filthy before," said Ellen from the chair. "You never even bothered to pick up your underwear before."

"I wanted to do it," he said.

Then I knew that I had had it with Jack. We had reached the final point and it was really clear in my mind now that he was hopelessly gay and would be dangerous to have around the place any longer.

"Jack," I said. "This is it, man. Either you walk out with your stuff now or I'll throw you out and shovel your stuff out the window."

"Like the plant," Ellen said from the chair.

"Shut up!" I told her.

I turned back to Jack, still on his knees, on the floor. "This is it, man. We can talk about the lease later. You won't have to pay anything, just get out *now!*"

I was really testing him then, because any straight fellow would raise hell about being put out of his own apartment, especially when his old man had already paid for it a whole year in advance. Only a real fairy wouldn't put up a fight. This was Jack's last test. And what did he do? He just looked at me, not wicked like he did in front of the fireplace the night before, but sad and like he was about to cry, just like one of those pet dogs. Then he got to his feet and walked to the door. Ellen and I watched him. Just before he went out the door he looked at me with that same hurt-dog look and said: "I'm not gay, Joe."

I didn't say anything.

He didn't come back for his stuff until that next week. I don't know where he went when he left. He didn't get any calls while he was away, either; he had lost all his friends in our crowd a long time before that. And when the word got around about the scene he had made he didn't have anything left. Even Katie, when she heard, put down the little feeling she still had for him. So there wasn't much I could say to him when he did come back for his stuff.

Ellen moved in with me after that. We really didn't need *two* bedrooms, but what the hell. She's a better roommate than Jack. She does all the cooking and she keeps the place really clean all the time. I think it's much better to live with a girl all the time than to live with another guy and only get to see a girl once a day, at night, or something like that. It kind of spoils a man. It makes him brood around and think too much. Thinking too much can be a bad scene. I guess that's what happened to Jack. His mind must have beat him out of the straight life.

It won't ever beat *me*, though. Ellen and I make it at least twice every night and sometimes some more, depending on how the day went. I don't have to feel sorry for anyone any more, and that helps a lot. It makes me more a man. But sometimes I wonder about Jack, about how he was trying to show me that he was making a comeback to the straight life. And sometimes I wonder what the hell it was in his mind that made him think that cleaning up the loft was a straight thing to do. I wonder how the hell that would have helped him. I wonder, and I still think it was pretty weird.

HUE *and* CRY

A joke is an epigram on the death of a feeling.
—FRIEDRICH NIETZSCHE

B UT IF THAT IS ALL THERE IS, what is left of life and why are we alive?"

"Because we know no better way to be."

"And are these our only options?"

"These few should be sufficient."

"But what of those who look for more?"

"One must either hate or pity them."

"Why hate?"

"Because they make us uncomfortable in their lack of loyalties to these options."

"Why pity?"

"Because we know that they must pay for our discomfort."

"But is it necessary that they should pay?"

"Always."

"On what authority?"

"For all of those who took the easy options; for all of those who are unhappy in their choices."

"And are there many of these unhappy?"

"Look around you."

"And what of those who look for more? Are they just as plentiful and just as unhappy?"

"Look around you. They live in dark and secret places, but one can see they are many and unhappy. And one can see how they pay."

"How do they pay?"

And then there was the getting to sleep. It would start with his moving across the double bed, slowly, for a position; and it would continue that way until he had moved to the edge of the bed, with the sheets still holding to his body, slippery and clinging at the same time. The sleep would come on him in the same slow way, like a very hot bath beginning to feel good and then getting cold too soon. Eric could not maintain the necessary consistency and would find himself still trying to reach sleep with his mind because his body had long before gone away. Then there was the telephone. Eric wanted it to ring, and he lay waiting for it. And then he did not want it to ring, and he waited for it not to. Besides these two things was his mind, which did not want anything but not being able to think. But he thought, in his double bed, in the night, in the dark. His thoughts were red behind his eyes, if he closed them, and if he held his eyes open in the room, his thoughts were black. Trying to keep his eyes closed was very hard, because then his mind was free to consider the old thoughts and the telephone. He willed that sleep should come, had to come, if only he were patient

and disciplined with his mind; and if he willed that the
thoughts should not come down on him. He shifted on
the sheet into a new position and prepared himself to
fight his mind. But the preparation was very hard. And
he began thinking again.

Eric got up and went into the bathroom for the bottle
of Librium. He found it in the dark and then cut on the
light and looked at the bottle. It was almost empty. He
held it in his hand and thought about the cigarettes and
the other bottles and the expense, and he knew it would
be no good. The bathroom light was very bright and it
hurt Eric's eyes when he looked into the mirror over the
washbowl and saw his own naked body reflected much
whiter than it actually was. Then he thought about the alternative to taking the Librium and, still looking into the
mirror, he felt ashamed of his body. He was not pleased
with darkness but he did not want to see himself or feel
himself or be aware of what he was, and the darkness
helped some with these things.

"It's no damn good," he said aloud in the dark and put
the unopened bottle on the washbowl. Then he wanted
to cry.

Going back into the bedroom, he picked up the telephone and brought it close to his bed, sat on the scattered
sheets, and dialed the number in the dark. The red glow
around the numbers on his clock showed it was almost
2:30 in the morning. After two rings he wanted to hang
up, but something—perhaps the idea of sleeplessness, he
thought—would not let him and seemed to dictate that
he let the telephone ring a third, a fourth, and then a fifth
time.

"Hello." He could tell that she had not been sleeping.

"Were you sleeping?" he asked anyway.

There was a little pause and some audible breathing. Eric knew she would not lie. "No," she said at last.

"I don't know why I called. I honestly don't know why."

"You couldn't sleep," she said.

"I was just thinking," he said. "Are you tired?"

"Yes."

"Are you alone?"

"Yes." Her voice was much heavier.

"Can I just talk to you?"

"What about? We've said all we have to."

"I'm sorry, truly I am."

"For what?" she said sharply. "What have *you* got to be sorry about?"

"For the way things are. Everything's just so messed up."

"And I'm black," she said. "That makes it messier." Her voice was not angry, just heavy, and Eric knew that if they talked longer she would be crying and he would have to go out walking all through the night. But he had called her, and he played with what he would say in his mind because he knew that if he was not careful he would begin to repeat himself.

"I'm sorry about everything. I'm sorry for the whole world and everybody in it. I'm sorry I'm alive." He had made his voice softer.

"Please don't do that, Eric," she said. "Oh, please, please don't start that. I just want to sleep."

He knew that he had said that too many times and

now she did not believe him. "Can I see you?" he asked, his voice very close to pleading.

She was silent for a moment and Eric thought about where he would go if he had to walk. "When?" she finally said.

"Tonight. Now."

"Why now? Because it's dark? Because *you* can't sleep and want to make love?"

"That's not it at all," Eric said quickly. "You know that's not it."

"But it's what we've come to, isn't it?"

Now Eric was silent. He could say nothing more without repeating himself and he did not want to do that.

"Is this all we have left, the night, and calling whenever one of us gets horny?"

"Don't," he said. "It was so beautiful. Don't dirty it. I know I deserve it but please don't say it now."

"When *will* I say it?" she said.

"I love you," Eric said. He said it soft in the telephone and he knew that he was repeating himself, but now it did not matter. "You know I love you and I love you so much it hurts to say it the way things are. I can't sleep. I can't take any more pills. I haven't even talked to another girl since last week and I don't know if I can ever talk to another girl."

"I hate you, Eric," she said.

Now there was nothing more to repeat. "I won't call again," he said. "It was rotten of me to do this anyway."

"Eric?"

"What?"

"You can come for tonight. I don't want anything beyond tonight."

"I don't want to use you. I swear to God I don't want to just use you."

"I know," she said. "It's just that I can't sleep."

II

MARGOT PAYNE HAD BEEN very bright in school and had never learned to dance. As a child, the brightness and the sense of superiority which she began to feel over the other, less intelligent, black children in her Cleveland school had not lost her many friends, but neither had it gained her any. And the dancing, which was never really important to her, had not mattered until she was much older, and until the other children became aware of her intellectual superiority and began to resent her because of it. Then the dancing became all at once very important to her. Margot's parents were very proud of her because of the reports, but secretly they worried over her integration in the community. They urged her to dance. And her mother, a cautious, sharp woman, counseled her in little nighttime bedroom sessions about black men and how important it was for a black woman of high intelligence to make it as imperceptible as possible, because they would resent it and her for having it.

She had tried very hard to feel accepted. And although she made great efforts to laugh and mix and dance, she still grew resentful and somewhat introverted because she found that she could not talk to anyone she knew

about the things that really mattered to her. She loved
to discover new ideas. She loved to think, and she loved
to argue. But she did very little of this. In her early teens
she began to date Ray, a fellow who loved his motor-
cycle better than anything else in the world and who had
quit school to prove it. She rode through most of Cleveland with him on the cycle, clinging to his back, and her
friends saw her and the rugged, green-shirted Ray, and
she was sad because she knew they had developed some
respect for her only because she was on the cycle, clinging to a boy who would always be intellectually dead.
And when she had tried to talk to Ray about ambition
and the dividing line, represented by the cycle, between
pastime and purpose, he would put her off and begin to
polish the chrome on his bike. Once, when she had suggested that he get a steady job so that he could afford a
car, he had looked at her from under his helmet, considered tremendously the suggestion, and said at last: "You
know, you *right*, baby! You stick with me and I bet you
can learn me a lot." Then she had known that it would
not work and she had stopped seeing him. Afterwards,
she was hurt when she saw other girls in her place on the
cycle, clinging to Ray's green back, and when she realized that it was not the chrome cycle or Ray's reputation
as a mover or the new girl's attractiveness to Ray that
had put her there; it was Margot's own property value
that had caused it, the secret, never admitted reverence
and respect which the other girls had for her intelligence
and her ability to choose a man of distinction. She was
aware that *she* had made Ray's reputation for him merely
by allowing her body and mind, and all they secretly rep-

resented to the others, to pause in idle proximity to his own native dullness as a kind of foil. And at first she thought it kind of funny, a sort of happy-sad commentary on the crass stupidity of people; but later, when she had to date boys who had no cars or cycles or even dimes for the buses, she did not think it so funny. She began to think harder about learning the dance.

She dated Hank, a big, self-assured fellow with a reputation for being mean to girls. She began to date him because in those late teenage years she had become more aware of her mind and its powers much superior to those of the people around her. She believed that she could control Hank, and in order to do it she had to be herself, smart, confident, superior, and she had to constantly remind Hank of it. In conversation she began to convince him of his own intellectual inferiority and she began to manipulate him in small ways. At first she was hesitant but then, when she observed her successes, she began to rather enjoy dictating to him where they should go, what they should do and how he should address her at certain times, and how to regard her in the company of other teenagers. In the latter part of the relationship, she took immense pleasure in constantly reminding him how much of an honor it should be for him to have a girl of her mind. The dull Hank complied, not because he was easy or grateful or a truly simple-minded person, but because he had only one motive in mind, one purpose in the total relationship for which he was firmly enduring these manipulations. Margot was a virgin, and the slow but crudely clever Hank had it in his mind that she should not be that way very much longer. And so he accepted, with a little pretense of fight, her spurts of self-assured mental superiority, her directions and daily increasing manipulations; and when the time was right for him to become conveniently angry, he did it with relish, beat her just enough to put her in her place, and then made love to her. As a final and absolute assertion of his manliness, he made her crawl naked on the floor of his room, crying and sobbing, placed one huge foot on her neck, pressing her face down, and compelled her to kiss the other. She did it. And in doing so, she forced from her mind all that she had known and all that she had ever expected to know about the dance.

III

ERIC CAME IN THE DOOR and she stood by in her night-gown, the short pink one he had bought her, waiting, her arm raised to the door frame, her breasts obviously firm and growing under the gown. They embraced and there was the sound of sobbing between them, and Eric did not know whether it was Margot's sound or his own. It did not matter. They clung and swayed together in the dark room and pulled away from each other, from time to time, to kiss, to breathe, to exchange deep, truthful looks into eyes that could scarcely be seen in the little light coming from the bedroom. They did not talk. And at the right moment Eric lifted her up and carried her into the other room.

In the middle of it she began to cry and he had to fight himself and the animal in him to stop his hungry thrusts, and he put his hand to her face to touch the tears. He did not try to stop them with his hand; she was crying for both of them and he knew it and was grateful.

"If there was any other way," he said very carefully, "I'd take it. I do want you to be happy."

She said nothing.

"I'm sorry I came," he said. "But I *had* to."

"For this?" Her eyes were closed.

Eric thought about the truth and how, when he was younger, he had always tried to use it to ennoble himself. "Yes," he said, "for this." And now he did not feel so noble.

Margot opened her eyes and looked at Eric. He was now holding his head down, touching her breasts with his hair without meaning to. He wanted very badly to move his body again, but he did not want to be the first to start it because he knew that he would not think much of himself afterwards.

"What are we going to do?" Margot said.

"I don't know," he said.

"I don't want to marry you now," she said. "I did, I really did once but I don't want it now."

"I wish we had done it before," he said. "Before everything got all mixed up."

"I want your baby," Margot said.

Eric pulled his head up and looked at her. "What baby?"

"The one we could have now."

"How could we?"

"I haven't taken anything for a week."

Eric caught himself pulling away. Then he said: "Why didn't you tell me?"

"I want it," she said. "I don't want you but I want it. Please don't move. Please don't. Just stay here with me."

"But I don't want you to do this, not for me."

Margot began to move slowly on the bed and Eric could not help himself. "When you think about it," she was saying, "nothing in the world matters at all."

Eric did not say anything. He was caught in his hunger and it increased. He felt thirst and heat and cold, and the melting and hard feel of himself far deep inside, close, and then far away, now above him, now down there and up again. He wanted to drink, he wanted to feel himself flow all over the bed, he wanted to cry, he wanted to moan, and he felt hunger. He knew, as she did, the right moment to press closer and deeper and where to put his arms and hands and lips, and where to expect hers, and how to receive them and all there was to know about the very last delicious moments before there would be an afterwards.

"WHY DO PEOPLE MAKE LOVE?"

"Because for some things they do not know how to talk."

"What does it do for a man?"

"It makes him feel very big and then it makes him feel very small."

"Why does he feel small?"

"Because sometimes he does not know what to say afterwards."

"Is it really necessary to say anything?"

"For some men it is necessary."

"Why should a man talk when he has gained everything a few minutes before?"

"Some men do not see it as a gain."

"Are there such men?"

"Many. But you will never know them in public."

"How is it that some people make such bad matches that they can only talk at night?"

"It is because they chose inconvenient options and will not admit it at least part of the time."

"Are such people crazy?"

"No. They are only people."

"What can be done for them?"

"Nothing."

"Is that really enough to have?"

"No. But see what they have in the night."

IV

ERIC CARNEY WAS A QUAKER, and had been taught all his life to look for causes. His father, in their little New Hampshire town, had called it "having a sense of purpose," and Eric had looked for this sense all through his life, and had taken the search with him to college. The tremendous social sensitivity he had inherited from the ideas of his people caused him to have a great number of false starts and a great deal of hurt during his first days. But he had learned, through trial and error, to be less a do-gooder and more a genuine person. And he had learned to live with being a genuine person and to this extent he was a social pacifist. He had gone to a good college in the East, a rather conservative college, and at first there had been few causes or few opportunities for him to feel and exercise his own sense of stewardship. But he contented himself with committee work, which he found dull, unproductive and routine.

Then the Southern marches began. Eric went down with the very first car to leave the campus. It was a very small, very backward, very grievously sick Mississippi backwater town, and Eric walked in the dangerous parts of it for a semester and a summer, becoming very busy and very purposeful. Even after going into that town became a badge for people from other schools, much like himself, and even after he sensed the dissatisfaction of the local blacks with the many people of his maudlin sensitivity and perpetually understanding nature, he had tried to keep up his voter registration, community organization and other works. He was proud that he had come early, before the rush, and he was especially glad that he had not in all his time there grown a beard or used anything stronger than pot. But, for all his care, he still sensed that the locals, after having surveyed the novelty of the mass migration of innocents and the heavy smell of absolute goodness in the thick, hot air, had slowly and subconsciously rejected the bounty of spiritual munificence and did not really want him, or any of the people like him, in their primitive places. It was, he thought, not because he lacked sincerity, but because he had too much of it. When he realized this he had got angry at first; but then he also realized that there was an inverse relationship, in that town and perceptible to the natives in all their sublime innocence, between the quality of goodness and the number of people contributing to it. Then he had known that staying longer would be no good.

He returned to school in the fall, his sense of purpose shaken but just as strong. He took a black roommate in an apartment, and was extraordinarily nice when he brought in girls who were not like him. The black fellow hated him for this, but Eric never knew this or understood why.

These were the autumn days when the dialogue over making a revolution and a truly democratic society flowed loosely and desperately in the air, and hung over night-time bull sessions with heavy cigarette smoke, and when everyone felt he had to make some movement, however slight or inconsequential, toward the attainment of goals not yet defined. Everyone was seeking something better, but there was no piper, no steady drumbeat or distant shield to lead them on to that better thing. There was only dialogue, and pamphlets of many colors to hand out, and more dialogue, albeit much more heated, and an occasional break for coffee or sex or pot, and then the words continued. There was a sense of quiet, a very heavy sound, and then there was a sense of motion, rapid and yet subtle, and slow: there were long heated talks over beer mugs late into the night when young men would rise to their feet and shake their fists in the air while girls watched them, in squatting positions, cross-legged, their eyes excited. In secret places, very well publicized, there was talk of the Party and the essentials of making a revolution, and the first Che books (abridged) were coming off the presses. And then there were martyrs in the country, many more than were needed to truly make something rapid and re-forming come, the thought of which drove students to

near madness and frantic conversation. But nothing happened; and nothing came except the weekends, when they
relaxed, left off the dialogue and the books, and sought
quieter places, away, in the country.

V

ERIC AND MARGOT MET at a small party of people resting from the week's dialogue. At first Eric thought her extremely plain; for, unlike many of his socially conscious
friends, his sense of social purpose did not warp his perception or his sense of aesthetics. He had the only possible sense of beauty, having all his life been conditioned
to revere a certain standard. He knew there were valid
discriminations a man must make between fat girls and
girls of better builds, and he also knew that color did not
make any less valid these discriminations. The girl was
not really beautiful. She was a very smooth near-black,
with short hair, not *au naturel*, and large glasses which
shielded huge, arrogantly staring eyes that moved over
him and the people in the noisy room with a quickness
that, to Eric looking at her, seemed almost defensive.
There was a kind of stoop in her shoulders which did not
make her unattractive, but Eric was most of all aware of
a powerful intelligence behind those eyes which made
him uneasy, and the shape of her breasts under the white
blouse she wore. Much later, thinking about that night
in his bed, alone, he confessed to himself that it had not
really been her eyes at all that first attracted him. It had
been the determined lips below them.

"Will you introduce me to him?" the girl had said directly to Eric, indicating with her bold eyes Jerry, his roommate, a very well-built, very handsome and confident mulatto who had, a minute before, been conversing with Eric and who had just turned away to laugh with well-kept white teeth at something funny that someone in a small group next to Eric had said.

"His name is Jerry," Eric had said.

"Will you introduce me?" she said.

"What's your name?"

"Margot."

He had turned to his roommate. "Jerry," he said. "Jerry, I want you to meet a friend of mine."

Jerry turned away from the group and looked at Margot. "Hi," he said.

"Her name is Margot," said Eric.

"Hi, Margot," said Jerry. "Glad to know you." Then, because she did not say anything but only stared at him, making him uncomfortable because he had been laughing with three white girls, Jerry turned away again.

Eric shrugged his shoulders, as if to bear responsibility for and to dismiss the discourtesy.

"It really doesn't matter anyway," she said before he could say anything. "He wouldn't be a nice person to know."

Hearing this served to reinforce Eric's initial impression of the girl's perception, for he suddenly realized that, truthfully, Jerry was not a nice person to know. But he had never let himself admit it to his mind. He got her a drink and they talked and Eric was impressed by her very excellent command of the language. Unlike many of the blacks he knew, she did not slur her words or sing-song them, or talk rapidly, or self-consciously give crisp, overdone enunciations to prove her command; she pronounced each word with a cool precision that was natural and unpracticed. She was well read in contemporary literature, and was a science major at an all-girl school which, she said, was very fine and proper but which reeked with decadence. She had a number of good ideas, all her own, so that at no point in the evening was there ever the need to retreat into the inevitable racial or revolutionary dialogue. Eric was a good listener, especially with blacks, and the evening passed without his ever having to interject into the conversation any fuel to keep it going. And then he found himself responding, talking about himself, his school, his family, his Southern mission, and the things that made up his life and the things that really mattered to him. He noticed that the girl had a peculiar method of listening: she never nodded in agreement or shook her head in disagreement, but looked severe, as if she were instantaneously evaluating in her mind all that was being said and placing him in a category. Eric felt uncomfortable, defensive, slightly agitated, and he had a sense of lacking something, for in all his previous dealings with blacks it had always been he who had felt the confidence and who communicated, in silence, the necessary understanding which made the other person feel comfortable. But now the old situation was reversed. He wished that she would smile; he wished that she would not. He did not want her to look that directly into his eyes; and then he did want it. Her expression carried an air of superiority, of absolute belonging, of something nicely like condescension about it; and alternatively, through the first part of the evening,

Eric liked her very much and was afraid of her. Perhaps, he thought, it was because she really regarded him as an equal. Perhaps she thought of him as her inferior. This was a new feeling for Eric. And he liked it. Then, after their third drink, and after she had told him some funny things about the housemothers at her school and their monthly uses of *Playboy*, she smiled and there were two dimples in her face and her chin stood out, and her lips parted and Eric was not afraid any more. And then it came on him that all along she had been very beautiful and had waited, testingly, until now to show it to him.

VI

ERIC HAD NEVER HAD a steady girl during his three and a half years at college, although he had had his own share of the total sexual experience. Now he found himself fighting longings for something steady, something certain, something in opposition to the uncertainty of the times. He thought about Margot a lot during the week, and then he put her out of his mind and got back to the dialogue. But on Thursday night she called him and the decision, which he later justified as his own, was made.

They began to date on weekends. At first he would go to pick her up at school and bring her to town on Friday nights. He tried to be very proper about it because he was aware, as he was sure she was, of the expectations which inevitably cloud this special kind of relationship. He wanted very much for it to be different. On the first three weekends he got a room for her with friends, and he kissed her only three times during all of this. At the beginning of the fourth weekend, however, he very cautiously and matter-of-factly invited her to spend the time in his apartment. She was very direct about her acceptance and it had surprised him, and even frightened him a little. The early part of the evening they spent talking to Jerry, the handsome roommate, who slyly glared at Margot whenever Eric was not looking. Jerry was that unhappy kind of person who wanted everything in the world without having to deserve it. He made certain comments involving witless sexual innuendo and laughed considerably before he went off on his own date, leaving them alone in the room. Eric was very uncomfortable and embarrassed. He sat away from her, on the floor.

"Don't feel you have to stay," he said. "If you don't want to stay, I'll understand."

"I want to stay," she said.

"Jerry is really a well-meaning person."

"You don't have to apologize for him. I know his type."

Eric had been aware for a long time, perhaps even since that slight hint at their meeting, that she did have the ability to perceive and categorize people. This confirmation, now, gave him considerable discomfort and very little to say.

"At first I thought I liked Jerry," Margot went on, "but I don't. I can't respect him."

"Why not?"

"He doesn't seem to have a purpose or anything to care about."

Eric leaned toward her on the floor. "What do *you* care about?" he asked.

"You," she said quite frankly. She was being honest because she could be no other way with him.

"Why?"

"Because you love me."

Eric thought very carefully and then found that he too could be no other way but honest. "I do," he said. "Margot, I really do."

Then she was close to him on the floor and they were kissing.

Much later that night, in the close, warm darkness of his bed, they talked. They exchanged childhoods, truthfully. Margot spoke of Ray and Hank and all the people like him who had made her very afraid to love anyone or to feel anything. Eric talked of his sense of social purpose, of stewardship, of right, and of too much wrong in the wrong, of what he had tried to do in life and what was still before him. He spoke of inequalities, racial and intellectual, of making a revolution, and of the responsibilities of his generation and the changes they must make. Margot did not care for causes: she had had a single one all her life, and she knew in her mind, in the single bed pressed very close to Eric with her breasts against his body and feeling his breathing inside herself as he talked on and on, that, unlike him, she had come closer to her singular goal in the last five hours than Eric would ever get to all of his during his life. She was happy. And she cared no more for talk of causes, even as Eric's voice went on beside her. To bring the talk closer to herself, she told him how she disliked school and how his coming had saved her from becoming an academic animal. Eric was sympathetic. He stopped his monologue and allowed her to talk. He found that her talking, her carrying the conversation, made him feel at ease and he knew that he would try very hard to keep the racial thing from touching them. Then he touched her in the dark, ever so gently, in a neutral place with his hand, and knew that the same thought was with her when she covered his hand with her own.

GOING TO THE BATHROOM late that next morning, Margot passed through the living room where Jerry was sitting, apparently waiting for just this opportunity. He smiled knowingly and she pulled Eric's blue cloth robe close about her throat.

"Sleep good?" Jerry said. He smiled.

"Fine," she said.

"How was it?"

She thought of ignoring him and the comment. But then she could not because she quite suddenly had the thought that now should be the time to put Jerry in his place for the duration. "Very good," she told him.

Jerry smiled confidently. He was handsome and he had always known it. "I can do better," he said. He maintained the smile so that she could see his very white teeth shine beneath his black moustache.

"Shall I tell Eric that?" she said. "Or will you?"

"What the hell," Jerry said. "He knows it." He smiled some more. Then he added, almost an intentional afterthought: "I'll call you sometime this week."

Now she looked at him and smiled, indicating with her eyes not flattery but amusement. "Don't bother."

"You can't be serious about *him*. He's a crazy liberal. He doesn't even know what he's doing yet."

Margot remembered the evening she had first seen Jerry from across a room and how she thought he was very striking. She remembered how he had snubbed her, and the three white girls with him, and how they had smiled at her in amusement, confident that their handsome plaything could not be taken from all three of them by her. She disliked Jerry for allowing them to smile at her that way. Now she wanted to hurt him.

"How was your Anglo-Saxon last night?" she asked.

"Very good." Jerry's teeth flashed white again as he smiled.

"Do you think she'll call *you* again next weekend, or somebody else?"

"What the hell do you mean? I got her in my *bag!*"

"And she comes whenever you call?"

"Yeah."

"Why?"

"*She's in my bag!*" Jerry said. He was not smiling. He was getting very irritated.

Margot knew that she was winning. "Next time she calls," she told Jerry, "before you go running over, ask her to describe your face."

"What the hell is *that* supposed to mean?" said Jerry.

But she had gone into the bathroom and locked the door. And Jerry sat on the chair in the living room, thinking, not quite sure whether or not he had been cut. Then he laughed aloud, with an unnatural enthusiasm calculated to carry the sound into the bathroom and above the noise of the running shower. He had decided that the thing was not a cut. The idea of its being so was silly. His girl was the liberated daughter of one of the oldest and wealthiest families in the East, and a sufficient amount of its three generations of money was firmly invested in his car, his clothes and his pockets.

"Silly bitch," Jerry said aloud. "What a silly bitch this is."

VII

MARGOT FOUND THAT SHE COULD NOT bring herself to study even a little during the week. She found that she did not want to do anything. She found that she loved to spend the week thinking about the weekends. She liked to lie on her bed during the day and play with ideas, both his and her own, carefully held over and salvaged from the last weekend. She liked to glance up at the framed picture of him on her dresser and discover new ways of seeing his face. She liked to have other girls come in the room and watch them become uneasy when they saw the picture. She especially liked it when they felt they had to say something nice about his looks: the sharpness of his nose and how well it sat on his sensitive face, the thrust and determination and sensitivity of his chin, the warm eyes, the way his mouth was sad but almost smiling. She liked the way they would inevitably ask if they were going to get married, and the way some of the girls made little impromptu social observations, almost in apology, when she said that they were very seriously considering it. And she tried not to see the way some of them would smile, secretly, and look at other girls in a knowing way.

She waited for weekends and did nothing else. And when they came they were very beautiful, and she always brought new ideas away from them back to the campus and her room, to be selectively considered and tested against her own until the next weekend. She failed two final examinations, but did not care because she knew that she did not want to pass them. And when, in June, there were no more weekends, they went away together to a California town, very small and colorful and very close to the beaches, for the summer. They did Eric's community work by day, and walked the warm-sanded beaches by night. Eric wrote small poems for her in the wet, white sand and she learned to memorize them very quickly, in the moonlight, before the white foam, pushed in by the inevitable sea, came up the beach to wash them away. Sometimes they lay in the quiet of the warm night, the waves coming up to their naked feet, and talked and kissed and looked up at the stars and out to where they met the distant waterline. Again he spoke of his societal obligations, and again she listened selectively to what was said. She did not want to think of society or community, at night in the dark warm wet sand, or anything beyond herself and that part of him which gave her happiness.

"We ought to get married," he had said close to her ear one night. "We ought to do it while it's still summer."

She thought of the girls and their social commentaries, and had said: "Everybody thinks we're in for it."

"I don't care," Eric said. "I know what I want."

"I wouldn't want you to hate me later, when it hurts."

"I can't hate," he said. "It's not in me."

"But people can put it there."

He kissed her ear. "Everything's changing now. In a few years nobody'll give it a second thought."

"It's nice to think that."

"But it's true," he said. "You'll see. As soon as everybody over thirty-five dies, it'll be a new society."

"I don't want to trap you through an idea, Eric. You could be wrong, and then you'll hate me for it."

Eric had never thought about being wrong himself. Only fighting what he believed to be wrong was in his conception of stewardship. "You'll see," he assured her. "Only people over thirty-five have this thing. If we can't change them, we'll just wait them out."

"Listen," Margot said, "please don't make me a crusade. I just couldn't stand being that."

"How can you say that. I love you."

"Just don't."

He had kissed her again and then they lay very still and quiet in the night and waited for the bigger waves to drive them further up onto the beach.

VIII

THAT FALL SHE HAD LEFT school for good, telling her parents that she could not bear its isolation any longer and that she could learn more on her own, reading, meeting intellectual people, and working for a time in the city. She found a secretarial job, very close to where Eric lived, and together, armed with a list of fair housing subscribers, they found a small apartment for her. At first they had considered living together, but she had rejected the idea because of her parents, two extremely class-conscious, fatally middle-class people, and the grief she had caused them by quitting school. They both agreed that living apart for a while would be better, and that they could always move into her apartment if they found separate living quarters too inconvenient.

The domesticity began. Eric went to classes and she went to work, and they met every day for lunch. Then Eric went back to study and she went back to work, and they met again, in the evening, at her apartment, for dinner and the afterwards. She taught herself to cook and she learned to invent new things in her kitchen, just to surprise him. He would always be very happy when he came in to something new she had done, and sometimes they would cling to each other in that happiness for so long that they did not eat until late into the night.

One weekend he drove her to New Hampshire to meet his parents. They were Quakers and had known that their son was bringing a special girl home, but when they arrived the father was away in the woods, hunting, and the mother, a slim, well-preserved woman of fifty with brown hair like Eric's, had given them tea and then sat across the room in a single cushioned chair and looked at Margot, politely, but very close to tears.

"We'll get married tonight," Eric had told her driving home in the car. "We've got to do it now if we're going to."

"No. Not now," she said. She had been cut, and knew that whatever dignity she had managed to bring away from that house would not let her take advantage of Eric's embarrassment. "We'll wait."

"They're over thirty-five," he said. "They can't understand."

She was thinking very rapidly now. "Half the world is over thirty-five," she said. "What are we trying to prove?"

"Nothing. It's just that we've got a right to live."

She was silent as he speeded along the turnpike. She wanted him to go much faster. She wanted to get out of the car and run much, much faster than it was moving. She wanted to cry. "Let's drop it for a while," she said abruptly. "It might be good if we both started seeing other people."

"Why?"

"It might just be good."

"I don't want you to see anybody else."

"It's no good this way."

"Then let's just get married."

"No."

"You don't love me."

"That's not it," she said. "I'm just scared of your ideas."

He looked over at her, next to the window. She was looking out at the blur of black and dark green trees in the forests along the road.

"What's wrong with my ideas?" he said.

"I don't know. I don't know if I'm a person to you or an idea. Right now, back there, I felt like a damn cause."

"That's silly," he said. But he said it very slowly. "You know that's silly."

Margot made no reply. And they drove the rest of the way into the city in almost total silence. Leaving her at the door to her apartment, Eric held his head down and put his hand on her arm.

"We'll wait," he told her. But he held his head so that she could not see his eyes.

IX

THE STUDENTS HAD got a fresh dialogue going because there was a war being fought somewhere, for no reason at all. The unabridged Che books had now come into the stores and many people were making a living printing anti posters of different colors. People were fasting now who had never known hunger in their lives, and they did these things in groups and wore badges so that they would be known. This was a great inclusive dialogue and it had room for the words of many people. Everyone had to contribute, everyone could contribute, there was a solid front of words. The same people who had been very good in the South a few years before and who had faded with the exodus and with the coming of black awareness, now came back, more colorful, more determined, more aggressive in their new goal. In college communities up and down the East Coast, people shunned parties where there was no dialogue. There were great migrations of these people across the country, displaced by a hard depression that was not economic; rootless, searching people, coming and going in the night, sleeping in basements and grouped in parks, cross-legged, long-haired, talking, always talking and plotting openly the fall of something secret. Everyone had hair, everyone grew it long, as if in this there could be some statement of self-assertion, an affirmative break with tradition. But everyone began to look alike, and for some, it, and the dialogue, became no good.

Eric did not grow his hair long. He was too much of a thinker. He saw insincerity and infidelity to the cause in the crowd, and he kept clear of certain of its elements. It had always been his philosophy that deeds should be the proper advertisement of a man, and so he kept his hair brown and short and his chin clean, and said very little. He was also selective about groups and certain people who espoused impossibilities. But the dialogue he loved, and he kept close to it, because it helped him to forget other things, things it would do him no good to remember. He was waiting. But he did not know or bring himself to understand just what he was waiting for. Sometimes he thought it was Margot; and sometimes he knew it was not. Sometimes he thought it was a vigil, his self-created wake for everyone over thirty-five. And then he sometimes thought it might be that he was waiting for everything and everyone about him, and not just those people over thirty-five, to end.

But waiting for something, waiting for everything to end, was very hard; especially at night. Eric had to take pills in order to wait. And still nothing happened. Going, always going, to the antiwar dialogue was not enough; something was still missing. He began to have truthful talks with himself, in his mind, at night, in bed, alone. And he recognized that he loved and needed Margot, not because she was black and married by nature to a cause that had once been very close to him, but because for over a year he had been making room for her inside himself through a slow and secret process of which he had not, until now, been aware; and now there was all that room, reserved and waiting, and he had nothing to fill it. Talk of the Revolution and the War was not enough; the words had no substance at night, when there was no group, when all those who talked went away in couples, boys and girls, enchanted with the ideas that had flowed and determined to carry the discussion further when they were alone, again in couples, again boys and girls. Eric had a void in his mind, an empty space in his bed, and a nothingness in that special place he had made that ate at him, especially in the night. He had the capacity; but nowhere was there a girl who could fill all the space inside him. It would take at least two, or perhaps three girls to do it, if it could be done at all. But he wanted only one, and he could not call her, he thought, because of the profound dilemma with which he found himself confronted. Both horns of it touched on marriage. If he asked her again, he knew that she would think it was for the same old reasons that frightened her: the cause, his slightly paternalistic attitudes, his reaction against his family and his crusade against people over thirty-five. She would refuse and he knew that he could never convince her that it was any other way with him because he did not know himself what his real motives were. On the other hand, if he saw her again without ever proposing marriage, it would intimate to her that she had been right all along, and that he thought of her only as a cause, an idea, a purpose, and that when the time came for an affirmation of his motives, his silence would make him seem guilty of a recognition in himself of these, the very suspicions she held against his motives. He could not call her and yet he could not get her out of his mind.

And then one night he had called her after a week of rationalizing in his mind that he could no longer sleep until he did it. And later, in her bed, she had wanted his baby and he could not give it to her because he was afraid of the dilemma and how it could get to be very complicated if that should come about. He had left the next morning, very early, before she came awake. But before he left the room he paused over the bed and looked down at her, asleep and, in her own secret way, very beautiful. He wanted to touch her or do something, leave something there in the bed, in the room, to show her when she woke that he remembered all the good that had been and still existed, however far away it went at times, and that he still had the capacity within him, waiting. But if he touched her he knew that she would wake up and talk, and there was only that one thing he could leave, the complicating thing, and so he could only look down at her, and then walk away.

X

"Eric? *Eric*."

It was morning and he had gone. Margot did not move from the bed. She knew that he had gone and she did not want more hurt by looking in the kitchen or the bathroom. She also knew that he would not be back; if he came at all, ever again, it would never again be the way he had come in the night, just before dawn, five hours before.

She did not want to go to work, although she was very

late; and so she remained in bed. She was empty and she could not bear being empty and covering the space she felt with clothes and walking streets crowded with fuller people, people going someplace important to them and doing things essential to them in these places, and then returning, much later in the evening, to better places to meet the valued persons who were the very reason for their coming and going and living each day just for the end of it. She had none of these things and did not want to be near people who felt something more than the nullity she knew was within her.

She fell asleep. And when she opened her eyes again it was late afternoon by the sound of the homeward traffic outside her bedroom window. She looked up, in the bed, and watched the white ceiling getting to be darker shades of white, and she was trying in her mind to draw some philosophical lesson and relevance to her own situation out of the way the ceiling was getting when she fell asleep again. When she awoke this time the room was quite dark and it was late night outside. Voices were calling other voices, and someone, a girl, was laughing from far away down the street. Then she started to cry. Being in the darkness made her sob even harder and soon she could not control her movements on the bed and fell out of it, slowly, uncaring, onto the floor, where she continued sobbing. Such was the heavy sound of her own voice in the totally dark room, that she scarcely heard the banging on the door and the loud voice behind it.

"HOW LONG WILL THIS GIRL cry?"
"Until she is quite sure she can feel nothing else."

"For whom does she cry?"

"For herself, and all those like her who come into the better options."

"But see her now. Is this a better thing?"

"At least she is suffering. Cowardly people never suffer."

"How can practicality be cowardly?"

"It stifles growth."

"Can one say that she is growing?"

"Yes. She is building something."

"What?"

"Something inside herself."

"But will it help her?"

"Come and see what it will hold out. And note also what it will hold in. Come and see how she will grow."

XI

MARGOT PAYNE BEGAN TO DO volunteer community work in a ghetto Housing Office three nights a week and all day on Saturday. She was very efficient with the poor who had dealings with her; but no one of them could say that he had ever seen her smile. The Revolution talk had drained the ghetto of its once plentiful store of volunteer workers and her coming to the inefficiently run Housing Office had a double advantage: first of all it provided her with as much work as she wanted for as much time as she needed to give, and it gave the office the benefit of her desire to accomplish as many things of a material, substantive nature as she could handle. Secondly, it allowed her to come into her blackness again.

She was intelligent, alert, and far more efficient than most of the paid employees in the office. But the high school graduates, the girls, did not envy her because she never said anything of a personal nature or smiled at any of the men in the office. This made her somewhat mysterious and extremely interesting to many of the men who worked there. One of those, who was very interested in her and her reasons for working so long and hard in a place where most people merely pretended to work and found excuses to get out of the office most of the time, was Charles Wright.

Wright was a plodder, a fellow of average intellect and even less perception. He had taken a rather dubious degree in history and political science at a very small, very unknown college somewhere in the South, which qualified him to do nothing at all. But having this small badge, and being black besides, *was* more than adequate credentials to qualify him for a job in one of the many federally sponsored ghetto projects, where he was paid rather handsomely to administrate promises and frustrate the lives of poor people. This was not intentional on his part; he saw it rather as his taking advantage of an unchangeable system full of cynical blunderers, incompetents and do-gooders before someone else took advantage of it. To him it was a matter of trying to make the best possible life for himself in an organization which would retaliate against anyone who genuinely tried to make things work.

Because he was a plodder, very few girls had ever been nice to him, and his primary purpose in taking such a job had been to earn the necessary capital to purchase a car, prestige whiskey, a good apartment, and well-tailored clothes; all of which he expected to use in luring a wife. It had not worked; and now he was seven years out of school and wifeless. Although he wore a full beard and stylish clothes and tried to maintain the image of a rather reserved swinger, inwardly he was desperate and searching and still a plodder. He was almost twenty-eight. And the girls to whom he was nice, and from whom he patiently expected eventual reciprocation, saw that he was an old plodder and knew that they did not have to be nice to him. He was persistent in being good when dealing with reluctance and was persistently used by girls of even very slight social significance. He got very little sex because most of the girls with whom he shared an evening in his apartment could sense, in his eagerness to please, that he was the nondemanding kind of fellow who, if put down on the first or second or even the third date, would nevertheless call again, always once more, for another evening.

Margot had refused his first invitations. But then, on weekends and sometimes late at night, the loneliness got into her and she knew that she needed something. She had perceived all there was to know about Charles Wright during her first few weeks in the office and knew that it was only necessary to be nice to him, with certain reservations set out beforehand, and he would be all right. In her misery and in her re-creation of something solid within her, she recognized that she needed someone to be very interested in her; someone always close at hand over whom she could exercise some control. She had called Charles Wright at first, some six or so weeks after his last invitation to dinner in his apartment had been extended. He was in the exact state as when they last talked and was very, very eager to cook dinner for her.

And it began that way. They began to date very frequently, and being nice to Charles and knowing that she was giving him her company out of charity rather than any genuine interest in him as a man, made her feel a little good. She tried very hard to lose what was still left of her old self in him. And he was grateful for her company, and for that alone. Of course he tried from time to time to seduce her, but each attempt, and they were relatively few, ended with his pathetically begging her for something she knew she could not give. She pitied him, she did not love him, and she could not make herself give anything to him, although she pitied his pleadings. They went out, they sat and talked, they kissed, they smiled and held off and then kissed some more. But all of it made her feel nothing.

"I don't want to take advantage of you," Charles told her once in his bedroom after being put off again. "I won't take advantage of you."

"I know that."

"I really like you a lot, you know that?"

She was silent.

"In fact," Charles said, "I love you."

"You shouldn't," she had said. "You shouldn't love anybody."

"All I want is to get married," said Charles. "To be honest, that's all I really want."

Again she said nothing.

"Do you want to marry me?"

She thought about it for a minute, how it would be to

see his face for year after year and to know his mind before he even knew it himself. "I can't marry anybody," she said at last.

"Is it because of Eric?" Of course she had told him about Eric.

"No. That's really all over now." She made her face very firm. "I think I hate him now."

"You ought to get married or something. Go back to school. If you don't, you're bound to get used by other guys."

"I don't think so."

"You know I wouldn't use you, don't you?"

"I know." She put her hand on his knee and thought about Eric and their last night and the eternity of a day afterwards. And then she thought about how she was crying in the dark and the banging and voices from her apartment door that made her stop crying. She had gone to the door with a sheet wrapped around her body. It was Jerry, Eric's roommate, drunk, loud, insistent that she sleep with him now that it was all over between Eric and herself. Jerry had even brought a friend along. Both of them knew that it was all over. Both of them insisted that she sleep with them. She had slammed the door and fallen to the rug on the living-room floor. And then she had really cried.

"I can't marry anybody," she said to Charles. "I can't love anybody."

He kissed her on the forehead, very tentatively and with the greatest tenderness, lest she should misconstrue his meaning.

"I do like you," she said. And then she kissed him back, and in her mind decided that she should be nice to him in the only way possible to prove the little affection she was holding out to him.

It was not very hard to like Charles Wright. He had in him a store of affection and tenderness, possibly saved from all the girls who had never been nice to him, which he poured over her. He was a very violent and very satisfying lovemaker, as though she represented to him all the women he had never had and would ever have in this life. He was satisfying and he was kind.

Sometimes, in the night, when a nervous spasm went through her body and caused her to wake, she would look up and see him, eyes white and genuinely concerned in the dark, his hand stroking her body, not sensually, but paternally and soothing.

"What's the matter?" he would ask.

"Nothing."

"Do you want to take something?"

"No."

"Was it a bad dream?"

"It wasn't a dream. I get that way sometimes."

"Do you really love me?" he would ask.

Now she would feel good toward him because he was there and so desperate in his eyes for some certain affirmation of even the slightest affection. "I really do," she would tell him. And then sometimes they would make love, or just lie close together and sleep in his bed, because he did not want her to be away, for a single night, in her own bed.

"I really do love you," she would say again, and make it the last thing said before sleep came. And when it did come, in her thoughts all night, she believed it and came close to the border territories of happiness.

XII

FEW WOMEN HAD EVER BEEN NICE to Charles Wright. It was not because of his lack of looks or status: he had both these things. His many failures before, during and even after college when he had arrived at a comfortable station in life might have come because, like so many other plain people, there was very little about him that was exciting. He represented stability at its very worst. And while this condition might have worked well to his advantage with older women, it did him very little good among the girls to whom his appetites went; girls much younger than himself. In his thoughts was a sad obsession, a kind of deadly flirtation with capturing all the youthful pleasures he had missed while he had been making his way up in life. He poured his feelings freely onto girls who, because of their age and the excitement of the times and environment, had very little use for men of stability. He could have had many younger girls, if that was all he wanted. But he craved more; he wanted very desperately to marry one and pull her out of the crowd. And marriage, to the girls who represented the most excitement for him, was something to be put off for years, or until they could do no better. Charles still had all his hair, and a beard, but he no longer liked to dance or experience new things. He was older and almost set in his ways and had created a life-style that, while not totally unpleasant, was extremely ritualized. And Charles found it very difficult to make the slightest variances in it. He went to work and ate at set times, he went to bed before 1:00 A.M. and he preferred to date only on weekends. Although he had a relatively new convertible, he would never drive it with the roof down. He watched certain dubious shows on television, preferred classical music to jazz or folk-rock, and liked to talk, in open conversation, about his personal problems rather than those of the times. As a husband he would have been a very good find for some girl in her late twenties, but as a companion for a girl barely into her twenties, he had very little property value.

Then, quite rapidly, he began to undergo a sort of metamorphosis that came about primarily through his relationship with Margot. She made him go to places where, a few months earlier, he would have felt quite inadequate. They frequented discothèques, secret parties where pipefuls of marijuana and stronger drugs were passed about; they walked in the woods on weekends and mingled with people who eagerly talked of riots and the making of a revolution. In going along with Margot in her desperate sallies to forget and to live her life to the fullest, Charles Wright began to alter his life-style, and his property value increased tremendously. He grew his beard fuller, which made him look younger. He dressed less conservatively, and he talked less of himself and more of the problems of a generation that was no longer his own.

Quite suddenly, he was no longer the same dullard that he had been. His property value was up and he began to notice it. He began to think more about enjoying himself for the moment and less about entertaining with the idea of possible marriage always in his mind, quite close to his present plans. And what was even more remarkable was the happy knowledge that other girls, younger girls, seeing him in this blissful state with Margot, began to take an interest in him. Very soon, younger, permissive, exciting girls, the ones he had always wanted, became available for dates; for by pure chance, he had fallen thankful victim to that peculiar desire of uncertain, searching young girls to want only what other not-so-searching young girls have. Charles Wright now received flirtations and invitations from girls who only three months before would not have looked at him once. And typically, like so many of those who have been denied all the things they think they have always wanted and then fall over facsimiles of what the old ideas had been, Charles began to take advantage of as many accessibilities as he could touch. This newly blown popularity bubble went quite to his head and he began to make some radical changes in his style. While he had always been a weekend dater, even confining most of his outings with Margot to weekends, he now began to sneak out during the week, after work. He suddenly discovered why coffeehouses were made dark, and he joined those who frequented the coffee circuit and the luncheon-date route; and he also found that he too had a touch of a certain form of wit which some girls found exciting and pleasing and entertaining. Now he began to bring girls into his bed on nights when he had very carefully arranged for Margot to be sleeping in her own.

He was nervous about this at first, he had been really moral and was new to rationalizations. The first girl's name was Marsha, a girl not black, but who was looking to drown herself in blackness. She was from a very rich family and was, predictably, in revolt against its money and status and traditions. She was seeing a psychiatrist, like many, many girls caught up in the nebulous ideas of the times, and she catered exclusively to black men because, she told him, they were just beautiful.

On the first summer night in his apartment he had played for her a very old, scratched album of an obscure black jazz pianist from his youth. The picture on the cover of the album showed him a very old, toothless, dissipated man.

"Oh he's *so* beautiful," Marsha had said. "Look at his color. See how his face changes colors when you look at it from different angles."

"Yeah, he is," Charles agreed.

"*You're* beautiful," she said.

"Thank you," said the uncertain Charles.

"Everyone in your race is beautiful. Everybody but me. I'm not at all pretty."

"But you are," he protested.

"No, I'm not," she said sadly. "I don't tan well."

"But you don't *need* a tan. You look good the way you are."

"I'm pale and ugly. All of us are too pale. Everybody in the world ought to be black or at least brown."

This was a notion never before touched upon in Charles's mind and he gave it good consideration. "I don't know," he finally said. "Being brown never did *me* much good."

"I know," Marsha said. "It's a dirty shame. Don't you hate us for it?"

"No."

"Well, *goddamn!* You should!"

Suddenly the idea registered in Charles's mind and he knew the vocabulary he should use to make the evening go all right.

"I guess I do," he said slowly and seriously.

"I know you do and I'm sorry. Truly I am."

"That's all right."

"Do you hate me?"

Charles looked at her: hair long and brown, eyes very green, lips nice and pulled down at the corners, sadly, in anticipation of his answer.

"I'll try real hard not to," he said.

She was very grateful. So much so that she was very nice to him that night in his bed.

Is it a bad thing to feed on sickness?"

"If everything grows from it, feeding becomes necessary in order to live."

"Does it make one feel bad?"

"Only if one spends time thinking about it."

"Are we all as ill as we pretend to be?"

"No. But it is still better for the mind if one does pretend."

"Why?"

"In order to rationalize appetites."

"Are appetites everything in life?"

"Almost."

"Then what is left of fidelity?"

"Very much. But only when it is convenient."

"Then this is not the first moral man to fall?"

"No. But he will flatter himself by thinking that."

"Is he *really* a good man?"

"A long time ago he was not. But now he is about to be. He is coming into his morality."

AFTER THAT it was not very hard for other girls to get to be nice to Charles. He began to rather enjoy letting them. He began to enjoy the ways he was learning of lying to Margot. He began to enjoy the way she seemed to worry when he was late and unnervous meeting her after work in the evening. And when he was with her at parties or in groups of their friends, his private ones among them, he began to enjoy the secret looks he could exchange with certain people without her ever knowing who, and why it was being done.

One night Margot found something unfortunate in his bed and sat thinking for a few minutes. She looked at him, wrapped in a towel, just out of the shower and regarding himself in a mirror. He took a long time before the mirror combing his hair and picking at his thick beard. He took a long time just looking at himself. Then, after she had picked up the thing in the bed and looked at it closely, she quite suddenly began to reconsider the advantages of having Charles, even as he reconsidered his own advantages in the mirror. She brushed another brown hair off the pillow and behind the bed.

"We ought to get married," she said. "I've been thinking it over and you're right. I guess I'm ready for it now."

Charles turned from the mirror but did not rush over to the bed and embrace her thankfully, as she had expected. He just looked at her. She waited for him to speak. He said nothing.

"Don't you want to marry me?"

"Sure," he said. "Sure I do. And we'll do it too. In a few years."

"But just two months ago you were *begging* me to marry you."

"I still am. But I've been thinking about it. We don't really know each other yet."

"It's been ten months already. How long does it take to be sure, anyway?"

Charles came over from the dresser and sat beside her on the bed. He touched her face. "Look," he said. "I tell you the truth. I need a better job before we can do it. I want to give you everything I can when we do it."

"That's not the real reason and you know it," she said.

"What other reason *would* I have?"

She thought about the brown hair and about Eric and the girls at school, and she felt about to explode. But she had made something solid inside herself from all her sufferings, something that took complete control just before emotion came; and so it allowed her to sit there while he talked on and on about the guilt he felt over his job, about how he wanted them to live in style, about how hard it was for an almost confirmed bachelor to change his habits quickly, about the summer riots and the possibility of concentration camps for blacks and his daily musing about leaving the country. But he said not one word about the brown hair.

"What does that leave for us?" she had said after Charles had run quite out of excuses.

"We'll do it for sure in a little while," he said. "When everything's settled."

"Maybe I won't be around then," she said flatly.

Charles smiled, his newly acquired confidence shining through his teeth. "You'll be around," he said.

And she was always around after that. Margot made it a point to always be around, unexpectedly, after work or late at night when she knew he expected her to be at home. She made a very special point of telling all their friends that they were planning to be married, and was especially decisive in announcing to a fellow who called her at home when Charles was there, that she was now engaged and expected to be married within a month, or two at the most. Charles, sitting at her table and pensively eating the dinner she had cooked for him, was very nervous and said nothing after she had hung up. That night he went home early and when she called him later, at 1:30 A.M., she could tell by his breathing and carefully worded sentences that he had been drinking and that he was not alone.

Seeing Eric when she was with Charles was the hardest part. He would always be alone, and looked always sad. And she would know that, had it not been for the hard, careful thing that was growing inside her, she would not have slighted him or refused to smile the many times they met by chance at a party or a lecture or in the street, when she had done just that. He and Charles always spoke and were extremely polite to each other, and she did not think it fair that they should be so resigned and without any indications of rivalry. But they were always friendly, and though they said very little, she knew that they respected each other; although that respect was uncomfortable and maintained, she liked to think, for her benefit. That irritated her. But what irritated her most was Eric's never offering congratulations to them, as if he did not know they were to be married. She wanted him to say something, to call her aside and plead with her not to do it, to offer threats against the marriage, against Charles. But, in the streets or at parties or wherever the three of them met, he only waved or made polite small talk, his eyes only suggesting to her own what she knew, what she expected, what she found herself wanting him to say.

Now she became obsessed with the idea of marriage. She pounded at it in bedtime talks with him; she repeated the announcement to her friends, his friends, to all the people he respected, that their ceremony was imminent and just a matter of months away. On three occasions she took him to her home in Cleveland to meet her family, and they liked him. They seemed to like him more after each visit. And she reminded him of this, constantly, persistently, encouragingly, along with promptings that he should set a date as soon as possible. She found herself driven to having a date, set and certain, waiting for her to meet it, waiting for it to meet her, and save her from something hard and cold and lonely, something around which she could not form words. It was something beyond love now, or something below it, or something that had nothing at all to do with love. She did not know.

"I don't care about you having other girls," she told him one hot August evening in his bedroom. "It really doesn't matter to me if you have all the girls you think you need until we get married. I really don't mind at all. Just tell me *when*."

"We'll do it one day," he had told her, thinking about a new girl he had met, a friend of Margot's, who had made certain intimations that, if given the opportunity, she would be very nice to him. "We'll do it one day, soon too."

"September? October? *When?*"

Charles thought about it. About all of it. "Maybe I better get a new job first. I'm not making enough at the Housing Office."

"That's stupid," she said. "You don't even *work* at the Housing Office. You get paid twelve thousand dollars a year for doing nothing." She looked into his eyes. They were moving away from hers in the dark room. "That's plenty for two people to live on."

"What do you know?" he said. "I do my part. What are you trying to do, run my life?" He sat up in the bed and reached over to the table, feeling for a cigarette.

She knew that he was trying to get the start of an argument out of her. And she knew why he was doing it. "No," she said resignedly. "I'm sorry."

"Don't think you can walk into my life and run it. I got along good before I met you. I can still do it too."

"I'm sorry," she said again.

"You're not the *only* girl in the world that wants to get married."

She did not answer.

"I'm about the best thing that ever happened to you. And I know it."

Now she was looking up at the darkness on the white

ceiling. It was in gray and black patterns, and the gray was hard to distinguish from the black. Charles puffed on his cigarette. He was not angry and he knew it. He was just safe.

"Charles?" she said, still lying back and looking up at the patterns on the ceiling.

"Yeah."

"*Please* marry me."

Charles could feel himself getting angry. He tried not to be but it seemed no good to try. He felt like he had just run over a rabbit or a squirrel or a bird in the dark with his car and he was angry because he could not stop at once to see if it was still alive. He felt bad.

"We'll talk about it," he said.

THE NEW GIRL'S NAME WAS KAREN. She was chubby and aggressive but she had a certain laugh and a mind quite a lot sharper than Charles's, and he was very interested in her, although he did not want to be seen with her in public places because she was chubby and because she was a friend of Margot's. After the first time she came up she had suggested that they live together. She had already been quite nice to Charles and, with the suggestion of cohabitation, promised to be even nicer. This suggestion had frightened Charles at first because he did not know how to accept anyone beyond Margot in his bed in the morning. None of the other girls had ever stayed over because Margot had a key and sometimes stopped at his apartment for coffee on her way to work; and he tried to be cautious enough to remove all evidence of the previous night's visitor and to always wake up alone, just in case Margot came in before he left for work or after he had gone. But the thought of having someone permanent, albeit chubby, in his bed in the morning without matrimonial ties or the threat of them was a new one for Charles, one that merited some consideration.

"Think about it," said Karen. "Just don't think too long. I can always go someplace else."

"I'm thinking about it now," he told her.

Karen leaned closer to him on the sofa. "Of course you could have other girls just like I would see other fellows. But neither of us should have any regulars."

"Why do you want to move in?" Charles asked.

"I like you," she said. "I like men who know what they're doing. There're too many boys around. You can't grow with them."

"But you don't want to marry me?" said Charles. He was thinking very fast, almost faster than his capacity to think.

She looked him full in the face and then went all sad around the mouth. "Not now," she said. "You know how bad the times are. My parents might bitch about it. They aren't bad people, but they honestly aren't ready for it yet. I really want to do it. I really might do it someday, but just think about the times and all the trouble I'd be inviting."

"It was just a thought," said Charles.

The girl was relieved. She put her hand on his knee and looked directly into his eyes with some sad indications of passion in her own. "One day it'll all be different," she said. She patted his knee, reassuringly.

"Yeah," said Charles. "It was just a thought."

"But we could still live together."

"Yeah," Charles said. "We could still do that."

"And no regulars for me and no regulars for you."

The thoughts were very hard for him to face now and he wanted to stop thinking about the rabbits and birds he might crush and never see for the speed of his car. He wondered if birds had an awful lot of blood in them. He wondered if birds bled after they had been crushed and were dead. He wondered if Karen cared or whether she would stop her car if she should ever crush something. And he wondered if, after being with her, he would care. But he was tired of thinking.

"We'll talk some more about it later," he told her.

Karen smiled at him and then moved very close to Charles on the sofa.

MARGOT PAYNE DID NOT SLEEP well at night. She did not want to lie on her back because then she would have to look up at the ceiling. And if she lay on her belly her face would be pressed down into the pillow, and before she knew it there would be a wet spot on the pillow. She was losing control over her crying and now seemed to do it whenever she was in bed alone, or whenever something not human pressed close against her breast and body. Now she found that the bed was responsible for the tears and there was no way open in her mind to rationalize their coming when they did. Earlier, before Charles had undergone his metamorphosis, she had been quick to assign the cause of them to Eric. But now, with this thing happening to Charles and with the growth of her dependency on him, she was able to make other assignments for the crying. It was Charles's fault, and it was the fault of many of her friends, girls who, unsuspecting of the consequences to her, took him to their breasts for a while because he seemed to them, for the moment, an exciting thing to have, and taking him for the moment seemed like an exciting thing to do. And while she understood this and the way they were, it gave her small comfort knowing the causes, and it did not help sleep come any easier. She found it very difficult to approach sleep.

She was thinking about Charles Wright all the time now. She could not help herself. He was very little like Eric, but, like Eric, she could sense him slipping away from her. And like Eric, there was nothing she could do to hold him. This was especially hard to understand because she knew that, having a mind that was by far superior to his, she should have had very little difficulty. But she did. The marriage bothered her too. She did not know if she really wanted the thing itself or just the comfort which she expected to draw from the mere idea of a date, a point, something on which her mind could be fixed and something that promised an afterwards and at the same time an end to the uncertainty she was feeling. She did not know exactly why she wanted it; but she wanted it.

Sometimes in the night when she could not sleep she would watch the late show or listen to the radio or read textbooks from school which she should have read two years before. And sometimes she would walk, not with direction, but aimlessly, wherever her mood carried her body. She did not walk to be picked up by boys on the street or men in passing cars; she was faithful, she told herself, to what she was; and she was, she told herself, a girl about to be married or about to know when it was that she was going to be married. She walked because she could not sleep.

And walking one night the idea suddenly came to her that a certain airline offered special honeymoon flights to Bermuda for hesitant people who chose to wait until September to get married. It was still late August and there was still time to get married and make the special rates for September honeymooners. She thought that she should tell Charles about this immediately and not stop over for coffee the next morning with the news, when it would not be as fresh and exciting and inspirational. She went to his apartment, content with the idea that more than justified her coming to wake him after twelve, and only a little apprehensive over what she might find there. Charles was a long time coming to the door, arriving at least five minutes after her third knock. She did not want to use her key.

"What do you want?" He had opened the door only a little way and stood behind it in his robe looking out at her, with something in his face quite a long way from sleep. "What do you want?" he said again.

"Let's have a cup of coffee. I have something good to tell you."

Charles held the door firm, opened only as much as would allow his face to show. But that was enough to tell her everything.

"Aren't you going to invite me in?"

"It's late. If I drink coffee I won't be able to get to sleep and I have to work tomorrow."

"We can just talk, then. Can't I come in?"

Charles made his words very precise now. It took a great deal of control because there were hundreds of words in his mouth all trying to say different things about the different feelings that were going through him. "I really wish you wouldn't," he said, selectively. "I really wish you would just go home and come back tomorrow morning for the coffee."

She stood in the hall and understood what was in the house and why his head had to be held against the edge of the door. And she also understood now just why she had come. The special rates for honeymooners was no new thought; her mind had just made it convenient.

"You have company?"

"No. Of course not. No."

"Can't I spend the night here?"

"I really wish you wouldn't."

Then there was the sound of someone's yawn from the bedroom; a sound, it seemed to Margot, that was deliberate and domestic and possessive at the same time. It was a bored sound and it made her go all tight inside when he, in some play at slyness, shifted his eyes momentarily from her face to the direction of the sound.

And now something went out of her, away, distant, ghostlike in its passage from her as she stood there. But Charles did not see it go and for a moment she felt sorry for him, almost as sorry for him as she was feeling for herself.

"I just came by to tell you," she began. Then she made her voice louder. "I just came by to say that you're right. There's no sense in playing marriage. If we're not going to do it we might as well stop playing house."

Charles just looked at her.

"I just wanted to tell you," she went on, "there wasn't much left in me. But what there was, you could have had."

"What are you trying to say?" Charles was afraid now of losing the peg that was solely responsible for holding his new self together. He was afraid of looking at the bird just after it had been crushed. And he was afraid that Karen, in the bedroom, would hear the sound of fear in his voice and not think him a man from whom she could learn things.

"What are you trying to say?"

"Nothing."

"Why don't you just go on home. We can talk tomorrow."

"No."

"We could have breakfast. I don't really have to go to work if I don't want to."

"No."

"Anyway," he said very rapidly, "we'll talk about it later."

"Sure."

He stood, embarrassed, expectant, waiting for her to look away or turn away so that he could feel justified in closing the door. She looked at him, in a way very much like pity, for an entire minute and he saw that something very important had gone out of the way she looked. It made him uneasy.

Then she turned her back, walked a few steps, and heard the door close and the lock turn and the chain push into place behind her. And she stood there, in the hall outside his door, waiting for the inevitable voices, just to give him every benefit. And when they came, it was as she had perceived they would be: his voice beginning, low and nervous and very fast, talking, soothing, perhaps apologizing. Then a second voice, which did not say very much, but which brought on a hurried response, unintelligible to her in the hall, just after its every few words. Margot pulled the last loose part of herself together and walked heavily down the hall, the sound of her shoes like a steady drumbeat on the floor, and out into the night.

JERRY HOWARD FANCIED HIMSELF A man about town, although that was far from what he actually was. He liked to think of himself as one of the very rich, that very special kind of self-possessed rich person who would be welcomed at any door among those of his acquaintances, at any time in the night. This night he was drunk. He had been drinking all week, in fact, because he had very little else to do until his friend returned from her European holiday. Earlier that evening he had decided that he did not want a girl; for he had made the very disconcerting discovery that girls, most girls, were beginning to bore him. He was only twenty-two and sometimes he worried about what would happen to him when he got older and found that girls still bored him. Secretly, he had certain fears of becoming a homosexual in later life, and this is what brought him away from his drinking sometimes late at night when he felt the fleeting need for having a girl. He wanted to exercise the need before it passed because he was very much afraid of what would happen to him after he lost all contact with it. And this is what brought him, once again, to Margot Payne's door at three in the morning. And this is what caused him to pound on the door and call her name and laugh aloud at what he was doing, and hope that she would not be in. Margot opened the door.

"What do you want?"

"I want to come in." Jerry smiled his old white smile.

She held the door open for him and he paused for a moment in disbelief, and then passed into the room. Then she closed the door and turned, and looked at Jerry; her face hard, her eyes staring as always, her arms locked behind her back as she leaned against the door.

"What do you want?"

"I thought you'd be glad to see me."

"I'm not," Margot said.

"My former roommate Eric sends his love." He smiled some more.

She made no reply.

Jerry walked about the small living room. He was very nervous under his eyes. He tried always to look away from her. "Why aren't you in bed?" he asked, brushing his fingers lightly across the tabletop.

"I was walking," she said.

"You horny?"

"No."

"Can't sleep, huh?"

"Yes."

"I guess you want to go to bed, huh?"

"Yes," Margot said.

Jerry walked over to the door where she was still leaning.

"With me?"

She looked him in the face and he lowered his eyes to her breasts not because he wanted to look at them at that moment, but because he was afraid that she would see in his face the fear he had of the thing possibly waiting for him on the other side of twenty-two. "Want to go to bed with me?"

"Why not," Margot said.

Jerry stepped back, away from her for a moment and brought his eyes up to a neutral part of her face, below her eyes. In her face there was nothing: not the slightest movement of her lips, not the barest hint of breathing about her nose, not the least movement of her chin. Jerry was not accustomed to this; there was no passion and it frightened him. He considered her and he considered the absence of passion in her face. He also considered what possibly waited for him on the other side of twenty-two. Then he smiled, still uncomfortable but confident that he had won something. "What a silly bitch you are," he said. "What a real silly bitch *you* are."

Then he touched her and she did not resist.

"Between my eyes I see three people and they are all unhappy. Why?"

"Perhaps it is because they are alive. Perhaps it is because they once were. Perhaps it is because they have to be. I do not know."

"But all around them is the smell of something dead and yet each of them is with someone. Why then are they unhappy?"

"Perhaps they have found a better way to be."

"But *is* this way better?"

"I do not know."

"Then what have we gained from seeing all this?"

"Nothing."

"Then what have *they* gained from doing all this?"

"Nothing."

"Then what will they feel tomorrow and the next day?"

"Nothing."

"But if this is all there is, what is left of life and why are we alive?"

JAMES ALAN McPHERSON, was the first African American to win the Pulitzer Prize for Fiction. A MacArthur Fellow and American Academy of Arts and Sciences inductee, McPherson was born in Savannah, Georgia. He was a graduate of Harvard Law School and held an MFA from the University of Iowa Writers' Workshop, where he later taught for thirty-five years. In a writing career that spanned forty years, McPherson was a contributor to publications, including *The Atlantic*, *Esquire*, and *Playboy*, and was an editor of *Ploughshares* and *DoubleTake* magazine. McPherson's works include the short story collection *Elbow Room* and two works of nonfiction, *A Region Not Home* and *Crabcakes*. He died in Iowa City in 2016.